DESPERATE MEASURES

Also by Jo Bannister

DESPERATE MEASURES

JO BANNISTER

MINOTAUR BOOKS ✠ NEW YORK

DESPERATE MEASURES. Copyright © 2015 by Jo Bannister. All rights reserved. Printed in the United States of America. For information, address St. Martin's Press, 175 Fifth Avenue, New York, N.Y. 10010.

www.minotaurbooks.com

Designed by Omar Chapa

The Library of Congress Cataloging-in-Publication Data is available upon request.

ISBN 978-1-250-07566-6 (hardcover)
ISBN 978-1-4668-8709-1 (e-book)

Our books may be purchased in bulk for promotional, educational, or business use. Please contact your local bookseller or the Macmillan Corporate and Premium Sales Department at (800) 221-7945, extension 5442, or by e-mail at MacmillanSpecialMarkets@macmillan.com.

First Edition: December 2015

10 9 8 7 6 5 4 3 2 1

DESPERATE MEASURES

CHAPTER I

Laura Fry drove through the wet night as if lives depended on it. Possibly they did.

It was a long time now since emergency calls had been part of her daily routine. She saw her clients in a comfortable office overlooking Norbold's Jubilee Park, during office hours, over coffee and the occasional shortbread. They were all people with problems in their lives, and though as a therapist she did her best to help them, and believed she was broadly successful, it was only realistic to acknowledge that sometimes people on the edge totter over.

This wasn't the first time she'd had a client do the mental equivalent of bungee jumping on knicker elastic. It wouldn't be the first time if the outcome was a nasty mess on the pavement. Usually, though, it was someone else's job to clean up. A psychiatric emergency response team if the client was still essentially intact, an ambulance if he was badly broken, a meat wagon if all the urgency had already gone from the situation. Laura would expect to hear what had happened sooner rather than later, but it was unusual these days for her to be involved while a crisis was still in progress.

This was different for two reasons. Gabriel Ash was certainly a client, had been for two years, and remained in need of her professional services, but he was not in fact mentally ill. His problems didn't originate within himself; they'd been inflicted on him. And, perhaps because of that, she'd come to think of him as a friend as well as a client. So when he needed her, she came. If that meant coming out in the early hours of a Sunday morning, no sign yet of the midsummer sun, virtually no vehicles on the roads, only herself and the traffic lights and the streetlamps reflecting off the rain-washed tarmac, so be it.

She drove straight to the big stone house in Highfield Road, abandoned her car in the drive, and hurried to the front door. It opened before she reached it, and a young woman wearing a checked shirt and a worried expression ushered her inside.

"It's good of you to come."

"Where is he?"

"In the kitchen. I've got the range going. He's icy cold."

"That's the shock."

The big man was hunched bearlike in a fireside chair. Someone, probably the girl, had put a blanket around his shoulders, but it wasn't enough. Gabriel Ash was shaking like a man in an epileptic fit.

The dog was there, too, pressed against her owner's legs, as if the only comfort she could think to offer him was the warmth of her slender body.

"Gabriel," said the girl. "Laura's here."

He looked up, dark eyes sunk deeper than normal, all the color gone from his face. He nodded spasmodically. "Thank you." His teeth chattered on the words.

"Good grief, Gabriel—you look like you've seen a ghost!"

It had taken Laura Fry six months to get Ash to start talking to her. He'd never been the sort of client to gush out his woes at the sight of a psychiatrist's couch. (In fact, she'd dispensed with her couch when she found clients getting too comfortable, helping themselves to the shortbread and settling in for the afternoon.) She didn't expect he'd be able to tell her anything useful now. She turned to the girl. "What happened?"

W here to begin? Five years ago, when he was a government security analyst, a man with a wife and sons and a scheme for combatting Somali piracy? Four years ago, when the pirates struck back by kidnapping his family? Six months ago, when he was a shattered wreck of a man, living like a recluse in the house where he was born, barely venturing out except when the white dog he'd taken in required it?

Or nine hours ago, when he talked to his wife by video call on a computer in Cambridge?

Hazel Best took a deep breath and tried to put it into some kind of context. She knew, and was grateful, that Laura Fry was familiar with the background—that she didn't have to start by explaining everything that had happened to Gabriel Ash, only what had just happened.

"He was following up old leads. People he'd talked to before Cathy and the boys disappeared. One of them pinged on his radar, so we followed him. To Cambridge. Gabriel was right: the man was involved—*is* involved. He wasn't just in touch with the pirates, he was working for them. Sending them information on arms shipments. That's his business—arms exports."

Laura looked at her in astonishment. "You did call the police? Please tell me you called the police."

"I *am* the police," Hazel reminded her wryly. "Except when I'm on leave, like now. And no, we didn't. For the same reason Stephen Graves didn't. The pirates have a hostage. They'll kill her if we don't do exactly what they want."

Laura was shaking her head. Casual acquaintances thought her a severe woman, with her narrow face and upswept hair and statement spectacles. None of that was for effect, but it wasn't all there was to her. She was a strong-minded woman. She was also, even beyond the demands of her profession, a caring one.

"It doesn't have to matter," she said slowly and precisely. Her sharp jaw came up, daring them to argue. "It's a horrible thing to say, but in hostage situations it comes down to damage limitation. What's the best thing for the greatest number of people? You pay a ransom, and more people get kidnapped. You refuse, and one person dies, but that's probably the end of it. You cannot make it a worthwhile strategy for terrorists to kidnap people. It's one of those lines you have to hold, whatever the short-term cost."

"It's Cathy Ash."

When you drop a bomb, it radiates force and matter, and light, but most of all it radiates sound. Imagine dropping a bomb that radiated silence. That was what Hazel Best had done: she'd dropped a bomb that blasted silence into all the corners of the shabby, shadowy room. Under the table and chairs, behind the dresser, into the awkward gap beside the range where Ash had squeezed a dog basket although Patience had expressed a preference for the sofa the first time she entered the house. More than that: this silence seemed to bundle within it the impossibility of sound. For longer than a man can hold his breath, it seemed impossible that any of those present would find a way of breaking it. Of returning sound to the world.

Of all of them, perhaps Laura had been in this position most often before. Startled wordless by a development unpredictable even as the expression of a damaged mind. She recovered quicker than most people would have done; and she knew that what was important now was not that she said the right thing but that she didn't say the wrong thing.

She said carefully, by way both of clarifying and of inviting clarification, "Gabriel thought he was talking to his wife?"

Ash looked up at her. "It *was* Cathy."

"You saw her? You recognized her?"

He nodded fitfully.

Laura bit her lip. "Gabriel—is it possible that you saw what you wanted to see? If this woman was being held by the people who took your wife, it wouldn't need a great leap of imagination to think it was her. I've seen these video transmissions—they're not great quality, even if they're coming from somewhere much closer than Africa. And it's been four years. If she's alive, if she is with these people, Cathy won't look like she looked four years ago. . . ."

Hazel said quietly, "She recognized Gabriel, too."

This was not par for the course, even in leading-edge psychotherapy. It was the equivalent of a patient who thought he was a duck actually laying an egg. It was a game changer. Laura Fry didn't often feel out of her depth, but she did now. "You *have* to go to the police." Even to herself she sounded breathless.

"No." Ash's tone was not the one she was familiar with. His tribulations, the breakdown they had provoked, had left him desperately uncertain of the world and his place within it, and all the time she had known him that was how he spoke: softly, troubled, afraid of drawing attention to himself. This abrupt determination was something new. At least new to her. A flash of intuition suggested that this was how he had been, always, before the sky fell.

"This isn't something you can cope with alone."

"Maybe not. But I'll decide what we do about it, and when. No one else is better equipped to. And no one has a better right."

Laura felt her jaw hanging and shut it. He looked like hell. He was still visibly shaking. But something inside his mind was standing up on its hind legs for the first time in four years, and she had the distinct feeling that if she tried to stand in front of it, to catch or corral it, it would run her down.

She turned to the girl. This was the first time she'd met Hazel Best, but she knew a fair bit about her. The fall from grace of Norbold's senior police officer had been documented by the local newspaper; certain aspects of it were not public knowledge, but were the preserve of an informed inner circle to which Laura Fry belonged; and some of the details were known only to those who were there when Superintendent Johnny Fountain met his death. Hazel Best was one of them. Gabriel Ash was another. And Ash told Laura things he would otherwise confide only in his dog.

So she knew that Hazel was, at twenty-six, a little older than the average police probationer—not, indeed, a girl at all, despite the initial impression created by her fresh complexion, unimproved by cosmetics, her wide green eyes, worried now into a frown, and the mass of fair curls partially tamed by an elastic band at the nape of her neck. In jeans and a red-checked shirt, she looked as if she might work on a farm.

The first hint that the whole might be greater than the sum of the parts came when the clear green eyes sought out Laura's own. There was a depth there that, primed as she was by her uncommon knowledge, still managed to surprise the therapist. A depth of intelligence that was nonetheless open and honest and strong. These are not characteristics that inevitably go together. But that brief clash of gazes told Laura Fry that Ash hadn't imagined anything that he'd told her about Hazel Best. This was a young woman purposeful enough to shoot a gangster dead when the alternative was something worse.

Laura cleared her throat. "You were there? You saw her, too?"

"I saw her." Hazel nodded. "I didn't recognize her. I'd only ever seen photographs."

"So—can you be sure it was his wife?"

"She recognized him," Hazel said again. "She said his name."

"It couldn't have been . . . ?" But Laura didn't bother to finish the sentence. There was no credible alternative. She made a helpless little gesture with her hands, a sort of low-level shrug. "I didn't think she was still alive. *Nobody* thought so, except maybe Gabriel, and I think even he only believed because he couldn't bear not to. What did she say to him? What did he say to her? How did he"—she groped for a word, could do no better than this—"handle it?"

Before Hazel could answer, Ash growled at her: "He probably handled it very badly. He was a bit gobsmacked, to be honest. But he's sitting right here, and he hasn't gone deaf, and he can probably talk to you himself if you keep the questions simple."

Laura felt her eyes popping, made the effort to blink. "Jesus, Gabriel," she exclaimed, "you need a therapist like I need a personal astrologer. I'm sorry. You look like shit. But obviously you're thinking fairly clearly."

Gabriel Ash vented an unsteady sigh. "No, I'm sorry. And I don't know how clearly I'm thinking. But I know what I saw and heard. I know what it means. Cathy is alive. Somewhere, my wife is alive. In Somalia, being held hostage by men whose only use for her is as a human shield, but alive."

Laura didn't know how to ask tactfully. But worse than saying it wrong would be not saying it at all. "What about the boys?"

He shook his shaggy mane of dark hair. "I don't know."

"You didn't ask her?"

His deep eyes burned like coals. "Of course I asked her. They didn't let her answer. They moved the camera off her. They—I don't know—I think they hurt her. I could hear her crying." He could still hear her—the lonely, desperate wail that had less to do with fists or even guns being shaken in her face, and more because for a few brief seconds a veil had parted in the nightmare that had engulfed Cathy Ash and a face she must almost have forgotten had flickered there, and then it had gone. "When the picture came back, she was reading from a card. Nothing about the boys. Only that I had to do what they said or they'd kill her. If I went to the police, they'd kill her. If I went to the Foreign Office, they'd kill her. If I tried to find them, they'd kill her."

"Did you believe them?"

Ash wasn't a man to whom hatred came easily. But there was no mistaking the hatred in the whiplash glance he threw at Laura Fry. "Yes. I believed them."

"What are you going to do?"

"I don't know. Wait for them to tell me what they want."

"They'll contact you again?"

"I imagine so."

CHAPTER 2

THE DOG, PATIENCE, STOOD UP, ALERT, all long legs and point-ing nose. She was looking down the hall. The doorbell rang.

Surprised, Hazel looked at her watch. Even on a weekday the milkmen would still have been in their beds. She moved toward the front of the house. "Whoever it is, I'll get rid of them."

This soon after the solstice, a paleness was already creeping into the sky. But the streetlamps were still lit, and light from the hall spilled out as she opened the door. If there had been anyone standing on the step, she'd have seen him. There wasn't.

If she'd taken another ten seconds to reach the door, she'd never have known who'd rung the bell. Thinking better of it, he'd retreated as far as the gate and was disappearing behind the hedge, a grubbier than usual teenage boy in a rugby shirt for a team that wouldn't have let him into its clubhouse.

"Saturday?"

Hazel got the distinct impression that he wished he hadn't come. But now he'd been spotted, he had fractionally too much pride to make a run for it. He ground to a reluctant halt, waiting outside the gate.

Hazel hurried down the path. "It *is* you. How are you? We haven't seen you since . . . well, for weeks." She glanced uncertainly back at the house. "Listen, I'd ask you in, but we're involved in a bit of a crisis."

The boy looked at her, all eyes, like a famine victim. His thin lip twisted in an ironic grin. "Another one?" On a good day he looked about twelve, on a bad one about forty. This was not a good day. In fact he was sixteen. He looked thin and cold in the early-morning chill, and more than that he looked . . .

She beat the thought back. If she admitted to herself that yes, that skimpy sixteen-year-old boy who lived in squats and had as near nothing as can be measured but still once risked it all for Gabriel Ash looked afraid, regardless of what was going on in the house behind her she could not for shame have him turned away—would have had to make the time to find out what he needed. As long as she could remember he'd been a street kid, a survivor; she could leave him on the back burner while the difficult events of today were dealt with. There would be a moment for Saturday later.

She returned his grin wryly. "Yes, another one. Can I tell you later? It's all hands to the pumps in there."

The boy nodded. "Anytime. Catch you." He let go of the gate and it rattled a moment before the latch fell.

Deep inside herself Hazel knew she was behaving badly. Saturday deserved better. He hadn't come with the first light of a summer's day because a gap in his social diary had prompted him to look up old friends. He'd needed something. Ash wasn't the only one with problems. She knew this boy, and owed him more than to tidy him out of the way until she could spare the time to help him.

Guiltily, she called after him. "Saturday—do you need any-thing? Money? Anything?"

Already she had only a back view of him shaking his head. "I'm fine."

Hazel knew it wasn't true. She knew she should have gone after him and found out what was going wrong in his life. What more was going wrong. But she told herself that his problems were probably the ones he'd always had and could wait, while Ash's demanded that decisions be reached pretty well immediately. She bit her lip, but she went back inside.

"Who was it?"

"Saturday."

Laura Fry looked confused.

So, for a moment, did Ash. So much had happened since then. So much had happened even in the last twenty-four hours. "Oh—yes. Was he all right?"

"He looked all right." Hazel knew as she said it that it was disingenuous.

"What did he want?"

"He didn't say."

Ash nodded distractedly. "I'll . . ." The sentence went unfinished because, even one word in, he knew he wasn't going to be doing anything about Saturday anytime soon. Instead he looked at Laura. "Thank you for coming. Hazel thought I was going into meltdown. Perhaps I was. I feel steadier now."

"I can give you a bit of sedative, if you think it would help."

He shook his head. "No. Thank you. I need to think. Can I call you later, if I need to talk?"

Her V-shaped smile was solemn. "Of course you can. Anytime. I mean that, Gabriel—anytime. But if there's nothing more I can do here, maybe I'll grab another hour's sleep before breakfast." One uptilted eyebrow made it a question.

Ash nodded. "Next time I go ape I'll try to do it during office hours."

Hazel saw her out. Laura paused in the doorway. "You were right to call me. Call me again if you think you should."

"You think he's wrong, don't you?" said Hazel. "About handling this himself."

After a moment Laura nodded. "I'm concerned that, in trying to do what's best for Cathy, he's going to pull himself to pieces. I hope it ends well—that he finds a way of bringing her home. But there are a lot more ways this can go badly, and if it does, he's going to blame himself. If he can't save her, I don't know what he'll do."

A chill settled on Hazel's spine. "Suicide? Gabriel?"

"It's a possibility. We need to be alert to it. Or he may go the other way."

"Other way?"

"Try to destroy the rest of the world."

This was Gabriel Ash they were discussing, the gentlest man Hazel had ever known. It was impossible for her to imagine him going Rambo. But she knew Laura wasn't trying to frighten her for fun. "I'll keep in touch."

"Do."

CHAPTER 3

WHEN HAZEL WENT BACK TO THE KITCHEN, Ash was in the process of emptying the dresser cupboards. He didn't keep pots in there; he kept papers—vast quantities of papers, in box files and lever-arch files and concertina files and loose in stacks. It looked as if a tornado had hit the Public Records Office.

"What are you doing?"

"I'm going to need some help with this," he said tersely. "Not the police. There are people . . . I have contacts . . . I know people. People who can help. There must be *someone* . . ." The urgent activity ground to a painful halt, leaving him stranded in the middle of his kitchen floor, his arms full of paperwork, his face twisted with a tortuous combination of hope and despair as the realization dawned on him that the people he had known, the contacts he had had, those who could have helped him, inhabited a past to which he no longer had access. In the depths of his eyes he looked lost, as if he genuinely didn't know where he was.

Hazel took the papers from him and put them with the others on the kitchen table. Then she took his arm and steered him toward the stairs. "All that is probably true, and when you've slept, you'll be capable of making decisions about it. Until then, anything you do is likely to make things worse rather than better. Go to bed, Gabriel. I'll wake you in three hours, and we'll talk about what we do next."

Ash allowed himself to be packed off to bed like a child and offered no argument. Perhaps he could see the sense in what she said. More likely, he was currently incapable of making any decisions, even to remonstrate.

Hazel gave him ten minutes, then went to check on him. She found what she expected. He was sitting on the edge of his bed, still fully dressed. He'd managed to get one shoe off; now he was holding it in his hands and staring at it as if unsure where it might have come from.

With a sigh, she took the shoe from him and knelt down to take off the other one. Then she pushed him back on his pillows and tucked the quilt around him. "There. That's good enough." She pulled the curtains to keep out the growing day.

"She's alive." His voice was a wondrous whisper. "Hazel, Cathy's alive."

"Yes," said Hazel softly. "And that's all we need to know for now. Go to sleep."

She didn't expect him to. But half an hour later she looked in again, and he was dead to the world.

P atience wanted to go out. Hazel let her into the back garden, then sank into the old leather sofa with a cup of hot, sweet tea. She didn't like hot, sweet tea, but she'd heard somewhere it was good for shock. Though probably not when it was allowed to sit untouched in its mug until it went cold. While Ash slept upstairs, Hazel slumped into an exhausted doze on the kitchen sofa.

She awoke with a guilty start, and for a moment couldn't think what she had to feel guilty about. Then she remembered the dog. Even on a summer's morning, it was too early in the day for the chill to have left the air, and her thin coat and spare frame gave the lurcher little protection from the weather. Hazel levered herself up and opened the back door.

The step was unoccupied. Hazel went outside. "Patience?" She dared not raise her voice for fear of disturbing Ash. "Patience! Time for your breakfast."

Still no response, and Hazel knew with an awful certainty that she wouldn't find Ash's dog even when she combed the whole of the overgrown garden. So it proved. It was an old house with a stone wall around it that should have secured anything but a sex-starved rhinoceros, but the dog had clearly found a way out.

Back in the kitchen, Hazel debated her options. To do nothing was probably the sensible thing. Patience had found her way over long distances before now and would undoubtedly return when she was ready. In the meantime she could keep herself out of trouble. Hazel knew this because for six months the dog had kept Ash out of trouble, which was much more of a challenge.

Or Hazel could go looking for her. Probably Patience had headed toward the park, which was where she usually took Ash for his morning walk. But Hazel didn't want to leave the house. If she woke Ash to tell him why, he would worry; and if she didn't and he woke to find himself alone . . . then *she* would worry about how he'd react.

She settled for a compromise. From the front gate she had a good view down the length of Highfield Road, halfway to the park. She walked into the middle of the street, hoping to catch a glimpse of the slender white shape with its distinctive scimitar tail.

In fact what she saw was the whole dog, trotting breezily up the pavement toward her. Nor was she alone. Hazel recognized the rugby shirt before she could see the boy's face. She went to meet them.

"Saturday! Thank God you caught her."

Saturday looked puzzled. "She didn't need much catching." And indeed, the dog was walking amiably beside him without so much as a bit of string through her collar.

"She must have known I wanted to talk to you." Hazel grinned so he wouldn't think she really thought that. "I owe you an apology. Come up to the house, let's have some breakfast."

She noticed, and didn't let him see she'd noticed, that the boy took the chair nearest to the range. Hazel opened a can from the cupboard. Chicken soup isn't most people's idea of breakfast fare. But then, most people don't go to bed hungry, and she was pretty sure Saturday had.

By the time the soup was hot, and the butter was melting into the toast, and cold tea had given way to hot coffee, a bit of color was showing in Saturday's pinched cheeks. He looked nonchalantly around the kitchen. "Ash not here, then?"

Hazel shook her head. "I sent him to bed."

"He's all right, is he?" He wanted her to think it was just a casual inquiry. But his nonchalant manner failed to disguise his genuine concern.

Hazel didn't know what to tell him. Wasn't sure how much of a secret it was. Realized then that it hardly mattered what she said to Saturday, because he had no one he could tell. In the end, too tired to lie, she told him a simplistic version of the truth. "He received some news about his family last night. His wife is still alive. She's being held hostage in Somalia. Africa," she added, in case he didn't know.

"Jesus."

"Quite."

One of the few things she knew about Saturday was that his family, when he had one, were Jewish. It was where the nickname came from—"Excused Saturdays." But he'd been alone so long that his language, including his profanities, was the language of the street. The community of the half homeless—those who didn't sleep in shop doorways but in empty houses, derelict factories, and disused garages, and didn't appear in most statistics because on the whole they didn't annoy anyone—were his family now.

Hazel was about the closest he had to a friend outside that community. Now that she was safely back so Hazel didn't have to tell Ash his dog was missing, she was glad Patience had gone over the wall. "I'm sorry about before. There *was* something you wanted, wasn't there? Tell me."

He shook his head. "It doesn't matter."

She breathed heavily at him. "Saturday, it's quarter past six in the morning! *Anything* you do at quarter past six in the morning, unless it involves toothpaste or toast, *must* matter, because you wouldn't be doing it otherwise, or at least not then. So tell me. It's not like I'm in a hurry to be somewhere else."

"I've got this laptop," mumbled the boy.

Hazel stared at him. "A laptop? You haven't got an address. You haven't got a power supply. And I don't mean to be rude, but you also haven't got any money. What are you doing with a laptop?"

"It's not *mine*," he growled. Nothing she had said was untrue. That didn't mean he felt good hearing it. "I found it."

"Ah . . ." As a police officer, Hazel had some experience of people finding laptops. Mostly they found them on the backseats of locked cars.

Saturday read her thoughts through the back of her neck as she poured the coffee. Not much made him blush these days. Somehow that did. Knowing what she thought of him. Knowing she had every reason to think it.

"Where did you find it?"

"At the service station at Whorley Cross. In the washroom."

He also didn't have a car. "What were you doing at a service station?"

The flush in his cheek was not subsiding. "Having a wash, all right?" And looking to see if anyone had left anything valuable lying around. Both of them knew it.

"All right," said Hazel. "Did you give it to the people in the shop?"

"That bunch of thieves?" Saturday glowered. "They'd sell it for beer money, and blame me if someone came looking for it."

"And I'm guessing you didn't take it in to Meadowvale, either." No one in Saturday's position ever entered a police station willingly.

"I thought you could take it in."

"Why?"

"Because no one'll accuse *you* of stealing it!"

"If you handed it in, no one would accuse *you* of stealing it." But there was no point; she was never going to convince him. She sighed. "Okay, I'll take it in."

"Don't mention me. Tell them you found it."

"I'm not telling them I found it in the men's washroom of the Whorley Cross service station!"

"I don't care what you tell them! Just don't mention me."

She shook her head at him, exasperated—like his mother, like his teacher. She imagined both of them had tried to keep Saturday on the straight and narrow. Hazel had no illusions about the likelihood of succeeding where they had failed. But there was something about the boy, a certain grubby charm, an underlying decency, that made her want to try. "All right, I'll think of something. Where is it?"

He carried his life in an ex-army rucksack, slung from one thin shoulder because he thought that was cooler than carrying it on his back. It was lying at his feet now. He reached into it, past the personal treasures he kept wrapped up in his other pair of socks, and produced the laptop.

It wasn't big. But it was a good make with a good spec: someone had paid serious money for it. Someone else would have paid fairly good money for it, no questions asked. Hazel directed a quizzical eyebrow at him. "You didn't think of selling it?"

The boy shook his head, turned his attention to the food. "It's not mine," he said virtuously, leaving Hazel fighting the urge to laugh.

"Okay, leave it with me. I'll drop it at Meadowvale later today."

"Don't mention me."

"And I won't mention you." She smiled. "Now—bacon and eggs?" It was her turn to blush. "Oh—sorry . . ."

Saturday returned her smile with one of his own, a sweeter, clearer-conscienced thing than he had any right to. "Don't tell Granddad, but I don't keep kosher anymore. You'd have to be awful fucking selective about which bins you raided."

CHAPTER 4

HAZEL WENT UPSTAIRS QUIETLY. She met Patience coming through the open bedroom door and, a moment later, Ash himself. The sleep had done him good. He still had no more color than a ghost, but at least now he looked like a ghost that had worked out what had happened to him and what he had to do next.

"Has Saturday gone?"

Hazel nodded. "I gave him something to eat. Actually, I pretty well emptied your fridge. Sorry."

"What did he want?"

"He nicked somebody's laptop. Now he's thought better of it and wants me to hand it in as lost property."

The fact that Ash was in the boy's debt didn't blind him to his essential nature. "Thought better of it?"

Hazel gave a grim chuckle. "That puzzled me, too. He wouldn't say any more, just left the thing with me and told me not to mention his name."

"We don't know his name."

Hazel looked surprised. "Of course we do. It's Saul—Saul Desmond."

"You asked him?"

She stared at him. "You didn't?"

And that was the difference between them. Hazel was a people person, Ash was not. She was genuinely interested in who they were and where they came from. Ash wasn't, and never had been. He was interested in big pictures, not fine brushstrokes.

"Never mind Saturday and his thieving little ways," said Hazel. "What are we going to do about your wife?"

They were words that must have been said a million times, and probably never in circumstances like these. But they were both too troubled to note the irony.

Ash led the way downstairs. Or rather, Patience did and Ash followed. In the hall he turned to face his friend. "Hazel, I appreciate that more than you can know. What are *we* going to do. But the reality is, *we* are not doing anything. I'll tackle this on my own from now on."

If he'd slapped her face, she could hardly have been more hurt. Surprise and resentment turned her voice into a plaint. "You don't want my help?"

Ash swallowed, feeling like a worm. But it was important to hold firm. "Of course I want your help. But I won't keep risking your life to have it. These are dangerous people. We know that— we've already been shot at, Cathy's been held captive for four years, and God knows what's happened to my sons. Well, I have nothing to lose. But you have, and I'm not going to see someone else I care about harmed because I made a bad decision. Go home now, Hazel. Stay away from me. When it's safe, I'll let you know how it all worked out."

She couldn't believe what he was saying. Far from waning, her sense of injustice and her anger grew—like sunflowers, like fireworks. She felt her fists knot and a quiver of pure rage travel up her spine. "Gabriel Ash, how dare you speak to me like that? After everything I've done for you! All the crap I've taken, for you! Because we were friends, and friends don't walk out on one another when the going gets sticky. How dare you tell me to go home now?"

"I don't want you to get hurt."

"I've *been* hurt!" she yelled. She knew she was going red in the face and didn't care, or not enough to stop. "I've been knocked out, half drowned, and had my backside peppered with buckshot! I've been stood down from a job I love, and I don't know when or if I'll be allowed back. My colleagues think I'm a loose cannon, my friends think I'm crazy. And why? Because you needed my help. You still need my help. Don't you dare tell me I'm surplus to requirements!"

His big hands reached out for her. He had never held her before, or only to keep her face out of a ditch. He held her now, broad fingers grasping her upper arms. There was nothing remotely sensual about it, but she felt concern radiating from him. And a calmness she would never have believed, even as recently as a few hours ago. Hazel knew then that Ash had already decided what his next move would be, and that it would not involve her, and that nothing she could do or say would change his mind. She felt slighted and disappointed and relieved, and could not for the life of her have said which she felt most.

"I know what I owe you," Ash said quietly. "Everything that I am today that I wasn't three months ago. Specifically, someone who now has the strength to do what's necessary without having his hand held. I am more grateful to you, Hazel Best, than I will ever be able to say: for your friendship, for your patience, for sticking by me when wiser counsels would have told you I was past redemption and you needed to consider your own position.

"Well, I still need your friendship, and I need your patience more now than before, but it's time you listened to those wiser counsels and started looking after your own best interests. If you won't, I'll do it for you. What I need to do next I don't need help with, and I don't want to be worried that in trying to save Cathy I'm putting you in danger. I mean it. Go home. I'll keep in touch. When there's something to report, I'll call you."

Hazel looked into his face, into the shadows of his deep-set eyes, and saw that he meant almost every word of it. He would accept no more help from her. From this point, he would travel on alone. His tone was gentle, but the words were ruthlessly honest. The only lie he had told was when he promised to call her. She knew she wouldn't hear from him again.

"Gabriel . . ." She couldn't keep her voice from cracking.

"It's all right." He smiled solemnly, and put her away from him. "Go home now."

"I can't."

"Yes, you can. You have to. If you come back, I won't be here."

What do you do when the sky falls? When everything changes? When the doctor says, "It isn't good news." When the lover says, "There's someone else." After your heart has clenched tight like a fist around broken glass, and the roller-coaster sensation in your head has passed, and the sun is still rising and setting to its appointed rhythm and the tide is still caressing a million nameless shores, and gradually it dawns on you that life will go on. That even *your* life will go on. Well, you pick yourself up, and you dust yourself down, and you check for missing limbs and the sort of bloodstains that might upset other people, and then you look for some point where you can reinsert yourself into your recent history. Where you can hope to pick up where you left off; and it won't be the same, it'll never be the same, but your screams will be silent ones and people who know you a little will think how brave you're being. How sensible. And never guess that you feel like you're bleeding all over.

Hazel stumbled blindly back to her car. It wasn't tears tripping her; it was too soon for that. It was pure undiluted shock that had bleached and narrowed her perception like the tunnel vision of a near-death experience. Gabriel Ash was not the beginning and end of her existence. She had had a life before she knew him; she would find a way back to it now he was gone. There were plenty of things she could be doing—*should* be doing. Just, offhand, she couldn't think what they were. She got into the car and sat still, panting softly like a hard-run deer.

The laptop was on the seat beside her. There was that. Maybe Ash didn't want her help anymore, but Saturday did. She sniffed determinedly. When you can't find a cure for cancer, sorting out the filing cabinet is a good plan B. Setting Saturday's mind at rest could be plan B. She'd head home, if home she must go, via Meadowvale and tell some innocuous lie about how the device came into her keeping.

It was now some weeks since she'd passed the portals of Meadowvale Police Station. They were surprised to see her. Even Sergeant Murchison, who'd seen most things at least once, blinked when she stood before him, friendly smile pinned firmly in place, the laptop in her hands.

"What can I do for you . . . er, miss?"

The smile didn't flicker, but Hazel heard the edge on her own voice. "First, Sarge, you can stop pretending you don't recognize me. Then you can find out if Detective Inspector Gorman's in his office."

It might have been Sunday morning but he was, and from the speed at which he appeared down the stairs, he at least didn't need reminding who she was. "Hazel! Come on in. Come upstairs, I'll get some coffee sent in." Instinctively, unaware that he was doing it, he ushered her up to the CID offices with an arm behind her shoulders, as if she might need defending. Of course, he was aware that she'd been stabbed in the back in this building before.

Hazel had expected to feel, and to make others feel, a little awkward. She was not prepared for how powerful the sensation of wrongness would be, or how urgent the instinct to cut and run. She made herself breathe steadily and keep walking. She'd had some difficult encounters in this building. But the facts had come out, and everyone who'd shunned her was now aware that she'd done nothing wrong. She had borne their hostility when they'd thought there was a reason for it, refusing to act as if she had something to be ashamed of. Now they knew the truth, it should have been easier. Somehow it wasn't. She was glad the place was quiet.

Gorman took her to his office and shut the door. He ordered coffee over the intercom. "How are you?" He peered into her face with every sign of concern.

"Fine," she lied breezily. "Just waiting for the word to get back to work."

Dave Gorman nodded. He was a squarely built man with a broad, low forehead and a much-broken nose. If you'd cut his leg off, it would have had the words *RUGBY UNION* running through it like a stick of rock. He was also an intelligent man, and a good one. "Give it time. What you went through, you don't get over in a week or two." He gave a sudden smile. "They're paying you to sit in the sun and do bugger all. Enjoy it while you can."

Hazel felt herself relaxing in his company. "I'll try." She put the laptop on his desk. "I brought you this."

He raised a bushy eyebrow. "Whose is it?"

"I don't know. I think it must be lost property. Somebody left it sitting on my car."

"Where?"

"Highfield Road. I came out and found it this morning." She didn't explain what she was doing at Gabriel Ash's house, and Gorman didn't ask.

"You didn't see who left it?"

Hazel shook her head. "No." It was a lie, but only a white one.

"Did you try to access it?"

"No," she said again. "We can now, if you want to. It's probably the best way of finding out who owns it."

"Okay." Gorman nodded. "Though isn't it a bit technical, getting past other people's passwords?"

Hazel had taught IT during her first career. "I'll let you into a secret about passwords," she said, opening the device and pressing keys. "Something like seventy percent of computer owners use the password PASSWORD." She entered the magic letters and the laptop let her in.

Automatically she called up the most recent document. But it wasn't a letter, as she'd hoped—something that would have the correspondent's name and address on it. For a moment she wasn't sure what it was. She tried tilting her head to one side in case that might make a difference.

"It's a map," said Dave Gorman helpfully.

But it wasn't, not exactly. "More like a blueprint," said Hazel. "The sort of thing an architect draws up to show how a building will sit on its site." Brow furrowed, she slowly resumed the vertical. "It looks familiar. Why does it look familiar?"

Gorman was shaking his head, bemused, when he recognized it and changed the side-to-side motion into an up-and-down one. "Dirty Nellie's."

Hazel turned to look up at him peering over her shoulder. "Pardon?" Her mother had thought it a vulgar expression, but she'd never quite cured her daughter of using it.

"The pub on the corner of Market Street. Former pub, I should say, it hasn't had a tenant for ten years. The sign says 'The Red Lion,' but everyone in Norbold calls it Dirty Nellie's. After a former landlady who ran it as a brothel."

"And they couldn't find a tenant for a pub known throughout Norbold as Dirty Nellie's? Amazing," said Hazel mildly.

"In the end the council bought the place to redevelop the site, just as the recession hit," said Gorman, remembering. "Nothing's been done about it because there's no money. Except"—he nodded at the screen—"it looks as if someone's finally taking an interest in it."

"Housing, by the look of it," said Hazel. "And shops." She scowled. "All very desirable, I'm sure, but it doesn't help us get this thing back to its owner."

"Yes, it does. The council will know who the developers are, and *they'll* know which of their employees has mislaid his laptop. A couple of phone calls, and you can expect a nice bunch of flowers from a relieved architect."

Hazel grinned. "That'll be the day." Flowers were optional, but she'd badly needed a success today, and this simple restoration of lost property would do. Already she was feeling better than she had an hour ago.

"Lunch?" suggested DI Gorman, reaching for his jacket.

Hazel looked critically at her watch. "It isn't lunchtime."

Gorman sniffed. "I am the senior CID officer and currently the second most senior officer in this police station. Lunchtime begins when I say it begins."

When the house in Highfield Road was built, good families kept their own carriage and horses and needed somewhere to park them. Around the back, accessed from a narrow lane referred to locally as a ginnel, was the stable block. For most of the last century, of course, it had been garages, and there was a car there now. It wasn't Ash's car. Ash had had a car, but he'd no idea what had become of it. This had been his mother's car until her death three years earlier.

For most of those three years he had felt no urge to drive. In the last six months, though, the notion had seemed less impossible than it once had, to the extent that he'd had a mechanic service the vehicle against the day when he might want to use it. Now he'd dismissed his chauffeur, the need to be mobile again was suddenly pressing. He turned the hall bureau inside out looking for the keys.

The white dog sat in the kitchen doorway, watching him.

CHAPTER 5

S TEPHEN GRAVES, TOO, WAS FINDING it impossible to sit still. Yesterday's developments had unsettled him more than he'd realized. He tried to catch up on some work, but though he had the Grantham office to himself, he was unable to concentrate well enough to achieve anything useful. In the end he did what most people do when the rug has been yanked from under their feet and they're not sure who's going to do the cleaning up. He went home.

His wife looked puzzled, unaccustomed to seeing much of him even at weekends. Graves assured her—lied to her—that all was well, and offered to treat her to an afternoon's golf. Then he had the house to himself.

Looking back from where he was now, it was hard to remember how it had begun. He'd been in the business of manufacturing arms for half his life; in a way, for all of it, since Bertrams had been established by a childless uncle with the clear intention that Stephen should succeed him. Most of that time it had been a complex, demanding, exciting, profitable business, one that he was proud to be a part of. Then, the thing with the pirates . . .

Even now it was hard not to smirk at the word. He knew, as

did anyone with a television and half a brain cell, that Somali pirates had been responsible for devastating losses to international trade and to life; still, the word conjured images of Captains Hook and Pugwash.

He'd known it was no joke even before he lost his first shipment. He'd been taking additional precautions since learning that the pirates were beginning to augment their maritime activities with attacks on air freight. Arms shipments held a particular attraction for them, so he and others in the industry had got their heads together to agree on a strategy, keeping details of destinations, routes, cargoes, and estimated times of arrival under wraps for as long as was practical. Maybe it helped, but it didn't solve the problem. Clearly there was a leakage of information somewhere in the system. But then, so many people had to know. Pilots had to be instructed; flight plans had to be filed. Somehow, the pirates found out.

That first time Bertrams was targeted, Graves couldn't believe how angry he felt. It wasn't just the financial loss, it was the sense of helplessness. Of knowing it could happen again the next week or the next month, and unless he could come up with an answer, he'd be just as helpless to prevent it then as he had been this time.

In due course it did happen again. Planes were seized off runways and flown away to God knows where. Planes disappeared in midair, between one refueling stop and the next. Planes reached their destination, only to be taken over while the paperwork was being completed.

They weren't all Bertrams shipments, of course. They originated in various parts of Europe and were en route to various destinations in Africa. Most of the competitors Graves had talked to seemed to be losing a shipment once or twice a year—not enough to devastate the industry, not enough to send otherwise-sound companies to the wall, but easily enough that there was no other topic of conversation when arms manufacturers got together.

That was when the government started taking it seriously. Not seriously enough to send gunboats—that sort of thing got ex-colonial powers a bad name in these democratic days—but enough to set up a dedicated task force in Whitehall to analyze the threat and propose countermeasures. Which is how Stephen Graves and Gabriel Ash first met.

Then there was the woman: Ash's wife. If Ash was functioning again, holding her hostage might be all that was keeping the pirates safe. He was, at least he had been, that good. Graves had known it the first time they met. His grasp of the situation, the threat he represented to a major criminal enterprise on another continent, was greater by an order of magnitude than that of any other experts Graves had talked to. Taking Cathy Ash had crippled her husband for four years. Knowing she was still alive might keep him on the sidelines for as long again. Or it might not. Graves didn't know.

The doorbell rang. Graves flicked on the security screen. An elderly gray Volvo, and a man leaning close to the camera. Gabriel Ash. Not entirely unexpected, but still enough to send a jolt through Graves's spare frame. He went to the door.

"May we come in?"

Graves looked toward the car, expecting to see the young policewoman. But the car was empty, and while Graves was still looking, Ash walked past him into the hall. So did the white lurcher.

Graves found himself staring, and dragged his eyes away and upward. "Mr. Ash. Is there some news?"

"What news could there be?" asked Ash. "I don't know where my wife is. I don't know how to contact the people holding her. You do."

"Not exactly," protested Stephen Graves. "I did explain. The pirates contact me. I can't contact them."

"They contact the computer in Cambridge?" Graves nodded. "Why not here, or at your office?"

Graves thought it was obvious. "My wife might see what I was doing if I spoke to them from here. Someone in my office might if I used a computer at Bertrams."

"So you use a computer in an empty flat in Cambridge that belongs to a friend who's abroad."

"Yes."

"How long has she been abroad?"

Graves gave a hunted shrug. "A while. She asked me to keep an eye on the place until she got back."

"How long ago did the pirates make contact with you?"

"About three—no, four—months ago."

"That's when they showed you Cathy?"

Graves bowed his head. "Yes."

"And said what?"

They'd been over all this the day before. But Graves wasn't surprised if Ash had been unable to take it in. "That in return for her life they wanted information about forthcoming shipments— ours, and any others I heard about."

"And you agreed?"

"No, I didn't!" The flash of temper subsided as quickly as it had flared. "I'm sorry. No, of course I didn't agree. I said I was going to the police."

"What made you change your mind?"

The manufacturer chewed on his lip. "Mrs. Ash did. Except that I didn't know her name. All I knew was she was some poor terrified Englishwoman who'd somehow fallen into their hands, who was sitting shaking in front of the computer with an assault rifle stuck in her ear, begging me to help her. To do as they said, or they'd kill her in front of me. And she said . . ." He glanced at Ash and the words dried up.

There was something implacable in Ash's expression, a thread of steel in his voice. "What did she say?"

"She said she had two little boys. That she didn't know where they were, but the pirates had said they'd use them as hostages if they had to kill her. They'd put them in front of the computer and hurt them to get what they wanted."

There was a lengthy silence before Ash spoke again. "So you agreed."

Graves nodded, defeated. "I didn't want to. I tried to think of an alternative. I couldn't. They meant it—I knew they meant it, the woman knew they meant it. In the end, I suppose it was cowardice that made me agree. I couldn't bear to think that I was her only chance and I was going to let her down. To watch her die, knowing I'd let her down."

"What about the aircrew? The men flying the planes carrying these shipments. Did you think they'd be set free?" Ash's tone was hard. As if it wasn't his wife they were talking about, and his sons; as if he wouldn't have made the same choice himself.

Graves gave a miserable shrug. "I didn't know them. And I didn't know they were going to die. Didn't know for sure. And if they did, it would be thousands of miles away and I wouldn't be watching. I'm sorry. It seemed a lesser evil than condemning one frightened woman and her children."

Another of those long, painful pauses. The white dog padded softly across the carpet; it took an effort of will for Graves to ignore her as she walked behind him.

Ash said, "How do you know when the pirates want to talk to you?"

Graves produced his mobile phone. "On this. They give me a time to be online in Cambridge."

"How did they get that number?"

"They found it on the paperwork when they hijacked one of my shipments."

"And you really have no way of contacting them?"

Graves shook his head. "They route the calls through different servers in different parts of the world. I don't think an expert could find them. I know I couldn't."

Ash nodded slowly. "Then we'll wait till they contact you again. I don't think it'll be long, not now they know I've seen Cathy." He was scribbling on the back of an envelope. "This is my number. Call me as soon as you hear from them, and I'll meet you in Cambridge."

"All right."

From the front door of his house, Stephen Graves watched his visitors walk out to the gray car. His heart was pounding in his chest. In fact, though, things could have been worse. Ash might have turned up here with a contingent from the Counter Terrorism Command. Even the girl seemed to have more important things to do. And Ash alone wouldn't be rocking any boats. He had too much to lose.

As they reached the car, Gabriel Ash looked down at his dog. He said quietly, "Well, what do you think? Is that the man who shot at us?" Who had forced Hazel's car into a ditch on a remote country road and would have killed them both but that the lurcher drove him off.

Oh yes, said Patience decisively. I never forget a pair of trousers.

CHAPTER 6

A DAY AND A HALF PASSED in which nothing much happened. Nothing important, nothing strange, nothing upsetting. This was close to a record in Hazel's recent experience, but she was constrained from even a low-key celebration by a sense of deep unease. Something *should* be happening. More than that, she should be *making* something happen. She knew as surely as if she'd read the script that Ash was walking into more trouble than he was capable of handling; and maybe he was right, maybe there was nothing she could do to help, but she ought to be there for him. Ready to pick up the pieces when his world imploded.

It would be different if he'd had any realistic chance of success. But his wife was the prisoner of terrorists in a lawless state that was geographically and culturally remote. The video link was misleading: it gave the impression that the person you were talking to was accessible. But today, with much of the world within the orbit of one satellite or another, being able to see and speak to someone didn't mean you could reach them. If Cathy Ash's captors were routing their transmissions so as to mask their whereabouts, Hazel couldn't find them, and she knew a great deal more about information technology than Ash did. And if he couldn't find Cathy, he couldn't help her.

It was a cruel joke that was being played on him. Like dangling a toy just beyond a baby's grasp, or showing a dog a biscuit and then eating it yourself. He would do what they said, whatever the cost to himself, but they wouldn't keep their end of the bargain. They would keep his wife after they'd promised to return her. Or they would kill her because he hadn't done everything they'd wanted, or hadn't done it quickly enough. Or simply because they were finished with him, and it amused them. The bitter truth was that Cathy Ash would have been better off if she'd died four years ago. She was never coming home.

If Ash had asked Hazel what she honestly thought, she'd have told him. She'd have sat with him while he dealt with it; and maybe it would have taken all the strength he had left, but in the end whatever survived would be standing on rock, not quicksand. After the grieving was done he could think about moving forward.

But he hadn't asked her. He hadn't wanted to know what she thought. If she'd tried to tell him anyway, he'd have refused to listen. That was why he didn't want her around anymore: he didn't want to hear that all he could do was make things worse. He was sticking his fingers in his ears like a frightened child.

There's only one way to help a frightened child: hold it until the monsters go away. But Ash didn't want holding, at least not by her.

Thinking thus brought a bitter taste to Hazel's mouth, not because she thought Ash was behaving badly but because she suspected she was. She was angry with him, and that wasn't reasonable. Three months ago the man had barely functioned as a human being, torn to shreds by his warring emotions. Now he found himself in a situation that would have challenged someone with no emotions. And she had the gall to resent the fact that some of his decisions were not the ones she would have made for him?

"Grow up, Hazel Best," she growled at herself, climbing the stairs to her rooms at the top of Mrs. Poliakov's Villa Biala in Balfour Street.

With her key in the door, she froze. It felt wrong. The lock turned, but reluctantly, as if something had happened to it while she'd been out. Something, possibly, involving little bits of bent metal and 22-'loid credit cards.

She knew what she should do next. She knew what the sensible response was, and whatever her strengths and failings, she had always been irredeemably sensible. She should have backed quietly away and called Meadowvale from the bottom of the stairs.

Instead she threw the door wide, hard enough to stun anyone standing behind it, and strode quickly inside.

You have to say something when you might be surprising a burglar. She went with "All right, who's playing silly buggers?"

But there was no answer, and when she'd had time to take in her surroundings, for a moment Hazel felt rather foolish. There were no upended drawers in the middle of the floor, no drifts of books scattered across the rug. Crossing the sitting room to the bedroom beyond, she found no piles of clothes on the bed. There was no sign of any disturbance at all.

She paused to catch her breath and take stock. At a much calmer pace she walked around the entire flatlet—two rooms and a tiny bathroom—and checked everywhere that anyone could possibly be hiding, after which she was content that she had the place to herself. And everything looked just as it had when she went out.

It would have been easy to think she must have been mistaken. But Hazel knew what she'd felt when she put the key in the lock, and she knew where she'd felt that before—in basic training, when her tutors were preparing her for the various situations she'd be dealing with. She had no doubt that the lock had been tampered with, and it followed that someone had been in her rooms while she was out. Not Mrs. Poliakov, who had her own key, but someone with the knowledge and the tools to force an entry, and the skill and also the motive to conduct a search without leaving any sign of it. Upending drawers is the work of seconds. A search that is both thorough and undetectable takes much longer.

But she'd been out for only some fifty minutes. So he'd known exactly what he was looking for and hadn't bothered looking in places it couldn't be. It was no leap of intuition to get from there to the laptop Saturday had left with her.

But there were problems with that, and they presented themselves one after another when she sat down on the little two-seater sofa, its many cushions still arranged as she'd left them, and thought it through. She didn't have the laptop anymore. Until she handed it over to DI Gorman, only Saturday had known she'd ever had it. By the time Gorman could have mentioned it to anyone, it was no longer in her possession, so there would have been no point for anyone to break into her flat to look for it.

Besides, who would Gorman have mentioned it to? Someone at the council, to get a number for the developer working on the Dirty Nellie's plans. But would he have mentioned Hazel's involvement even in passing? Some clerk would look up a file, Gorman would phone the number, and he'd get . . . another clerk, probably. So he'd leave a message: a laptop handed in as lost and found, some plans on it, anybody missing one? Before long the message would reach the owner, who would call back and claim it.

And say . . . and say . . . and say, perhaps, that he'd like to send some flowers as a thank-you; who was it who found it?

Strictly speaking, DI Gorman shouldn't have given either her name or her address. But he knew her, and maybe that altered things. Maybe he thought she'd appreciate a bunch of flowers. Maybe he couldn't see what harm it would do.

That should have been the end of the matter. The fact that it wasn't, that instead of sending flowers, someone had broken into her flat, could have meant any number of things, but what it meant for certain was that this was no longer a simple case of restoring lost property to its rightful owner. Someone was behaving as if he had something to hide.

Hazel spent a little more time going through the evidence before her, to make sure she wasn't overreacting. Then she picked up the phone to call DI Gorman.

Then she put it down again. The only one she'd spoken to about this was Dave Gorman. And after she'd spoken to him, someone had come and given her flat a thoroughly professional search. Did she really want Gorman to know that she'd noticed?

The answers to two questions would tell her a lot more about what was going on, and would mean she could judge the honesty of the answers she was given to any other questions she asked. The Town Hall could give her the first piece of information. And just thinking about it carefully enough would give her the second.

She phoned the Town Hall, asked for the Planning Department. "The developer on the Dirty Nellie's proposal—can I have the name and address?"

The planning officer was a bit sniffy, though not about giving out the information, which was a matter of public record. "We're not calling it Dirty Nellie's anymore. We're calling it the Archway."

"Of course we are," said Hazel encouragingly. The developers were Fenimore & Newman, with an address in Birmingham. "And was it Mr. Fenimore or Mr. Newman who was in Norbold last week?"

"Neither. It was their structural engineer, Mr. Charles Armitage."

Googling him didn't tell her very much more. He was a man in his late forties, married, with three children, who lived in the Clent Hills and had worked for Fenimore & Newman for eleven years. Nothing about his photograph suggested he was a man who'd break into other people's flats.

But if he had, or if someone had on his behalf, what had he been looking for? He'd already got his laptop back, or at least he'd been told it had been found and was waiting for him. He knew before someone took lockpicks to Hazel's door that she no longer had his computer.

So he wanted to know—she was working this out as she went along—if she'd had a look at the contents before she handed it in. With a password like PASSWORD, it was entirely possible. And the way he'd know that, without asking her, was . . . yes. If she'd seen something he didn't want her to see, she'd have made a copy. He, or someone working for him, broke into her flat, looking for memory sticks.

Hazel went quickly to her own computer, opened the drawer where she kept her peripherals. It looked undisturbed, but then, so had the flat. Had someone copied them? It would have been the work of moments if he'd come prepared. But he wouldn't have found what he was looking for, only photos of family and friends and copies of work-related documents she might conceivably need again.

The next question was, would that have reassured him, or the very opposite? Would he have waded through the pictures of her father digging his garden, Pete Byrfield driving his cows, and Patience posing smugly against a variety of backdrops—she had no images of Ash, who hated being photographed—and read her essays on the future of community policing in twenty-first-century Britain, then celebrated with a stiff drink the fact that nobody so boring could represent any kind of a threat? Or would he have been concerned that finding nothing didn't mean there was nothing to find; rather, that she'd been clever enough to hide it where he wouldn't look?

"Mr. Armitage, Mr. Armitage"—she sighed, gazing at his photograph on her laptop screen—"what is it you're not telling me? You mislaid your laptop, you got it back within a few days, and still you were worried enough to turn burglar. Why? Besides all those plans and drawings and things, what the hell else did you have on that computer?"

CHAPTER 7

"THEY WANT TO TALK TO YOU." There was an audible shake in Stephen Graves's voice.

"When?"

"Now. Tonight." In fact, it was already Wednesday morning, if only just.

"Where?"

"The Cambridge flat."

"You'll meet me there?"

"Yes." Even to himself, Graves's voice must have sounded hesitant, because he repeated the word with added certainty. "Yes."

"I'll leave now. But it'll take me a couple of hours to get there."

"There's time. Just."

Ash looked at his watch. For a long time after leaving his job, he hadn't bothered wearing one. Time hadn't had much meaning for him. Only days ago he'd felt the need to reintegrate himself into the temporal continuum that ruled most people's days and used to govern his. He'd gone to the chest of drawers in his bedroom, straight to the watch his wife had given him. He hadn't looked at it for years, but he knew exactly where it was. Now it was on his wrist.

"All right," he said.

The dog watched expectantly as he dressed. He avoided meeting her gaze. "I can't take you. I don't know how long I'll be. I don't know if I'll be coming straight back."

Patience said nothing, just held him in her steady golden gaze.

"I'll leave the back door open." There was little in his house that was worth stealing. "If I'm not going to be back by morning, I'll ask Hazel to come around and feed you. . . ."

That pulled him up short, like dropping a mental anchor. He couldn't call Hazel. He'd told her he didn't want her help. If he called now, to ask her to look after Patience, she'd think him a hypocrite for using her when it suited him, excluding her when it didn't. She'd say that he presumed on a friendship that he only ever acknowledged on his own terms.

And then she'd come around and look after Patience.

Knowing that didn't make him feel much better as he let himself out of the house, pausing only to check that he had his phone.

H e didn't even have the courage to speak to her. Eight o'clock that morning found Hazel sitting on her bed, fuming, with the text on her knee. After all they'd been through together. After everything she'd forgiven him for—and everything, to be fair, he'd forgiven her. And now he couldn't pick up the phone and say, "Look, when I said I didn't need any more help, I may have been a bit premature."

Instead he sent her a text. "Can you feed Patience? Possibly next few days. Will let you know. Back door open. Thanks." And he signed it *Ash*. That was all. No apology, no explanation, just a blithe assumption that she'd fit in with his plans.

Furious as she was, Hazel almost texted back immediately: "Busy—get someone else." But there was no one else, unless you counted Laura Fry and the perennially unreliable Saturday. If she refused, probably Patience would go hungry.

Scowling, Hazel put her shoes on and went downstairs and out to her car. But she was damned if she was going to call Ash to confirm that she was prepared to tidy up his loose ends once again.

Childishness is a contagious disease.

H azel looked at the dog, and the dog looked at Hazel. Hazel blinked first. "Well, you've had your breakfast and you've been out. You've got water, and you've got your basket, and, God help me, I've even plumped up the cushions on the sofa, which, if you were *my* dog, I wouldn't let you sit on. What else can you possibly want?"

Patience didn't answer. But she did continue looking at Hazel in the expectant way that a dog has when it knows that if it can be patient enough for long enough, its human will finally understand.

Hazel's forehead wrinkled in a doubtful frown. "You want to come with me?"

A wave of the scimitar tail suggested she was getting warmer.

"You want to come *home* with me?"

Dogs don't nod. A flicker in the steady golden gaze *suggested* a nod.

"You can't," Hazel said firmly. "Whatever would my landlady say? Anyway, Gabriel will be back soon enough. He'll throw a wobbly if he gets in and you're not here."

The lurcher wasn't giving up. There was nothing remotely aggressive about her stance or even her persistence, but she had the air of someone who would stand on the bridge as long as it took for the bodies of all her enemies to float underneath.

"No," said Hazel firmly. "I'll come back, I'll keep checking on you till he gets home, but you have to stay here. I can't do what I have to do with a damn great dog in tow!"

Ten minutes later they were driving back through Norbold, Patience on the backseat like the queen on a state visit, Hazel working out how she could do what she had to do with a damn great dog in tow.

She could have called Charles Armitage to ask if he'd sent someone to search her flat and, if so, what it was he'd hoped to find. But Hazel had learned her trade from some good teachers, men and women who'd policed Britain at a time when information technology was the landline telephone, the lapel radio, and a copy of the local A to Z; who hadn't grown up thinking that the answers to most questions should be no more than a couple of clicks away; and who therefore knew the art of discovering information for themselves, often from people who didn't want to part with it.

And one of the best bits of advice she'd been given had been: Try not to ask a question until you have at least some idea what the answer should be. Then you'll know if you're being told porkies, and who's worried enough to be telling them.

Or she could have swallowed her misgivings and gone to DI Gorman. Until she'd got home and found her key catching in her door, she'd never had reason to doubt his integrity, even at a time when the rest of Meadowvale was treating her as a pariah. The fact remained, the only connection between Hazel and the owner of the laptop was Dave Gorman.

Plus, of course, all the paperwork that attended even something as simple as restoring a bit of lost property to a careless visitor. Once Gorman had recorded who'd handed the machine in, almost anyone in the police station could have accessed the information. Still, she was reluctant to pour anything more into a bucket she thought might be leaking.

There was one thing she'd noticed that might lead her somewhere: the remarkable tidiness of her flat after the search. That wasn't a couple of local hoodlums hired for twenty quid apiece; that was a professional job.

The British police have an odd relationship with private investigators. Officially they're dismissive, on the grounds that anything that needs investigating is the preserve of the police and paying a private investigator to investigate anything else is like pushing money down a manhole. Unofficially, though, there is often a kind of guarded respect between them, not least because many private investigators are retired police officers.

A retired police officer would know how a search should be conducted, and would have the time to do it properly.

Hazel presented herself at the front desk just as Sergeant Murchison was coming on duty. She thought she saw him wince, but she might have been mistaken. For one thing, he owed her. Until she worked out how the recent death in custody had come about, much of the responsibility had hovered over Donald Murchison's shoulders. One day he would be grateful to her.

Perhaps it was a little soon for gratitude. But as long as she stayed this side of the counter, she was a member of the public and he was there to serve her. Worse, she was a member of the public who *knew* he was there to serve her.

"Hazel," he acknowledged cautiously. "How can I help you?"

"I need the name of a reliable private investigator. Ex-job. Discretion and professionalism more important than cost. Anyone come to mind?"

If a genuine member of the public had asked him that, Murchison would have referred her to the Yellow Pages rather than make a recommendation. But Hazel Best was still, more or less, a colleague. He'd need a reason not to help her out, and he couldn't think of one quickly enough. "What's it to do with?"

She was ready for that one. "Lost property."

Sergeant Murchison relaxed, just a little. "I suppose. . . ."

"Yes?"

"I suppose you could try Martha. . . ."

Martha Harris wasn't everyone's idea of a private investigator. But then, she hadn't been everyone's idea of a detective sergeant either, certainly not twenty years before, when she first came to Norbold on promotion from Newcastle. She was a woman at a time when most detectives were male; even in her twenties she was somewhat stocky, at a time when women were still judged first by their looks and only then by their abilities; and finally, though a quick temper had got her into trouble on a number of occasions, she was plainly a kind woman. No one raised on cop shows expected that of an ambitious female detective.

Now she was twenty years older, significantly fatter, and curious to discover what Hazel wanted. While she waited, she pushed the second half of a box of chocolates across the desk in her visitor's direction. "Help yourself, pet. Them ones in gold foil are good."

Hazel put on her friendliest smile and took a strawberry cream instead. "Ms. Harris, do you know who I am?"

The other woman considered for a moment before nodding. "Aye, pet, I do."

"Then you know I'm a police officer."

Another thoughtful pause. "Who you are, what you do, what you did."

Hazel's smile never wavered. "Did you know that when you broke into my flat?"

This time the pause was much longer. Martha Harris reached out and took another chocolate. It was the last one in gold foil. "I didn't break anything," she said eventually.

"That's how I know it was you."

It's a sad fact of policing that almost the only compliments you get are from other police officers. Those who go solo forfeit even that meager source of appreciation. Ms. Harris offered half a smile in acknowledgment. "Off the record?"

"For now," conceded Hazel carefully.

"I didn't know you were job when I took the man's shilling. When I realized, I gave it back."

"I don't suppose it would do me any good to ask what man?"

The smile broadened. "No, pet."

"What were you looking for? When you didn't break into my flat."

The investigator considered at length before answering that one. She decided that she could, in a general way, because she had not identified the client. "Photographs."

Hazel wasn't expecting that. "Photographs of what?"

Martha Harris shrugged. "Digital ones, on any sticks and discs I could find. But actually, it was the photos on your mantelpiece that told me who you were."

Hazel frowned. "How?"

The older woman gave her an old-fashioned look. "The dog, pet. I've lived in this town for twenty years, but if I'd only lived here six months, I'd have recognized that dog. Gabriel Ash not so much, but his dog? Easy. And who was going to have pictures of Gabriel Ash's dog? Gabriel Ash's friend. Constable Best, who took on Norbold's senior police officer *and* its last godfather, and won."

"It didn't feel much like winning," said Hazel wryly.

"You're alive, aren't you? And they're not. From where I'm sitting, that's a big-time win."

"So what did you give him?" asked Hazel. "This client you're not going to identify."

"Nothing," said Martha immediately. "I told you. As soon as I realized you were job, I was out of there. I didn't copy nothing. I didn't even look at anything that you didn't have framed and on show. I returned his retainer and told him to think again. I haven't heard from him since. I'm not expecting to."

"And that's all he asked you for—digital photographs?"

"Aye. I had a bloody great EHD with me, so I could copy everything I found. But I never got it out the bag. I wasn't in the flat five minutes."

Hazel nodded slowly, taking it in. An explanation of a kind, but more questions raised than answered. And apart from the one thing she knew Martha Harris would never tell her, and Martha didn't know that she already knew, she didn't think the woman was holding anything back. "All right. We can leave it there, for now.

"Just one thing," she added, turning in the doorway. Martha

raised an interrogative eyebrow. "You're a neat worker. But next time you break into someone's flat—"

"I didn't break anything," interjected Martha firmly.

"*Next* time you break into someone's flat, don't leave it tidier than you found it."

CHAPTER 8

CHARLES ARMITAGE HAD MISLAID HIS LAPTOP, Hazel had handed it in to the police, and within days the structural engineer had it back. But instead of sending flowers as a thank-you, he'd hired a private investigator to search her flat for photographs. The only possible conclusion was that he had pictures on that laptop that he *really* didn't want people seeing.

Hazel had bought herself a box of chocolates on the way home. The ones in gold foil were indeed particularly good. The white dog was curled up at the other end of the sofa, not begging—which she clearly thought beneath her—just close at hand if anything happened to be going spare. Hazel knew chocolate is toxic to dogs. Every so often, as she mulled over what she knew and what she thought, she offered Patience one of the little pink wafers, and the dog graciously accepted.

The plans for Dirty Nellie's might be commercially sensitive. But did structural engineers resort to burglary to protect commercially sensitive information from someone who wasn't even a competitor? Burglary was a panic reaction that seemed less like a company defending its legitimate interests and more like an individual caught with his pants down.

Mr. Charles Armitage, successful professional and family man, had been doing something he shouldn't with someone he shouldn't, and had been unwise enough to keep the evidence as a file of photos on his laptop. And now he was afraid he was going to be blackmailed.

As simple as that? He had a bit on the side, he'd taken photographs of her—maybe he'd taken photographs of them together—and now he thought he'd lose everything if copies reached his wife? Hazel sniffed indignantly. Did Armitage really think she had nothing better to do than point out his shortcomings to a wife who was almost certainly aware of them already? With very little encouragement, Hazel would have called him up to tell him so.

But as she thought about it, and took a certain amount of satisfaction from the panic she would hear in his voice before he realized this was as bad as it was going to get, wiser counsels prevailed. It was one of those "Least said, soonest mended" occasions. If, like Patience pretending she'd never liked chocolate anyway, Hazel exhibited no interest in Charles Armitage's affairs—in both senses of the word—she fully expected he would lose interest in her. And that would be best.

They're alive, Ash. Your wife is alive. Your sons are alive."

"Yes." He'd seen them. After four years, he'd seen them, alive and, as far as he could see, well. He wouldn't have recognized the boys if he'd bumped into them in the park, but Cathy wouldn't have lied. She'd stood them in front of the Webcam for a minute, then ushered them away into some other room. She hadn't wanted them to hear what she had to say to him.

She'd been supplied with more of the cards. She sat down facing the computer and read them out one by one. Ash thought she already knew what was on them. Her voice was breaking before she got to the punch line.

"You don't have to do what they want." There was no emotion in Stephen Graves's tone, only the careful emptiness of someone who has passed through shock and out the other end. "It's asking too much. No one would blame you if you decided this . . . conversation . . . never happened."

"You didn't," Ash reminded him. His voice was oddly flat, as if it was a straight choice between that and screaming. "You decided Cathy's life was worth more than your business, more than your honor, and she wasn't even your wife."

Graves was dismissive. "A business is only money. Honor is only a notion. I wouldn't have given what they're asking of you."

"She's my wife," Ash said simply. "They're my sons."

Graves regarded him somberly. "You're serious? You're prepared to . . . pay their price?"

Ash didn't have to think about it. "I have no choice."

"You don't even know . . ." Graves had to stop and clear his throat. "You don't know that they'll do what they say they'll do. Even if you do everything they ask, how can you be sure they'll send your family home?"

"They'll have to convince me. Nothing will happen until I *am* sure."

Graves had no idea how Ash intended to get guarantees he could believe in. But he had no doubt that Ash could structure the deal to his satisfaction. This was the security analyst he'd first met five years ago, not the pale imitation who'd occupied his skin for much of the intervening time.

"But *how*? I heard what they had Cathy say, too. That they'll send her and your boys home as soon as . . . as soon as they feel safe. But for God's sake, man, you can't just take their word for it! What makes you think you can trust them?"

Ash regarded him with a fine scorn. The apologetic stoop was gone, leaving him a bigger man than Graves remembered. "I *don't* trust them, Mr. Graves. But I can ensure that they don't get what they want until I've got what I want."

Graves shook his narrow head in appalled wonder. "But how?"

Ash gave him a chilly, remote smile. "It's funny you should ask that. . . ."

Mrs. Poliakov regarded Patience gravely. Patience regarded Mrs. Poliakov in much the same way. Hazel held her counsel, and her breath.

Finally the landlady said firmly, "No dogs. It says in the tenancy agreement. No dogs."

"Yes, it does," Hazel had to agreed. "Which wasn't a problem eight months ago, because I didn't have a dog then."

"You said this is not your dog now." Mrs. Poliakov sounded suspicious.

"And that's true," Hazel said quickly. "She belongs to a friend of mine. He's having a really difficult time, he needs me to look after her, but it's only a temporary arrangement. He'll take her back as soon as he can."

"Your friend Mr. Ash."

Slightly stung by the implication that she might have only the one, Hazel nodded nevertheless. "Yes. Mr. Ash."

"The crazy man."

"He's not . . ." But there was no point. Hazel sighed. "It's not Gabriel Ash I want to keep in my flat for a few days, it's Patience.

She's very quiet, she's very clean, and if she causes you any problems, I'll think of something else to do with her. But I'd consider it a favor if you'd let me keep her here."

Mrs. Poliakov bent in the middle to take a closer look. She was a middle-aged Polish woman who'd lived in England for so long that it had required a real effort of will to keep her accent. "What sort of a dog is it?"

It was the first chink in her armor. And Hazel wasn't the only one to notice it: Patience waved her scimitar tail, just once, decorously.

"She's a lurcher. Saturday says she's a gentleman's lurcher—a pointer cross."

"Saturday?"

That was going to take too much explaining. And while Hazel thought her landlady just might soften to Patience in the end, she knew she'd chase the street kid down her steps with a broom. "Just someone I know. His granddad was a dog expert, apparently."

"A gentleman's lurcher, hmm." There was a bit of Mrs. P. that was unreconstructed snob. It wasn't a small bit. The magic word swung the balance. "One bark in the night, she goes," she said sternly. "One unmentionable on the carpet, she goes. She chew my furniture, you both go."

"It's a deal," said Hazel, relieved; and Patience waved her tail again, just the once.

Balfour Street, where Hazel shared the three-story Victorian villa with Mrs. P. and two other tenants, was on the far side of Norbold from Highfield Road, with its leafy gardens and nearby park. But the canal ran along the back, and since the Rivers Agency had restored the waterway and the council had tidied up the towpath it was a pleasant strip of open space, a rural finger tracing its route through the postindustrial town.

It was popular with narrow boat enthusiasts, with ramblers, and with dog walkers. Hazel lost no time introducing Patience to its charms.

Half a mile up the towpath, with the houses thinning as the eastern edge of town approached, Hazel was less surprised than she might have been to see the thin, always slightly shifty figure in its misleading rugby shirt strolling nonchalantly toward her, toes visible through a hole in one trainer.

"I didn't know you knew about this place," said Hazel by way of a greeting.

"'S public property," said Saturday defensively, shoving his hands deep into the pockets of his jeans.

"I didn't mean that," said Hazel, starting to apologize before she realized she had nothing to apologize for. "I thought the park was your preferred hangout."

The boy shrugged. "The park's good. The canal's good."

Hazel couldn't think what he found it good for. Even after the Rivers Agency's efforts, a hook dropped into the water was more likely to catch a shopping trolley than a fish; and anyone planning to mug the walkers had better be stronger and faster than the brisk, no-nonsense senior citizens who frequented the towpath, or he'd find himself tipped into the canal.

On the other hand, he knew where she lived. "Were you looking for me?"

"No," Saturday said quickly. He looked around him rather than meet her eye. "Jeez, a guy can't even get a bit of fresh air without being accused of something."

"Okay," she said mildly; but she knew she was right, and when he fell into step beside her, she knew it was only a matter of time before he told her what was on his mind.

Where a bridge took the Coventry road over the canal, someone had parked a chip van. The legend on the side read WINKWORTH'S MOBILE CATERING, but it was still a chip van. With lunchtime imminent, Hazel bought sausage and chips for two, then remembered there were three of them and asked for extra sausages. But she was damned if she was buying the dog a mug of tea as well.

Winkworth was doing a roaring trade in the sunshine, and all the nearby benches were taken. They wandered a little farther up the towpath and, on the far side of the bridge, sat down on the edge, dangling their legs over the water and defending their chips from a particularly determined swan.

Finally Saturday said, "You handed the laptop in, then." Hazel nodded. "Anybody claim it?"

"The DI worked out who it belonged to and sent it to him."

There was a longer than expected pause. Had Saturday been hoping to get it back? It wasn't as if he had anywhere to charge it. "So he got into it?"

Hazel dipped her sausage in ketchup. "There wasn't much of a password. There were plans on it, for a development here in town. It belonged to someone from the architect's office."

"And the coppers gave it back to him."

"'Fraid so," said Hazel, briskly unsympathetic. She could have gone on to tell him about her break-in, but there seemed no point. And Saturday would never be a reliable confidant. If she'd wanted any more doing about it, she'd have done it herself; and if she didn't want anything doing, she certainly didn't want anyone gossiping about it.

There was a long pause. So long that she began to think the conversation was over and the youth was simply hanging around in the hope of getting an ice cream to follow his sausage and chips. But no. Saturday wasn't here because he was interested in narrow boats. He'd come looking for her, and he hadn't yet got around to saying why.

Finally, with the air of someone being forced to play both sides of a chessboard because his opponent was too dim to do her share, he said, "What about the pictures?"

Hazel hadn't guessed he was interested in architecture, either. She shrugged. "I told you. They're redeveloping Dirty Nellie's. Offices, shops, flats. Why?" She grinned. "Thinking of putting your name down for one?"

As soon as it was out, Hazel wished it unsaid. It had only been a bit of banter. If she'd said it to Ash, or Ash had said it to her, it would have been obvious as such. But both of them had homes, and Saturday did not, and that meant it wasn't a joking matter. You have to be a very close friend before you ask a man with no legs when he's trying out for Manchester United.

Saturday gave her a long sideways look. But before she could marshal an apology he said, with a kind of heavy patience, as if he was going to make her understand if it killed him, "Not those pictures. The other pictures. The pictures he shouldn't have had. The ones he had hidden behind the second password."

CHAPTER 9

DISTRACTEDLY, HAZEL WENT TO GIVE THE REST of her chips to the swan. It was only the dog's reproachful look that stopped her. So she gave them to Patience, but really she didn't care who ate them as long as she could concentrate on Saturday's bombshell.

She turned to face him, and waited until his shifting gaze settled somewhere near hers. "There was a second password?"

"Sure," he said negligently. As if none of this really mattered. As if he hadn't been walking up and down this towpath, possibly for hours, in order to have this conversation with her.

"How do you know?"

"I hacked it."

This was the first she'd heard about the boy as computer wizard. But then, he was from the generation that had grown up with computers. Before he was a street kid, he was just a kid, going to school and doing IT classes and learning even more from his mates behind the bicycle sheds.

"How?"

He looked at her askance. "A guy who uses PASSWORD as

his password, he's not suddenly going to use a quadratic equation to lock his vault."

Hazel thought about it. Children's names, pets' names, birthdays—most people used one or another of them, but Saturday wouldn't have known that sort of information about Charles Armitage. So . . . "DROWSSAP?" she asked faintly.

Saturday grinned. "Tragic, innit?"

All this was a little beside the point, except as evidence that the rest of it, the important stuff, was not a figment of the boy's imagination. "All right. So you got into his vault, and it was full of pictures. We're not talking family snaps here, are we?"

"Jesus, I hope not!"

And they weren't talking about Mr. Armitage's mistress, either. Saturday might have spent an inordinate amount of time studying pictures like that, but he wouldn't have involved Hazel if that was all he'd found. He'd found something that even someone with a street kid's flexible morality felt he had to do something about.

"Children? Saturday—were they pictures of children?"

He wasn't grinning now. He nodded and looked away.

"Children being abused?" Again the nod. "Sexually?"

"Yes!" he shot back, angry and embarrassed. "All right? Little kids, some of them. And girls pretending to be all grown-up, except they're clutching a teddy bear in their free hand. It isn't right, Hazel. Not when they're that little. I don't want to be a prude, but . . . that's not right."

"No, it isn't." It never occurred to Hazel to doubt the truth of what he was telling her. She knew he was perfectly capable of lying, cheating, and stealing, but she didn't think he was lying about this. It was too serious—a thing even Saturday regarded as beyond the pale. "How many pictures did you see?"

He shrugged. "A fraction of what was there."

Child protection is a specialist field, online child protection even more so, but Hazel had covered the basics in training and—with her IT background—seen more of it than most probationers. More than enough, though if she returned to policing she would undoubtedly see more. She understood now why the boy had been so determined to pass a valuable piece of equipment on to the police. It had been a good and brave thing he'd done, when much the easiest thing would have been to drop the thing in the canal.

Because it was a police matter. The children could be half a world away, possibly beyond any help Hazel could hope to send them, but the men fueling the trade—and they were mainly, though not exclusively, men—were everywhere. They were in England; they were in Norbold. They were in nice houses like the ones in Highfield Road and in modest flats like hers. They had jobs and friends and workmates, and most of them had families, and hardly any of those people knew about their little hobby, or would have believed if they were told. They were someone to have a drink with, to play darts with, to have around for a meal. They were the men who didn't mind dating a girl with kids. Sometimes they were the husband and father who was happy to keep coaching the junior swimmers, though his own kids had now left home.

They were that nice professional gent in the architect's office who'd pick your kids up from school if you were running late.

"Saturday, we have to take this to Meadowvale. To DI Gorman."

The boy's eyes flared, afraid. "No way!"

"We have to. It's too serious to ignore."

"I didn't ignore it. I gave the laptop to you."

"I thought it was just lost property! I didn't know it was evidence of a crime!"

They were shouting at each other, enough to draw curious glances. Hazel lowered her voice. "It never occurred to me that you wanted me to pick it apart. When we saw the drawings and realized where it had come from, we thought it was just a matter of getting it back to him. I'm sorry, Saturday, but we need to see DI Gorman right away."

"You tell him." There was a nasal whine in the boy's voice.

"I will," promised Hazel. "I'll explain everything. But he'll need to talk to you. You saw these things and I didn't. He won't be angry with you. Why would he be?" She got to her feet, pulled Saturday to his.

And it was through her hand on his arm that she felt his spare muscles bunch, ready to flee. She said softly, "If you run, I will come after you. We have to deal with this, and we have to do it now."

After a moment, Saturday nodded. They walked back to Balfour Street and collected Hazel's car.

Detective Inspector Gorman had them shown up right away. It was almost, Hazel thought, as if he was expecting her. But the boy trailing reluctantly behind her like a pram dinghy behind a frigate took him by surprise.

He had his mouth open to say one thing, then thought better of it and shut it. He waved them to chairs on the opposite side of his desk. "Er . . ."

Hazel waited another moment, politely, before embarking on the explanation she'd prepared. "This is my friend Saul Desmond.

You may know him as Saturday. He's the one who left that lap-top for me to bring in." She was pleased with that. It was perfectly accurate, without contradicting anything she'd told the DI previ-ously. "And the reason he wanted us to have it instead of selling it to some guy in a pub"—Saturday kept his eyes averted—"is that he's got better instincts for criminality than the two of us put to-gether. He accessed it the same way we did. But instead of seeing who the owner was and shutting it down, he found a second set of files behind a second password. Those were the ones he wanted you to see."

Dave Gorman blinked. He'd thought, when he heard Hazel was at the front desk, that he knew how the next few minutes were going to go. But it wasn't like this. "Why?"

Hazel turned to Saturday; Saturday remained fixated on a tear in the left knee of his jeans. Hazel sighed. "Because they're full of images of child pornography. Scores of them."

Police officers dedicated to the pursuit of criminals and the prevention of crime cannot decently admit to smacking their lips at any lawbreaking. Among themselves, though, a certain relish may be detected at the prospect of a good jewel heist to solve or a clever art robbery. There are those who positively look forward to working on a good old-fashioned bank job or a brilliant con.

But nobody wants to investigate child abuse. They do it be-cause decent police officers, like all decent people, want it dealt with as efficiently as possible, and the perpetrators put where they can do no more harm. No one wants to work on cases like that, but when they do, no one has to ask them to stay late. Detectives who can normally stretch a lunch hour until three can be seen eating sandwiches at their desks. They abandon all hope of a private life until they're sure they've done everything they can.

"You didn't see these images?" Gorman asked Hazel.

"No."

"And he didn't tell you about them when he gave you the laptop?"

"No," Hazel said again. "Mr. Gorman, I know this boy. I know he isn't lying. He's got nothing to gain by lying. He could have sold the laptop and neither you nor I would ever have known. Fifty quid, eighty quid in his pocket. That's a lot to someone like Saturday. He'd need a good reason not to do that. Well, this is it. What he saw on that computer. He may not be your idea of a model citizen, but this struck him as important enough to do the right thing."

"Why didn't you tell us what was on it?" This time the detective was looking straight at the boy.

Saturday mumbled something in reply.

"What?"

The boy looked up with a sudden hawklike fierceness. "Because," he enunciated sharply, "it never occurred to me for one frigging minute that you wouldn't frigging look!"

Gorman had Saturday repeat in grueling detail exactly what he'd seen. He prepared a witness statement, which Saturday, under a kind of weary protest, signed. They had a certain amount of difficulty with the witness's address, until Hazel volunteered her own, fervently hoping that Mrs. Poliakov would never get to hear of it.

"You going to arrest him now?" asked Saturday, adding with a fine disdain, "The dirty bugger."

"I'm certainly going to bring him in for questioning. And seize his laptop." DI Gorman glanced at Hazel. "The problem is, of course, that he's had time to cover his tracks."

"It's pretty hard to erase things from a hard drive so completely that an expert can't find them," Hazel pointed out.

"This isn't some middle-aged creep running a second life from his back bedroom," said Gorman shortly. "He's a professional man." He might have said more, but there were things he would say to Hazel that he wouldn't say in front of the teenager.

"I know who he is," retorted Saturday. "Charles Armitage. Every file on the desktop had his name on it, for God's sake. I also know what he is."

Gorman scowled. "All right. Well, Mr. Armitage is also a well-connected professional man. If he needs technical help, he can buy it. If he needs the kind of technical help that'll keep its mouth shut afterward, he can buy that. And if he needs a steamroller to flatten his old laptop and give him an excuse to buy a new one, well, he works on building sites every day, doesn't he?"

"We'd still have Saturday's statement." Doubt was seeping into Hazel's voice.

"Yes," said Dave Gorman. He said nothing more. He didn't have to. If it came to a straight choice between believing responsible, professional, middle-class Charles Armitage and believing a street kid who needed to borrow an address to put on his witness statement, a jury that found Saturday's evidence credible would probably believe in unicorns and the tooth fairy as well.

The DI got up. He opened his door and waved to a passing constable. "Show Mr. Desmond the way out, will you?" But as Hazel went to follow, he shut the door again, almost in her face. She turned, startled, and his expression took her completely off guard. Intense, concerned, a hint of dread pinching the small muscles beside the eyes. "You don't know, do you?"

Hazel stared at him in astonishment. "Know what?"

"It's been all over the Internet all morning." Gorman pursed his lips. "But I suppose you've been busy. . . ."

"*What's* been all over the Internet?"

"Your friend Ash," said Dave Gorman, and Hazel's stomach dropped into her boots.

She dragged up a heard-it-all-before voice to hide behind. "What's he done now?"

CHAPTER 10

FIFTEEN MINUTES LATER DAVE GORMAN leaned forward and turned the screen off. The absolute silence that washed back into the small, untidy room was almost tangible.

He waited for her to say something. But Hazel had lost the power of speech. She'd almost lost the power of thought. She just sat there in stunned silence, staring at the blank screen with gritty, dry eyes, as if she, too, was waiting.

For what? For Gorman to give a sudden chuckle and say, "Don't look so serious, it's just a joke"? For the door to bang suddenly open and all the people who thought they owed her a slap to pour through it blowing whoopee whistles? For the DI to advance a kindly hand as far as her trembling wrist and say, "Don't worry, we won't let it come to that," and mean it?

None of those things was going to happen, and somewhere in her tiny icy heart Hazel knew it. Those few brain cells that were still operating knew it. It wasn't a joke, and it wasn't a mistake, and it wasn't Meadowvale getting its own back, and Dave Gorman wasn't going to say that he was in a position to prevent it. The most he could say, the very most, was that he'd try to prevent it; and though she waited, achingly, he didn't even say that.

What he said eventually, when one of them had to say something and it was becoming clear that Hazel wasn't going to, was, "It may be some kind of a delaying tactic. He may not intend to go through with it."

Hazel blinked. Then she cleared her throat. Her voice still didn't sound much like her: thin and frail yet utterly convinced. "He intends to go through with it."

Gorman leaned closer, studying her face. "How can you know that? Have you spoken to him?"

"About . . . this?" She shook her head, the girlish fair hair tossing. "About his wife and sons, yes. He was always ready to do anything that would bring them home. He told me once he'd have gladly killed himself if that would bring them home. The only thing stopping him was that he wouldn't know if it had worked. If the Somalis would realize he was out of their way.

"Well, he knows now." She swallowed, looked up at Gorman. "I'm understanding this right, am I? They've contacted him. They've said Cathy and the boys can come home if he . . . if he . . ." She couldn't say the words.

"Yes," said the DI, and his naturally rather coarse voice was gentle. "That's what they say. Why would he believe them?"

"Because they have nothing to gain by holding his family if Gabriel is"—this time she got it out—"dead. They were hostages to his good behavior, the means of keeping him off the pirates' backs. If he's no longer a threat to them, they don't need to hold on to the people he loves."

"They could still kill them," warned Gorman. "It would be easier than sending them home."

Hazel nodded. "Gabriel will know that. He'll make sure he's getting what he wants before he gives them what they want."

"How?"

"I don't know. But he'll find a way. Don't underestimate him. People around here think he's a fool. He's not. He never was."

Gorman was nodding slowly. "I know that. But it's a big ask, to outwit people as ruthless as that when they're holding something so important that you're prepared to die for it."

The immediate shock was passing. In its wake Hazel felt a terrible sense of urgency. "We have to find him. He will do it, when he's sure Cathy and the boys are safe. He'll do exactly what he's agreed to—kill himself, live on the Internet. We have to find him and stop him. Where did that package come from?"

"The IT guys are working on that right now," Gorman assured her. "Only . . ."

This was Hazel's field. "Only, it may not be possible to establish exactly where he was talking from; and even if it is, he may not still be there when we get there."

"In a nutshell," agreed Gorman. "Hazel, you know him better than anyone. Where would he go? If he needed not to be disturbed while he worked on this? He must have known we'd hear about it as soon as it went viral, and he'll know we're trying to find him. Where would he go if he didn't want to be found?"

"I don't know!" When she first knew him, Gabriel Ash's world had shrunk to a half-mile radius centered on his house and extending no farther than the park, the nearest shops, and his therapist's office. She knew he'd had a life before that, and friends, and probably places he went. But the life had collapsed in on itself when his family disappeared; the friends had been defeated, their attempts to help or console rejected, and had drifted away; and in the months she'd known him, the only times he'd left Norbold he'd been with her. "Is someone watching his house?"

"Of course."

"What about the house in London? Covent Garden, I think. Does he still own that?"

Gorman made a note. "I'll find out. Even if he doesn't, I'll have the Met check it, just in case. Good. Anywhere else?"

"The flat in Cambridge?"

"What flat in Cambridge?"

So she told him. She kept the explanation brief and to the point; even so, there was time for his expression to grow from compassionate to thunderous. Laura Fry had been right: she should have told him before.

"You're telling me the CEO of one of the arms companies that lost shipments was helping the hijackers? And you've known this for four days, *and you didn't see fit to share it with me?*"

"I'm sorry." She meant that. "He said they'd kill her. Ash's wife. Graves said if we went to the police, the pirates would kill her."

Gorman went on glaring at her, but there was nothing he could usefully say. He knew that the only responsible reaction to a hostage situation is to ensure that the kidnappers gain nothing by it. He knew Hazel knew that. He also knew that, when it's personal, all the responsible, moral, above all *right* arguments in the world aren't worth a row of beans. Confronted by a sobbing, terrified image of the wife he'd thought was dead, Gabriel Ash had been incapable of entrusting her fate to the police; and what Ash couldn't do, Hazel Best wouldn't do. Gorman was entitled to be angry; but he knew that if the same situation arose again, the outcome would be exactly the same.

The same situation was never going to arise again.

He reached for the telephone.

Hazel didn't know the address of the Cambridge flat. She

described, to three different people, how to find it. None of them shouted at her, but the strain of not doing so came right down the phone line at her. Like hands clamped around her throat, it left her white-faced and trembling because she knew now that she'd been wrong, and what being wrong on this scale was going to cost.

By the time Gorman had finished making phone calls, some of his anger had subsided. She was a young, inexperienced police probationer who was on extended sick leave because previous traumas had left her emotionally fragile. He was surprised that she hadn't behaved like a hardened officer of ten years' standing? That she'd behaved like a human being and a friend instead?

"Cambridge will have someone at the flat in five minutes. Do you think they'll find him?"

Hazel chewed her lip. She desperately wanted to be able to say yes, but she couldn't. "I don't think he'll be anywhere I know about. He may have gone there once more, to tell the pirates how to contact him directly, but after that, all he needed was access to the Internet. He can get that anywhere—why would he risk going somewhere I could find him? He knows I'll stop him if I can. He'll be in a motel somewhere, or a lockup that he's hired for cash down, or . . . hell, if he was a bit more up-to-date he could do it all through a smartphone. I don't know how we're ever going to find him in time."

Gorman said slowly, "Maybe he isn't the one we should be looking for."

Hazel almost managed indignation. "Of *course* we should be looking for him! However hard it's going to be, we can't just abandon him. These people are *killing* him—murdering him. The fact that they're using his own hand to do it doesn't alter that!"

"That's not what I mean," said the DI quickly. "What I mean

is, Ash is going to need help. To make sure his family is safe before he does anything . . . irreversible. Someone to meet them and let him know they're okay. That person may be easier to find. Who would he ask? To do something that difficult, that dangerous, that emotionally demanding. Who would he turn to?"

There was no stopping the tears now. It was the final straw, the ultimate betrayal of their friendship. Hazel felt as if the last thing Gabriel Ash had done before organizing his public suicide was slap her face. "Me," she sobbed. "I didn't know there was anyone else."

Gorman brought her coffee in a horrible little waxed-paper cup. She used the time it took to drink it to pack her emotions back in the box and hammer the lid down.

Finally, when her composure was more or less restored, the DI said, "Hazel, you know we'll do everything we can. But if we aren't successful, promise me faithfully that you won't blame yourself. None of this is your fault."

And perhaps it wasn't. But she was a compassionate young woman, and if she couldn't save Ash, if this happened despite her best efforts, she would feel all her life that she'd let him down.

"And the other thing we might want to consider," murmured Gorman, "is that maybe Ash is right and we're wrong."

Hazel didn't understand. She frowned at him, perplexed, so that he had to grit his teeth and say aloud what he'd hoped she might recognize intuitively.

"I mean, maybe a man has the right to make a sacrifice—even this sacrifice—for the sake of his family."

Hazel stared at him in astonishment. "Kill himself? In front of the world's online community? To protect a bunch of murderous pirates? *Are you insane?*"

But he wasn't ready to back down. "Give it some thought. Would you stop him from diving into a river to save them if their car went off a bridge?"

"It's different," she insisted. "To risk your life is one thing. To throw it away is another."

"He's prepared to sacrifice himself for his wife and children. Lots of people would see that as a pretty noble thing."

"It *is* noble," Hazel conceded. "Being willing to do it is noble. It wouldn't be very noble of us to let him."

"Would he forgive us if we stopped him?"

"Probably not. Who cares?"

"Would he forgive *you*?"

That made her pause. But it didn't make her change her mind. "I don't imagine he would. Too bad. This is too important to go along with what somebody else thinks is right, even if it's Gabriel. *I* think he's too distraught to be making life-and-death decisions, and if I can stop him making this one, I will. If we can stop him, we must."

It was hard to tell what Gorman thought. Perhaps he wasn't allowing himself the luxury of an opinion. To a great extent, his duty was clear whatever he thought. Suicide isn't a crime in Britain, but assisting one is. If he could save Ash from his own best intentions, he was bound to try.

Hazel's brow was creasing again with thought. Suddenly it cleared. She knew, as surely as if she'd overheard the conversation, to whom he would have turned in preference to Hazel herself. And Stephen Graves would have agreed because, his own involvement's being so problematic already, the last thing he wanted was Ash angry enough to go to the police.

"Find Stephen Graves," she said breathlessly. "If Gabriel

needs someone to fly out and negotiate Cathy's freedom for him, at least he won't have to explain it all to Graves. At least Graves won't try to stop him."

That night, when she was alone, she watched the thing again. Patience, curled up on her sofa, seemed not to recognize the image on the screen and paid it no heed. Hazel envied the dog her blissful ignorance.

Hazel was an optimist at heart. She always looked for silver linings, always believed that there would be one even if it took a bit of finding. Driving home—Dave Gorman had offered to have someone take her, but she didn't want company and most of all she didn't want the company of police officers—she'd almost managed to persuade herself it was a trick. Norbold in general and Meadowvale in particular knew Gabriel Ash as an idiot. They called him "Rambles With Dogs." Hazel knew a very different Ash, a man with a highly intelligent and analytical mind damaged by the events that had overtaken him. She had to trust that he was still capable of putting together a package that would give him what he wanted—the return of his wife and sons—without giving the kidnappers what they wanted. She had herself more than half convinced that when she watched the video again, that was what she would see: a clever man outsmarting his tormentors.

And it wasn't. Try as she might, hard as she looked, Hazel could see only what everyone else had seen: an exhausted man driven to despair, offering up his own life for the safety of his family. His deep eyes were drained, no hope left, and over the broad bones his face was drawn gaunt, dark shadows gathered in the hollows of his cheeks.

Despair. Not desperation, which at least allows the possibility that a situation may still be salvaged and hunts frantically for the hidden way. Despair is not frantic but chill, the slow cooling that follows the death of all hope. Despair knows there is no happy ending. Nothing left to chase, nothing to strive for. That was how Gabriel Ash looked now, staring out of the screen at her like a stranger. Like a dead man captured forever in the moments before his death. The vacant-eyed Tommy photographed in the muddy trench in Flanders, repairing his kit while even now another soldier of the Great War is loading the shell that will kill him.

Sobs juddered in her throat. She twisted her hands in the hem of her shirt, wringing it beyond rescue. Grief tore her insides. He was her friend, and she was about to lose him, and he was alone. If he'd been where she could reach out to him, nothing would have stopped her. Certainly not the fact that he was somebody else's husband. She wasn't in love with Gabriel Ash. That had never been an issue. But, however much he exasperated her, she had come to love him, in a way. To care for him, to worry about him, to hope things would work out for him.

But they weren't going to, and he knew it and now she knew it, too. And she wanted to be with him. To stop him, if she could; to plead with him that the sacrifice was too great, whatever the prize; to insist that there was another way, *had* to be, and beg him to look for it; to cut the plug off his computer and the jack off the phone line so the essential element of proof that the pirates were looking for couldn't be provided, at least until he got to a hardware shop. And if all that failed—and Hazel knew in her heart that it *would* fail, that the most she could do now was delay him—to be with him at the end. His witness, his comfort, his friend.

But she wasn't with him; he'd made sure of that. He

hadn't wanted to listen to her arguments or her pleas, and he hadn't wanted her to witness what he was going to do. That was why he had left Norbold and not told her where he was going.

She sat up most of the night, miserable, lonely, and afraid, waiting for news that never came. Around dawn, exhausted, still in her chair—and yesterday's clothes—she fell into a troubled sleep. The phone woke her; she started violently enough to bruise her insides. It was DI Gorman.

"Stephen Graves has left the country. He was on a flight from Heathrow to Addis Ababa yesterday afternoon. Just him. Neither his wife nor his secretary knew he was going."

"He's gone to bring her home," Hazel said faintly. "After . . ." She swallowed. "After Gabriel is dead."

"That's what it looks like," agreed Gorman, his tone somber. "The pirates take Graves to Cathy, he calls Ash to say she's fit and well and ready to leave, and Ash carries out his side of the bargain."

"At which point the pirates slit Cathy's throat and Graves's as well," said Hazel. Her voice was thick as wormwood in her throat.

"It's possible. Though actually, it wouldn't gain them anything. With Ash dead, they might as well let them go. If only in the interests of future negotiations."

She hadn't thought of that. She hadn't thought that the business of piracy would go on after her own involvement had ended. That other hostages would be taken, if they weren't already being held in reserve, and their desperate relatives made to dance to the pirates' tune. There seemed to be no way of stopping it, not even with innocent blood.

"This isn't why I called," said Gorman. "Has Ash ever mentioned a café called the Copper Kettle to you?"

The sheer unexpectedness of it made Hazel bark an incredulous laugh. "You think he's negotiating his life away over coffee and scones in a tearoom?"

"No, I don't," said the DI levelly. "The café closed a year ago. But the building was owned by Ash's mother—the team searching his house found the deeds in a bureau. The last tenancy agreement lapsed, so the building is probably empty. Not a bad option if you need to be undisturbed for a couple of days."

Hazel felt her heart quicken. "This building—is it in Norbold?"

"Leamington Spa."

"Give me the address. I'll meet you there in"—she did a quick calculation—"twenty minutes."

"Not legally you won't!"

"Dave, Gabriel Ash's life depends on it. We're not even *talking* about speed limits."

And of course he did as requested. If she hadn't asked him to meet her in Leamington Spa, he'd have asked her. He wanted her there if they found Ash locked up in his mother's little investment property with a computer and a double-barreled shotgun. Gorman didn't expect the man to put the gun down and come quietly because *he* asked. He just might do if Hazel Best asked.

Back in Balfour Street, Hazel was heading for the door, taking the car keys off the dresser as she went. The white dog stood in her way, gazing at her hopefully.

Hazel shook her head impatiently. "No, we can't go down the towpath, there isn't time." The scimitar tail waved. "No, you can't come with me. I don't know how long I'll be." But actually, that was a pretty good reason not to leave even a well-behaved dog alone in Mrs. Poliakov's house.

Hazel took a steadying breath. "And I don't know what I'm going to find."

Patience kept on regarding her with those calm toffee-colored eyes.

There also wasn't time for an argument. "Oh, all right, then," Hazel growled, and the lurcher led the way out to the car.

CHAPTER 11

STEPHEN GRAVES HAD LEFT THE COUNTRY eighteen hours earlier, openly on his own passport, flying from London to Addis Ababa in Ethiopia, three hundred miles from the Somali border. Of course, three hundred miles in Africa is not like three hundred miles in England. It was probably as close as he could land to Somalia without risking the same fate as Cathy Ash.

As she drove, Hazel tried to make sense of everything that had happened. Gabriel Ash had sworn to kill himself, live—she wished she could think of a better word—on the Internet, where the pirates could watch, as the price of freedom for his wife and sons. But he wasn't going to do it until he knew they were safe. Stephen Graves, who'd been the pawn of the same pirates, had left for the Horn of Africa. Internal flights and a hired Land Rover would take him from Addis to any of a hundred points along the Somali border where an exchange could take place.

What then? He'd speak to Ash, by phone or video call. "They're here. I can see them. They seem fine. There are three machine guns aimed at them. There are two half-tracks and a helicopter, and maybe fifteen men. They have a laptop in one of the half-tracks, picking up your feed. What do you want me to do?"

And Ash would say, "Exactly what I told you to do before you left. Ask to speak to Cathy. Have them bring her within earshot. Ask her if she's all right. Ask if the boys are all right. Ask her if she's been told they're being freed."

A pause. Then: "She says they are, and that's what the kidnappers told her. She wants to know why. Should I tell her?"

"On no account." Hazel could almost hear the steel in Ash's voice. "She'll find out soon enough. Keep her away from the Internet for as long as you can."

"What do I do now?"

"Ask them to release Cathy to you as a show of goodwill. Point out that she was separated from her sons for four years, she's not going to leave them behind now."

Then: "Cathy's with me. They still have the boys on the other side of the checkpoint. We're all within machine-gun range. They say no more concessions until they've got what they came for. They say it's time to do what you promised."

"I know."

And then—what? What did Ash intend? A bullet in the brain, a knife across his throat? It had to be something pretty unarguable. He couldn't take an aspirin, tell them it was strychnine, fall over, and expect to be believed. In exactly the same way that Ash wanted proof that his family was alive, the pirates would want proof that Ash was dead.

And then a good man, a loving husband and father, would do what good men have been prepared to do since humanity was in its infancy: render up his own life for the sake of his family. Men hunting dangerous beasts, men fishing wild seas, men mining the depths of the unkindly earth—all those men who risked death, and accepted it when it came, to put food on their children's table and coals in their hearth. There was nothing unique about what Gabriel

Ash was doing. The only thing that would set his death apart from all those that had gone before was the thousands, potentially millions, of people who would witness it.

And when was this meant to happen? The answer came from the marrow of Hazel's bones: sooner rather than later. The more time that passed, the greater the chance of Ash's being found and stopped; and he didn't want that, and the pirates didn't want that. The clock had started ticking as soon as that video went viral. In a very real sense, the eyes of the world were watching to see what Gabriel Ash would do next. Hazel didn't need to watch; she knew. He'd do what he'd said he'd do, unless she reached him first.

There was no motorway between Norbold and Leamington Spa. The most direct route was the A road, and it passed through a number of villages and around a couple of larger towns.

Hazel first saw them as she drove through Upper Lytton. And thought nothing of it, except that the July sales must have started. But it was the same in Beeswick and on the Ashbury bypass: clusters of people standing on the pavements, staring into shop windows. Not going into the shops, just staring through the windows. When she realized they were all electrical shops—shops with computers and tablets in their windows—she knew what they were looking at.

Her heart leaden within her, she looked for somewhere to stop, hurrying to join the little group outside Bright Spark Electricals on the Ashbury bypass. People at the back of the gathering shuffled aside to make room for her. She was struck by the awful silence.

If she hadn't already known what she was going to see,

Hazel wouldn't have recognized Gabriel Ash. The strain had sapped every ounce of color from his face, and he sat in front of the computer as rigid as an artist's model. Only his lips moved when he spoke, and the top of his chest, visible in his open-necked shirt, rose and fell with his shallow, rapid breathing. He looked—the thought drove knives into her—frightened to death. And also utterly determined.

There was a young couple standing beside Hazel. The girl said, "I think he's going to do it." And the young man said, almost breezily, "No, it's a scam. There's money involved somewhere, bet you anything."

Hazel found herself spinning on them, ready to vent her misery and frustration. But then she saw that the girl was crying. There were slow tears wandering down her cheeks. And the young man, a protective arm around her, was saying anything he could to comfort her. He didn't think it was a scam. He wanted her to leave before the inevitable happened. But she wouldn't be drawn away. She seemed to feel she owed it to the broken stranger not to turn away.

A sense of obligation the rest of the quiet little gathering seemed to share. When the manager of Bright Spark Electricals realized what was going on, he hurried to the window display and started turning off the monitors. But the watchers insisted, quietly but resolutely, that he turn them back on. Not because they wanted to watch, but because they felt they should.

Hazel tried to look past Ash's gaunt face to the room behind him. Did it look like an abandoned café? There was nothing to see, only white walls with nothing on them. He could have been, almost literally, anywhere on the globe.

A phone rang, sending a shock wave rippling through the

little crowd outside the electrical supplier's. They had been wound taut waiting, and they hadn't been waiting for this, and the faint anticlimax drew sighs of relief and even a few wry chuckles.

Then they realized that the phone didn't belong to any of them, but to the man on the screen, the ring reaching them through the plate-glass window. The chastened manager had turned the sound up, almost as a public service for those who didn't have the equipment to follow these unfolding events. A detached part of Hazel's brain that was still capable of rational analysis supposed it was the same at all the electrical shops where the little crowds had gathered. Many more people—ordinary people, not natural ghouls—would be following the drama on computers, laptops, and smartphones in homes and offices up and down the country, and farther afield.

The phone was on the desk beside Ash's computer; in answering it, he brought it into the Webcam's field of view. The sound of his voice had more trouble penetrating the plate glass than the ring of the phone had, but in fact the sound was almost superfluous. Anyone could have read his lips for the few words he spoke, and those who couldn't could have read his eyes.

He said, "Yes?" And then, with a different inflection, "Yes." A much longer pause while he listened.

Then: "You're sure?" And finally: "Very well." And he rang off.

All her life Hazel Best had been an optimist. She had always believed the glass to be half full. She had always believed—really believed—all the things that little girls used to embroider on samplers: *Where there's a will there's a way. Every cloud has a silver lining. The darkest hour is just before the dawn. God never shuts a door but that He opens a window.*

She believed, at a bone-deep level and despite the evidence

all around her, that most people were fundamentally decent, and most disasters could be averted when people of goodwill worked together. And somewhere inside her she still believed that the tragedy unfolding before her eyes wasn't going to happen. That Dave Gorman would knock the door down in the nick of time. That word would reach Ash that his family was already beyond harm. That, in the last resort, Gabriel Ash wouldn't do what he'd promised.

So, in spite of everything that had brought them to this point, Hazel was not prepared for it—not really, not inside herself—when Ash put the phone down and picked up something else that was just out of view of the camera, and it was a handgun.

For a couple of seconds he looked at it as if unsure how it had got there, or what it was for. Then he vented a sigh, and a tiny, fragile smile flickered across his face. Then he put the muzzle in his mouth and pulled the trigger.

The explosion sprayed the back of his head across the wall behind him. His body lurched sideways out of the chair, and the computer's camera—unwinking, unmoved—continued to record the blood on the wall, the left shoulder and wide-flung arm of the body crumpled against the skirting board, until some innate sense of decency made somebody somewhere pull the plug.

CHAPTER 12

HAZEL BEST CONTINUED TO STARE at the blank screen long after most of those around her had drifted away. A couple of them, like the girl beside her, were in tears, but Hazel wasn't crying. A couple of them were trying desperately to find something smart to say to defuse the palpable sense of shock. Of course they failed miserably, crassly, but Hazel couldn't find it in her to resent them. Everyone deals with tragedy in their own way. There are no guidelines. You do what you can bear to, what you can live with. If a sick joke made what they'd just witnessed more bearable for some of them, Hazel wasn't going to tell them they were wrong.

And of course they didn't know—how could they?—that alone among the people watching Gabriel Ash kill himself, the quiet fair-haired girl looking over their shoulders knew the man personally. Cared about him, counted herself his friend. She could have told them. They might not have believed her. At moments like this, there are people who get a peculiar satisfaction from involving themselves in the story—claiming to have been on the wrecked train, to have seen the assassin, to have walked by the car bomb moments before it exploded. To have known the man who blew his brains out live on the Internet. What stopped her, though, wasn't that, but the obscure but persuasive sense that they didn't need to know. Telling them wouldn't make her feel better, and it might make them feel worse. She went on staring at the blank screen, her eyes stretched with shock, stripped of the will to do anything else, as the little crowd dissipated around her.

By the time she was fully aware again, she was standing on the pavement alone, and the manager was standing in his shop window waving angrily at her to go away. She dragged in the first proper breath she'd drawn for fifteen minutes, turned, and stumbled back to her car.

She was too late. She hadn't reached him in time, and Gabriel Ash was dead because of it. Sorrow filled her chest and rose up her throat, threatening to choke her. She hadn't known him that long. They'd never been more than friends. But somehow his passing carved a great hole in her world, one she didn't know how she'd set about filling. She'd have other friends, closer friends. But Ash had been . . . unique. Irreplaceable. No one would ever fill the gap he'd left, nor would the wound heal that he'd left by dying that way, hopeless and alone.

Hazel's only consolation was that, if there was any justice in the world, his death had accomplished more than simply shocking a bunch of people walking past electrical stores. If his sacrifice had bought the freedom of his wife and sons, he had paid a terrible price but one he at least had considered worth paying. Hazel wouldn't devalue his final desperate gift to his family by saying it wasn't. It was a decision only Ash had the right to make.

Still dry-eyed, she turned in her seat and looked at Ash's dog. What was Patience going to think when her master didn't come back? Would she think she'd been abandoned again? And would it be better or worse if she knew Ash was dead? Not that it mattered. Hazel had no way of explaining the situation to even a smart dog.

A more immediate problem was how she was going to explain to her landlady. Because whatever she'd promised Mrs. Poliakov, Hazel's first act after witnessing Ash's lonely death wasn't going to be to take his dog to a shelter.

An immeasurable amount of time passed. Eventually she was ready to get back on the road.

She might simply have turned and gone back the way she'd come. There was no longer anything to be gained in Leamington. But she couldn't bring herself to. It felt like a betrayal. She felt something almost like duty calling her on, to the address she'd been given, to the empty building on its unfashionable side street, which had once housed the Copper Kettle Café.

Until the moment she turned into that narrow street, she wasn't sure that this was where he had been. But half a dozen police vehicles filled the road, many with their lights still blinking blue and white although the need for urgency was now past. There were uniforms on duty at the door, admitting a few people with the right credentials, turning more away.

Which told her everything she needed to know. Still she found herself getting out of the car—carefully leaving the windows slightly open for Patience—and walking up the street to where the cordon was being controlled by a detective constable from Meadowvale. She steeled herself and hoped her voice would come. "Is DI Gorman inside?"

DC Rodgers did a classic double take. He'd hadn't seen her for weeks, was startled—though later he realized he shouldn't have been—to see her here. "Hazel? Er—yes. I'll call him."

"Don't bother. I'll find him."

Rodgers looked concerned. "I don't think you should go inside. It's pretty . . . messy . . . in there."

Hazel sighed. "Of course it is. But it won't be anything I haven't seen before."

"It's different when it's someone you know," warned Rodgers.

"I know it is. But, Jack, it really won't be something I haven't seen. I saw him do it."

"Oh, shit."

A moment later the front door opened and Dave Gorman emerged. He'd been watching for her. "I'm sorry. We were too late." He looked terribly tired.

"I know." She managed a brittle smile, to ease a little the guilt they all felt when they did their job but didn't do it quite fast enough. "I saw."

Gorman fisted both hands deep in his trouser pockets, dropped his square chin onto his chest. "I'm so sorry. That we couldn't stop him. That we didn't get here in time."

"I know. Thank you."

He looked past her. "Is this your car? You shouldn't be driving. I'll find someone . . ."

She held on to her car keys, politely but firmly. "I'm fine. I'll head home now. Unless . . . ?" She left the question mostly unasked.

Gorman heard it just the same. He shook his head. "You can't go up there. You wouldn't want to, Hazel. And you wouldn't want to hinder the investigation. The guys from the Home Office are here already. I suppose, because of who Ash was. They've pretty well taken over."

"Investigation?" For the first time since it had happened, her iron control wavered, the word booming like an overpressured dam.

"Dave, we know what happened! We know what he did and why he did it. The whole world knows, or at least as much of it as has access to the Internet. Tell me one thing. Are they safe? Are they really safe?"

The DI nodded somberly. "Yes. The British consul is at the checkpoint now. He's confirmed that Cathy Ash, her two sons, and Stephen Graves are all safe. They'll be on a plane home as soon as it can be arranged. Ash achieved what he wanted to, Hazel. If he thought the price was worth paying, then it was."

But Hazel still didn't think so.

She got back in her car and headed south. A few miles from Norbold, though, the weather turned unexpectedly dreary—mist shrouded the A road so much that she had to slow down, followed soon afterward by a downpour that stole the last of her vision and forced her into a lay-by.

Only when the windscreen wipers whined a dusty protest and failed to improve matters did Hazel realize that the downpour was highly localized. That the dam had broken, and it was tears blinding her, not rain.

CHAPTER 13

Two days later, on a hot Saturday afternoon, an RAF flight landed them in Coventry. Hazel was there to meet it. DI Gorman had conveyed the request from the Home Office, but she was glad to, felt she owed it to Ash to greet his family. He'd have been there himself if he could. She was a poor substitute, but no one else would have been a better one.

The first she saw of Cathy and her sons was three dots on the tarmac. Actually there were four dots—Stephen Graves was there, too—and it took them a few minutes to cross the open space, heat haze rising like a mirage from the surface, to where Hazel was waiting.

It wasn't a bad way to approach what was always going to be a difficult meeting. As the figures grew larger, the two women were able to adjust mentally to each other's presence. Hazel found herself vacillating between relief that Cathy Ash had found her way home after four years in captivity, so that her husband's sacrifice had not been for nothing, and a resentment so deep that she could hardly contain it, even knowing how unreasonable it was.

What Cathy thought of being met by this young woman who

had been her husband's friend, there was no way of knowing. Her face was closed, all her emotions tightly contained. For four years her life had depended on her ability to keep her thoughts to herself. To absorb developments and react, if she reacted at all, only after considering the consequences. Of course her ability to express her feelings had been compromised.

Intimidated by the wide-open spaces, perhaps, Ash's sons stuck close by their mother's side. The taller would be Gilbert, now eight years old; Guy was six. Gilbert was the most like his father, but both of them had inherited their mother's slender frame. Hazel had expected they would all be deeply tanned, but they weren't, only touched with a little gold, as if they'd been on holiday. The reason was obvious: they'd spent most of their time in Africa inside locked rooms. The boys glanced at her suspiciously, Guy clutching Cathy's hand, as Hazel went forward to greet them.

Graves performed the introductions. "Mrs. Cathy Ash, this is Constable Best." The faint emphasis on her title puzzled Hazel until she remembered that the last time they met she'd let him think he was dealing with someone very much more senior. "And this is Gilbert, and Guy."

Hazel smiled at them. "I'm here to take you home."

"Home?" Cathy sounded uncertain, as if she'd all but forgotten what one of those was.

"To Norbold."

But Cathy and her sons had never lived in Norbold. Their home had been in London. Hazel felt a twinge of embarrassment for forgetting that. "For now," she added quickly. "Until you get things sorted out. Gabriel kept your flat in Covent Garden, but he let it out. It may be a little while before you can get it back. In the meantime, we'll get you settled in his mother's house."

Cathy nodded. She was around Hazel's height but slimmer, would have been even without four years of living on kidnappers' rations. Her hair was cut short, the color somewhere between fair and brown, her eyes the washed-out blue of old denim. She wore no makeup. She was wearing a cream shirt and linen skirt, and though they had obviously been bought for the journey, they were hardly any different from what she'd been wearing when Hazel saw her last, on the computer screen in Cambridge. She looked around warily, eyes skating over Hazel, over the police officers, over the airport buildings, unable to settle for more than a moment at a time. She was free, and she was back in England, but Hazel thought it would be a long time before she lost that hunted look.

Turning to Graves, Hazel said evenly, "What about you? Are you coming back with us?"

Graves flicked her a somber little smile. "No. There are people waiting for me, too." He nodded resignedly at the police contingent. "I'm in a certain amount of trouble. Just how much remains to be seen."

"You did what you felt you had to do," said Hazel.

"I got people killed."

"And saved Mrs. Ash and her sons. Mr. Graves, I have no idea how this will all work out. But I do know that actions taken under duress can't be compared with those undertaken willingly. Get yourself a good lawyer. Make sure everyone understands why you did what you did."

"Thank you," he said. "I will. And . . ."

Hazel had half turned away. She turned back, one eyebrow raised.

"I'm sorry about Ash."

"Yes," she said after a moment. "We all are."

* * *

The easiest thing was to concentrate on Ash's sons. There was no ambivalence in how Hazel felt about them. She could see Ash in both boys, but particularly in Gilbert, who was dark, quiet, and solemn, and who watched the world carefully from a pair of deep, dark eyes exactly like his father's. He said very little. Hazel felt he was reserving judgment: possibly on her, possibly on England.

The circumstances in which he and his brother had been kept would emerge in due course. Even a sensitive debriefing would have to wait until they were capable of dealing with it. Hazel knew they'd been separated from their mother for much of the time, but neither showed the scars of either cruelty or neglect. Perhaps some local family had been given the task of caring for them, and over the years the barriers between the boys and their fosterers had blurred. Perhaps they felt that being made to return to a land neither of them could remember very clearly, and to a mother who was almost a stranger, was another abduction, more painful to them than events half a lifetime ago.

They wouldn't go on feeling like that, Hazel told herself. By the time they were old enough to understand what their father had done for them, to comprehend the enormous wellhead of love his sacrifice had sprung from, they would be old enough and settled enough to be grateful.

She made no attempt at conversation as she drove, left Cathy to set the pace. And clearly Cathy was worn-out—exhausted by the long journey, by the emotional upheaval that had preceded it, most of all by four years of living on a knife edge. For four years this woman had been the captive of utterly ruthless, wholly unpredictable men. They had snatched her from her safe, comfortable life in

London with a husband who loved her and sons she adored; somehow they'd smuggled her out of the country and across a couple of continents; they'd taken her sons away and made her plead for their lives with a total stranger on a computer screen. Now she had her children back and was bringing them home to a place she didn't know, to pick up a life she must hardly remember, without the husband who had bought her freedom with his death. Hazel couldn't begin to imagine how Cathy Ash must be feeling. But she understood why the woman didn't want to make small talk all the way to Norbold.

On the backseat, first one, then the other of the little boys fell asleep.

It was five o'clock before she turned into Highfield Road and stopped outside the big stone house near the end. "We're here."

Cathy looked at it out of the car window, made no attempt to get out.

"Have you been here before?" asked Hazel gently.

"A couple of times." Cathy's voice was colorless. "To visit his mother. When did he move back?"

"A couple of years ago, I think. It was before I knew him. You knew . . ." But of course Cathy didn't know how Ash had passed the time they'd been apart. How could she? Perhaps a hint from Graves, but he didn't know much more himself. Hazel made herself look Ash's wife in the eye. "Gabriel had a mental breakdown after you were abducted. He blamed himself. He was hospitalized for a time. He only came back here after his doctors thought he was fit to cope on his own."

And that, she added in the privacy of her own head, was a fairly doubtful judgment. But perhaps if he hadn't come back here, Ash would never have gained the strength to rebuild his life. In which case he'd still be alive, and you'd still be in a whitewashed room in Mogadishu.

There was a pause while Cathy considered. Then she said, "I didn't know that." Another pensive gap. Then: "Do you think that's why he . . . did what he did? Because the balance of his mind was disturbed?"

"No!" said Hazel quickly—so quickly, so vehemently, that Cathy's pale eyes rounded for a moment. "You mustn't think that. He knew exactly what he was doing. He finally found a way to help you. He was glad to take it."

Cathy managed a thin, pale smile. "You were a good friend to him, I think."

"I valued his friendship, yes."

Cathy Ash sighed, finally opened her door. On the backseat the boys stirred. "I suppose we'd better go in. See what we've got and what we need."

"I'll come back tomorrow, if you like, and help you shop," offered Hazel.

"Thank you. But really I need a car. Did Gabriel have one?"

"I don't know where it is now," Hazel had to admit. "The police may have it. I'll arrange a rental car for you. And I'll bring his dog around."

Cathy blinked at her. Hazel might have been proposing something faintly unsavory. "Gabriel had a dog?"

Hazel nodded. "Patience. They thought the world of each other. Because neither of them had anyone else, I suppose."

"I'm sorry," said Cathy stiffly, "I really don't want a dog in the house."

It was one of those moments when the world shifts very slightly to the left, and you just know that somewhere a tsunami is getting ready to wipe out some villages. Hazel tried to convince herself that Ash's wife hadn't understood. "Patience lives here. I mean, she's at my house at the moment, but she was Gabriel's dog. She's no trouble—she's clean and good-natured, and she doesn't chew things. . . . I'm sure the boys would like to have their father's dog."

"Oh no," Cathy said firmly. "I'm not having a dog."

Hazel felt as if she'd been floored by a pillowcase full of wet herrings. "But . . . what do you want me to do with her?"

Cathy shrugged. "It's at your house? Keep it, if you like. If not, I'm sure there's a shelter somewhere that will find it a nice home." She walked up the steps to her new front door, and the boys piled out of Hazel's car like weary puppies and followed her.

CHAPTER 14

MRS. POLIAKOV LOOKED AT HER as if she suspected Hazel, not the dog, of having designs on her furniture. So much so that Hazel, who had never in her life felt the urge to chew a cabriole leg, began to redden and talk faster, as if she had something to hide among the words.

By contrast, Patience sat demurely in the hall, unflustered by the increasingly warm debate on her future. Posing elegantly, her long tail curled around her long legs and her long nose directing the focus of her golden-amber gaze, she might have been one of those stone hounds that guards the gates of stately homes, except for the faint, not unpleasant aroma of prophylactic flea repellent. Hazel had spent a small fortune at the vet's only that morning. The dog's fine, thin coat offered a poor haven to hitchhikers, but Hazel didn't want to risk even one appearing. She felt sure that Mrs. Poliakov could zero in on a single flea on twelve square meters of carpet like a laser-guided missile, with similarly explosive results.

"A few days, I said," insisted the landlady, her tone that curious combination of outrage and aggression that women of her profession have developed as a defense against Being Put Upon. "Didn't I say that? A few days. We agreed."

"We did agree," Hazel admitted. "I expected Gabriel would be back for her after just a few days. I didn't expect . . ."

Mrs. Poliakov was not an avid reader of the popular press. Uniquely in Hazel's experience, she watched television for the adverts for cleaning products, then turned off when the programs resumed. She took a Polish-language magazine, but activities in middle England were low down on its list of priorities. She didn't know what had happened. "Expect what?" she demanded. "That your friend would vanish, leaving you holding his baby?" She thought about that. "Puppy?"

Hazel swallowed. "He's dead, Mrs. P. He shot himself. To save his wife and children. They were the only things in the world that mattered more to him than this dog. I can't—I won't—give her to a shelter. If you won't let me keep her here, I'll have to find somewhere else to live."

Mrs. Poliakov was still taking it in. Translating the English words, with which she was quite familiar, into her native tongue inside her head because even after thirty years things didn't seem entirely real until she'd absorbed them in Polish. "Your friend Gabriel?" she said eventually. "Mr. Ash?"

"Yes."

"He's not coming back? Never?"

"No," said Hazel. It still broke her heart to say it out loud. "And his wife doesn't want a dog."

Mrs. Poliakov started to say, "*I* don't want . . ." and then thought better of it. She thought of the hurt in Hazel Best's eyes, red-rimmed and smudged beneath with dark stains like bruises. She thought of how happy she'd been when she first came here, a bright, cheerful girl eager to embrace the challenges of her new job; and how that, too, had been snatched away. Her unlikely friendship with the strange man with the dog had been almost the only satisfaction she'd got out of the last few months. And now he was gone, too, leaving her with only grief and a white dog.

She leaned forward, peering with concern into Hazel's drawn face. "You think this through? I mean properly? You never want a dog before. You want this dog? *Why* you want this dog?"

The tears started again, more than she could blink away, more than she could blame on a touch of hay fever. But then, Hazel wasn't at work; she didn't have a professional facade to maintain. She'd lived under Mrs. Poliakov's roof for over a year. She counted her a friend. You can be honest with friends. You *should* be honest with friends. Her voice broke. "Because she's all of him that I have left."

Mrs. Poliakov had the right to keep her home a dog-free zone. But she knew that if she exercised that right, it would be a long time before she slept soundly again.

Instead she said, "All right. We give it a try. Any trouble"— she raised an admonitory finger—"she have to go. But she's a good dog, I can see that. We give it a try."

With Patience's immediate future secure, Hazel knew it was time for her to get on with her own life. She thought about visiting her father. But the only place she could get used to Gabriel Ash's not being around anymore was here, where he ought to be.

She needed something to do, something useful to occupy herself. She thought of the situation Saturday had dumped in her lap. First thing on Monday morning, she called Dave Gorman.

"What's happening about Armitage and his computer?"

"Er—what?" It was clearly not what DI Gorman had thought she was calling about.

Hazel breathed heavily down the phone at him. "Charles Armitage? The guy with the unpleasant little hobby and a casual approach to computer security? What are you doing about him?"

Gorman was recovering from the surprise enough for indignation to surface in his gravelly voice. "Today? Not very much. In case you hadn't noticed, I've been pretty busy with something else." But that was unkind, and anyway it wasn't a good answer. He took a deep breath. "Sorry. I haven't forgotten, Hazel. I will deal with this. Leave it with me a few more days."

For now anger, even misplaced anger, was easier to deal with than grief. "There are children involved, Dave." She couldn't remember when she'd started to use his first name; but if she was no longer a probationer at Meadowvale Police Station, she was damned if she was going back to calling him Mr. Gorman. "I don't know how current the images on that computer were, but some of that abuse may be going on right now. Today. The information that will help us put a stop to it may be on that laptop. Are you sure you've got more important things to do than getting it back?"

There was a pause while DI Gorman reevaluated. This was something Hazel had grown used to, as people who had her marked down as a nice, polite, responsible, well-brought-up young woman suddenly realized there was another side to her. It was the human equivalent of a sat-nav system spinning its gyros and stammering out "Recalculating . . . recalculating . . ."

Finally he said, "You're right. I'll get on it as soon as I can. Don't think I've forgotten about Armitage just because I haven't the manpower to deal with him this very minute."

She knew all about prioritizing. Any other week she'd have sympathized. But the anger was serving her too well to let it go. "And another thing. Every time I ask about Gabriel Ash's funeral, I'm told you're not ready to release the body. You never listened to him when he was alive—what do you think he's going to tell you now?"

That was easier to answer, although Gorman knew the answer wouldn't satisfy her. "Not my call, Hazel. The Home Office has him, they're calling all the shots." Invisible at the other end of the line, he winced at the unfortunate turn of phrase. "I'll keep you informed. As soon as I know something, you'll know it." There was another pause as he debated whether to ask his next question. But he wanted to know. "Have you seen much of Cathy Ash since she got back?"

"No." Hazel added nothing to that, though Gorman waited.

Eventually he tried again. "You should probably keep in touch with her. You're the best friend Ash had in Norbold—any questions she has, you're probably best placed to answer them."

"I don't think she has any questions," said Hazel shortly. "Or if she has, there are people she'd rather be dealing with. I don't think she wants me anywhere near her."

"Why?"

That could have been either of two inquiries. "Why doesn't she want to see me? I think she's got the idea there was something going on between me and Gabriel. There wasn't, but I think Cathy thinks there was. And why do I think that? Because she pretty well slammed the door in my face when I took her home."

Gorman gave a sad little sigh. "We need to make allowances, Hazel. The woman's had a hell of a time. For four years, if she slept at all, she woke up not knowing if she was going to survive the coming day. For a lot of that time she didn't know where her children were—didn't know for sure that they were even alive. Lord knows how she felt about Ash by the end—whether she hung on to the belief that someday he'd come and save her, or if she blamed him for everything. Either way, how he died must have put her emotions through the mincer. She'll need a lot of help to come to terms with it all. Until she has, we should try not to judge her."

Hazel needed telling none of this. She knew she had no right to resent Cathy. She bit her lip. "Has anyone suggested that she talk to Laura Fry?"

"As a matter of fact," said Gorman, "I did. Laura's happy to see her. Cathy's going to need a little persuading, but I'll try again when she's had a chance to catch her breath."

"What about the boys? How are they adjusting to being back in England?"

"I'm not sure," admitted Gorman. "Cathy's—naturally—very protective of them. I've tried to speak to them, but she won't let them out of her sight. As a matter of fact"—he had the grace to sound faintly embarrassed—"I had hoped you might succeed where I've failed. That she might let you take them for an ice cream and a chat."

"I wouldn't hold your breath," muttered Hazel.

"It's probably too soon," agreed Gorman. "But will you? If I can get her to agree?"

Hazel couldn't think of a reason to say no, so she said yes.

She knew that if she walked Patience beside the canal, Saturday would appear. And he did, barely ten minutes after they'd left Balfour Street. Hazel didn't particularly want to talk to him, because she knew what he'd want to talk about and she hadn't an answer to satisfy him. But she was damned if she was going to avoid him, as if she'd done something to be ashamed of. So she kept walking, and Saturday caught up and fell into step beside her.

He had a black eye.

There was nothing terribly unusual about this. Saturday and his associates traded casual blows the way normal people exchange handshakes. Sometimes when she saw him, he had a black eye; sometimes he had a skinned knuckle. She imagined he gave as good as he got, or at least had the sense to run if he was seriously outclassed. "What happened to you?"

The boy shrugged, unconcerned. "Nothing much. A misunderstanding."

"His? Or yours?"

Saturday grinned. At sixteen he was caught on the cusp of change, no longer a child, not yet a man. There was something knowing, ironic, in his grin that would not have been there six months ago. "His. I explained where he went wrong."

Hazel regarded him critically. He was small for his age, undernourished, not so much wiry as downright thin. She could only assume the other party had been skimpier still. "When are you going to do something with your life?" she demanded waspishly.

He looked surprised. "Like what? Brain surgery? Ballet dancing?"

"Like getting a job," snapped Hazel. "Like pushing a wheelbarrow around a building site and making the tea until someone thinks you're worth teaching some skills. Like buying a chammy and a bucket and cleaning people's windows until you've saved up enough for a mower so you can cut their lawns. Like anything that adds net worth to the human race instead of being a drain on it."

This wasn't a boy who was easily hurt. Or rather, he was so used to being hurt, in the normal course of every day, that it took something special to register with him. That, coming from Hazel, whom he had learned to trust, got through his defenses in a way she had not anticipated. He reared back as if she'd struck him; color flooded momentarily into his pinched cheeks.

Guilt flooded Hazel's. Her eyes dipped quickly—and met the golden gaze of the lurcher, watching with interest to see what she would do now. Hazel glared at her—she didn't need a dog to tell her when she was behaving badly!—then glanced apologetically at Saturday. "I'm sorry. I've no business taking it out on you."

He was still startled from the way she'd turned on him. Another moment, though, and he'd have fired off a fitting retort, something to leave her feeling mean and small-minded. And then he saw her expression and realized there was very little he could do to make her feel any worse.

Saturday didn't flatter himself that being unkind to him had reduced her almost to tears. He said quietly, "What's happened?"

Hazel stared at him in growing disbelief. "You don't know?" But of course he didn't know. He didn't own a computer or a television or a power-socket to plug them into. His only chance of learning what had happened to Ash was if somebody tossed him some unfinished chips wrapped in the front page of the *Norbold News*, because even if half the town was talking about it, nobody would think of telling a street kid. Nobody would think he might be interested. "Gabriel is dead."

Incredibly, the boy laughed. "Dead? Of course he isn't dead! Who told you that?"

"Nobody told me. I saw it."

Only then, when her expression failed to soften into a grin, did he realize it wasn't a joke. Something terrible happened to his face. Slowly the flesh—and there wasn't much of it to start with—melted from his cheeks, so that he aged twenty, thirty years in front of her. His eyes hollowed, sucked in by grief. His skin sallowed to the gray of old concrete, the flimsy dryness of archived paper. In the space of a few seconds he changed before Hazel's eyes from a skinny youth to an old man to something almost more like a mummy. A lifetime compressed by time-lapse photography.

She'd had no idea Ash meant so much to him. All she could think was that Saturday had so few friends, so few people in his life who even cared whether he lived or died, that losing one was devastating. "I'm sorry," she stammered. "I should have told you before. There were things to do, and I didn't think . . . I'm sorry."

The tears on Saturday's cheeks were like drops of rain among the freckles. "When?"

"Four days ago."

"How? What . . . How?"

So she told him, holding nothing back. The truth would hurt him, but he deserved to hear it from her, not as a bit of casual gossip tossed over a campfire in a condemned building.

By now they had lowered themselves onto the grassy edge of the towpath, legs dangling over the water. Hazel was plaiting stems of couch grass as she talked, her fingers deliberate and careful about the meaningless task. Moved by the same need for distraction, Saturday was stroking the dog, holding her in the crook of his arm. Patience turned her long face and licked his nose once, golden eyes all concern.

"What are we going to do?" the boy moaned when Hazel had finished her account.

"Do?" she echoed bitterly. "There's nothing *to* do. We get on with our lives. We've lost a friend. The world won't stop turning because of it."

She thought she'd managed to shock him. That Saturday thought she, too, should be crying for Ash. But four days had passed, and she'd done all the crying she could do for now. She straightened her bent back, threw the little plaited wreath onto the brown water of the canal, and stood up.

"Actually," she said crisply, "there is something we can do. Something I can do, and you can help me with. Something DI Gorman should be doing, except he's too busy and we're not. We can get that damned laptop back."

CHAPTER 15

ALMOST AS SOON AS THE WORDS WERE OUT, Hazel knew she was making a promise—or issuing a threat—that she had no way of keeping. They might know what Charles Armitage had been up to, but the only evidence was a bundle of electronics he'd had ample time to dispose of. In all probability the laptop no longer existed.

Hazel was aware that a hard drive is harder to wipe than most people outside the computer industry appreciate. But even a top nerd needed at least the remains of the laptop, and if Armitage— knowing what was on it, knowing the police had had it in their possession—hadn't dropped it in a lake a week ago, weighted with stones like someone who'd come second in a gang war, he needed his head examined. That was the real reason Dave Gorman wasn't beating his door down right now. Not that he was busy, although undoubtedly he was, but because there was no point. His time was too valuable to waste chasing wild geese.

But right now Hazel needed to be doing *something*. Anything would be better than sitting in her quiet room, looking at Ash's dog, wondering when it was going to strike Patience that he wasn't coming back. It was oddly upsetting that she couldn't explain what had become of him to someone—all right, to an animal—who'd loved Ash as much as anyone in the world. It was another small misery adding to Hazel's burden.

She needed a job to do, something worthwhile, to occupy her mind and tire her body, and give her some prospect of a success. Because right now she felt a failure. Gabriel Ash had been her friend, she'd taken satisfaction in what she'd been able to do for this clever, wounded, vulnerable man, but the bottom line was that she hadn't been able to keep him alive. He hadn't trusted her enough to tell her about his appalling dilemma and give her the chance to help him. Someone else might have seen that as his failure. Hazel saw it as hers.

She desperately needed a success to set against it. Not to erase it from her memory—nothing would do that—but to set against it in the great scale of deeds. She needed to be able to think, Perhaps I couldn't save Ash, but there are some miserable, abused young girls who are going to get back a bit of their childhood because of me, and a man who exploited and encouraged and enjoyed their degradation got his comeuppance because I know what to do and will do it.

And maybe Saturday needed that as well. Some small triumph of hope over despair. That, too, had been in her mind when Hazel made her rash pronouncement. But all she could see now, a scant half hour later, was that she was also going to let Saturday down. There was no possible way she could do what she'd said she was going to do.

But she wasn't going to tell him. She thought this was one of those few occasions when chasing the unattainable was better than letting it go, because just going through the motions would give both of them something to focus on. Hazel would have to pretend they were doing some good; but she was willing to do that, for Saturday's sake. The boy had been kicked in the face too often already.

The developers working on the Dirty Nellie's site were a Birmingham firm. Charles Armitage lived in the Clent Hills, less than an hour's drive from Norbold. Hazel had two decisions to make before she did anything. Whether to approach Armitage at his home or his office, and whether or not to warn him she was coming. There were arguments for and against in both cases.

She didn't expect a closet pedophile to be honest with her wherever they met, but was he more likely to be flustered into betraying himself by the presence of family or colleagues? It would be easier to throw her out of his private home than a public office, but then he'd have to explain to his wife. Also, it was more likely that the man pursued his grubby little hobby in his study than in his place of work, which meant that any evidence was more likely to be found at his home. If he left her alone long enough to look for it. If he let her through the front door in the first place.

The second decision also made itself. If she called him first, however quickly she drove he would have time to hide or destroy that evidence. If she turned up on his doorstep, she ran the risk that he wouldn't be there—but if he was, she could snatch the initiative because she knew now what she was looking for.

She could go this evening. She thought Monday night was probably as good a time as any to catch Armitage at home. If he'd been away for the long weekend that professional people take as their right, he would be back by tonight. Hazel still marveled at the way the moneyed classes got on a plane because there was nothing worth watching on the television.

Saturday wanted to go with her. Hazel thought it was a bad

idea. One reason was the same as Ash's for not taking Patience on important and delicate visits. If knocking at someone's door with your dog on a lead damaged your credibility, being accompanied by someone like Saturday would probably kill it off entirely.

But she wasn't a cruel person, so she gave him the other reason. "I don't want him to see you. He knows enough about who found his laptop"—you see: that was kind—"to recognize you if he sees you. You don't want him recognizing you."

The youth was full of a fine disdain. "Some ponce who wets himself over pictures of little girls? You think I can't take him?"

"Some ponce with money and connections," Hazel reminded him. "Maybe you could take him." Kindness again: privately she couldn't think of *anyone* he could take. "But he wouldn't come himself. What about the three heavies he'd send looking for you?"

"Hmm—three," murmured Saturday, as if he'd have expected to cope with one or two. "Maybe you're right."

Afterward, Hazel realized the ease with which she'd won the argument should have made her suspicious. As it was, she was approaching Warwick when a rustle of movement in a corner of the rearview mirror made her purse her lips thoughtfully and look for a lay-by. Safely out of the traffic, she turned around and lifted her coat off the backseat. It was her warm winter coat, which had lain there undisturbed for months.

Saturday sat up and gave her a sickly grin. So did Patience.

Plan B was where Saturday stayed in the car and kept out of sight. "Can you do that?" demanded Hazel.

"Course I can," growled the boy.

"You didn't do it very well just now."

"Well enough to fool you," muttered Saturday.

"Fooling me isn't the point," retorted Hazel tartly. "I'm not going to beat your head in if you get it wrong."

Charles Armitage lived in one of the many little rural churches converted into homes in the last thirty years, since congregations started to shrink and house hunters' aspirations to grow. This one was set amid the rolling greenery of the Clent Hills.

Hazel parked on the main road, staring at the quaint stone building in absolute horror. Somehow, until right now, she hadn't believed—not really *believed*—that this moment would come. She'd known it was a wild-goose chase from the start, thought she was just driving around the countryside to give herself something to do and Saturday something to feel positive about. Somehow she'd forgotten that if she kept following the sat-nav instructions, she'd end up at Charles Armitage's front door. Now she was here, she hadn't the faintest notion what to do next. Drive away again? She could imagine what Saturday would say. Patience would look down her nose at her as well. Patience could say more with the angle of her long nose than you could put in a short essay.

But the alternative was also pretty appalling. To leave her car and walk up this drive, alone, and knock on the door and confront Charles Armitage about the contents of his laptop's photo file. Knowing that she could prove nothing. Knowing that he was a well-to-do, well-connected professional man who undoubtedly retained expensive lawyers. If he denied everything, what would she do then? She couldn't produce Saturday—his credibility as a witness was too meager to justify the risk to him—and she'd never seen the pictures herself; and if DI Gorman had, it would have been him walking up the Armitages' front drive, and Armitage would know that. Hazel hadn't a single shot in her locker.

Sometimes, they say, nothing is a real cool hand. But usually it's not.

She found herself wondering what Gabriel Ash would have done.

Maybe he wouldn't have got himself in this position in the first place. It was, she had to admit, pretty stupid, and Ash was never a stupid man.

But nor had he been afraid of looking stupid if he thought he was doing the right thing. He'd confronted some grim situations himself—and to Ash, who'd found even casual conversation a trial, the prospect of a hostile reception must have been anathema—when he'd needed answers he could see no other way of getting. Gabriel Ash had always had the courage of his convictions. He was dead, and his wife and sons were alive, because of it.

Hazel felt a slow flush traveling up into her cheeks, and the die was cast. She wouldn't disappoint just Saturday if she turned around now. She would be letting Ash down, too, because he would have expected better of her. A serious crime had been committed by the man who lived in that church, and maybe there was nothing she could do to bring Charles Armitage to justice, but she could at least let him know that she knew. Mark his card. Make him aware that, whatever his social circle believed, however much they admired his talent and envied his success, there was a police officer (probably) in Norbold who knew exactly what he was. Maybe it would have an effect. Maybe the humiliation of having his secret discovered would be enough to make him concentrate such spare time and energies as he had on golf.

Hazel took a deep breath, marched up the gravel drive, and rapped on the lancet-shaped front door before she had time to change her mind.

Everyone knows what a pedophile looks like, don't they? Pale, damp, limp-wristed, washed-out eyes that avoid your gaze, a tendency to dress much as he had when his mother was buying his clothes. Except for the jolly uncle ones, of course, who are red-faced and round and never stop laughing, and have pudgy hands and wear socks with their sandals. And then there's the other kind, who . . .

And therein lies the problem. As a trained police officer, Hazel knew exactly what a pedophile looks like. He looks like everyone else. Certainly there are those who match the stereotypes, but there are more who don't. Who look like husbands and fathers, like teachers and clergymen and shopkeepers, like people you know and trust. You can't tell by looking at them. Hazel knew what he was, and still Charles Armitage didn't look like a pedophile when he opened the door with a yellow duster and a spray can of furniture polish in his spare hand. When his rosy middle-aged face with its laughter lines on the cusp of turning into wrinkles split in an amiable, slightly rueful smile and he said, "Yes? Can I help you?"

A uniform is a magical thing. It can turn a bunch of individuals into a cohesive group. It can make them fight for one another when, without it, they wouldn't fight for themselves. It can make them stand when all their instincts are screaming at them to turn and run. One made of soft blue cloth can stiffen a spine better than whalebone.

Hazel had been told this. Now she knew it was true. She'd had the protection of a uniform, and then she had lost it, and she knew what it was worth.

On the other hand, it isn't the uniform that does the job: it's the person inside. Hazel Best was still who she'd always been, and arguably more so. She stiffened her own spine, and looked him in the eye, and did what she'd got good at doing recently: lying without saying an untruthful word.

"I'm Hazel Best, from Meadowvale Police Station in Norbold. Your laptop was handed to me as lost property."

She paused there, watching to see the effect of this opening statement on Charles Armitage. It was reasonably gratifying. The smile died on his face and much of the color drained out of it. He took half a step backward and his eyes contracted around a little knot of worry at their cores. He knew what she was talking about all right, and she hadn't said anything yet.

Unsmiling, holding his eyes with her own, she continued slowly, picking her words with care. "It seems there may have been some . . . irregularity . . . in the way the hand-in was logged. You'll understand, there are procedures that need to be followed when we take responsibility for somebody's valuable property. There's some question as to whether we recorded all the necessary particulars."

It was a classic police tactic, hiding the weakness of her position behind a wall of official-sounding words that might mean anything or nothing at all. And it was entirely alien to the way Hazel had done her job, which was with the same openness and honesty with which she lived her life. But all the weapons in an armory have a use, and she went on holding his gaze remorselessly, daring him to look away. And he wanted to, but couldn't.

"So would you mind providing me with some information about the item now? For the record? Is it your personal property or does it belong to your company?"

"Er—it's mine," said Armitage. He was sure he'd covered this ground when the laptop was returned to him, but if covering it again was the price of getting rid of her, he was more than willing.

"But you were using it for business."

"Yes."

"When you lost it."

"Yes."

"At a petrol station."

"Yes. Officer . . ."

Hazel tilted her head imperiously, so that her nose came up like an admonitory finger. "One moment, sir. Let's get what we need first. Does anyone else use the computer?"

She saw his lips tighten. Oh yes, he knew what she was here for. "No, Officer."

"And do you use it for anything other than business?"

He took a deep breath. "Occasionally. I really can't see how relevant . . ."

"So all the files stored on it would be yours. And they would mostly be connected to your work as a structural engineer, but there might be some personal data on there, too. Would that be a fair assessment?"

Charles Armitage nodded once. "Yes." He managed to look both ill and obstinate.

"May I see the computer, sir?" asked Hazel, adding, from not much more than personal malice, "Again."

That, too, had the desired effect. Her meaning jolted through his expression. "You accessed it?"

"Of course we did, Mr. Armitage. How else could we find the owner?"

"But the password . . ."

"Yes," she reflected. "PASSWORD. Not the most secure I've ever come across. In fact, I read somewhere that it's the commonest password used in the English-speaking world. You might want to change it to something a bit more original." And then, having stretched the silence until it was ready to break like an elastic band, she added pointedly, "And DROWSSAP isn't much better."

If she'd expected him to fall apart in front of her at the dreadful realization of how much she knew, to fall gibbering at her feet, blaming it all on his upbringing and the public school system and the fact that his wife didn't understand him, Hazel had mistaken her man. He seemed to shrink in front of her; but things that get smaller without losing mass actually get denser, harder. Charles Armitage's eyes hardened to little steel balls and his lips compressed so much that they almost disappeared.

"Thank you for the advice, Officer," he said, expressionless. "I'll bear it in mind."

Hazel nodded slowly. "So . . . may I?"

"May you what?"

"See the laptop that was returned to you."

Of course, he'd had a week to work out what to do if this, or anything like it, came knocking at his door. He was on firmer ground here, and it showed. "I'm afraid not."

"Really?" said Hazel. She could hardly pretend to be surprised. "Surely you haven't lost it again?"

"In fact, I gave it away," said Armitage, lying easily because actually it didn't matter whether she believed him or not. "While it was missing, I treated myself to a new one. When it turned up again, I took all my data off it and passed it on to a charity. They send them to schoolchildren in Africa, I believe."

Hazel hadn't seen that one coming. "What was the name of the charity?"

Armitage pondered. "I don't think I can remember. I saw a flyer, it seemed like a nice idea, I dialed the number, and someone picked it up."

"Do you still have the flyer?"

It was a final sally from a position about to be overrun, and Armitage knew it. There was a tight smile in his voice. "I'm afraid not. I didn't expect to be asked about it."

There was nothing more Hazel could do. There wouldn't have been much more if she'd been here in an official capacity. She could make an accusation she now had no way of proving, or she could retreat with a small measure of dignity intact.

But she couldn't resist a parting shot. She knew what he'd been up to. Armitage knew she knew. If all she could do was give him a sleepless night, and maybe get him to stop surfing the Internet for a bit, it had to be better than nothing. "Not to worry," she said, the words casual but the message in her eyes entirely serious. "There can't be many people doing that in this area. I'm sure I can find them. Someone must remember collecting your laptop. From here, was it, or your office?"

"Er . . ." The thing about lying is, you need to think fast and remember well. The thing about structural engineering is, you take all the time necessary to do all your thinking long before someone picks up a trowel, and you write everything down. Charles Armitage was not a natural liar. "Here," he managed to say eventually.

It was the right answer—if he'd said the office, a colleague would have witnessed the transaction—but the time it took him to produce it, and the uncertainty in his voice, left her a small but definite triumph to leave on. "Good enough, Mr. Armitage," she said, turning from his door. "I'll let you know if there's anything else I need to ask you." A faint spring in her step, she returned to her car.

It was empty.

CHAPTER 16

I<small>T DIDN'T TAKE HER TEN SECONDS TO LOCATE THEM,</small> Saturday and Patience both, on a wide verge fifty meters away, playing a version of fetch in which the dog dropped a ball into the long grass and the boy beat around looking for it. But for those ten seconds she thought it had happened again. That she'd lost someone else for whose safety she'd assumed responsibility. That someone had seen Saturday waiting outside Armitage's house, guessed who he was, and taken him where he couldn't be a threat anymore.

When she spotted them, relief surged in her throat like vomit; but faster and sourer still came a furious rage. She'd told him to stay in the car. He'd agreed to stay in the car. And she couldn't pump the horn, let alone shout his name, without drawing attention to him. She got into the car, turned it around, and drove to where they were playing. "Get in," she said quietly.

They both looked at her innocently. "Finished, then?" said Saturday.

"Just . . . get in." Hazel was hanging on to her temper by the thinnest of threads.

They were half a mile down the road before she trusted herself to speak again. "I told you to stay out of sight."

Saturday seemed genuinely surprised. "I *was* out of sight. Unless there was someone sitting on the roof, hanging on to the belfry, and I'm pretty sure I'd have noticed if there was."

Hazel breathed heavily at him. "How can I get it into your thick skull that you could be in danger?"

The boy delayed answering so long that she thought he wasn't going to, that he'd accepted the reprimand to deny her the satisfaction of shouting at him. She concentrated on her driving.

But Saturday wasn't stumped for an answer. He was just trying to formulate it in a way that she might understand. "Hazel," he said quietly after a minute or so, "I'm always in danger. Not just me, we all are—all the people I live around. Every night from October to May there's the danger of a hard frost that means some of us won't wake up. Every time we strike lucky and find someone's unwanted lunch on a park bench, there's the danger it's been there longer than we thought and there's enough bugs in it to bring a buffalo to its knees. Every time we ask someone for his change, there's the chance he's had a really bad day and this is the last straw and he's going to turn nasty. A girl I knew was in hospital for three months after a pinstriped city type hit her with his umbrella and knocked her into the traffic.

"You know this. You know that if we arrange to meet, you're always slightly surprised when I turn up. If you want to feel safe, if you want some certainty in your life, you probably don't want to live the way I live. I'm not saying this so you'll feel sorry for me," he explained earnestly, "just so you understand. We don't feel the same way about danger as you do. Because it's always there, in our lives, pretty much everywhere we look. And because we have less to lose."

And then, having twisted the heart within her, he broke it entirely by adding, "But it's kind of nice that you care."

Another mile down the road Hazel asked, "Whatever happened to you, Saturday? You're a nice kid. Somebody loved you enough to make a good job of bringing you up. She should be proud of you. But here you are, sixteen years old—"

"Seventeen last week," he interjected, as if that was the bit that mattered. He was sitting not beside her but on the backseat, one arm round the lurcher.

"Seventeen years old, you're living in empty buildings, you own nothing that you can't carry on your back, and your idea of a day's work is leaning on a lamppost, sticking your hand out as people go past. You're capable of so much more than that. You're worth so much more. Whatever happened to make you think you weren't?"

"She died," Saturday said simply. "My mum. She died when I was thirteen. Breast cancer. She hung on long enough for my bar mitzvah"—in the rearview mirror a tiny smile crossed his face—"and then she died. My dad remarried. We didn't get on. I went to live with my grandparents. Then my gran got sick. My granddad didn't need to worry about me as well, so I moved out. I told him I had somewhere to go. I write to him sometimes, tell him I'm doing fine. Maybe he believes me. Or maybe he wonders why I never send an address he can write back to."

Hazel had let the car coast to a halt. Not because she had anything to say that required her full attention. She had nothing to say at all. And she knew he'd be utterly astonished if she leaned through the gap in the seats and hugged him. All the same, she felt the tears she'd all but managed to stifle in the last few days beating their fists against the inside of her throat. There had been a couple of times in her life when she thought she'd been really unlucky. But that left all the rest of her life, and moments like this she knew herself blessed. Perhaps she always knew, but it took moments like this to remind her.

She put the car back into gear and rejoined the traffic. She thought in silence for six or seven miles. She suspected that what she wanted to do was crazy. She still thought that it was right.

Finally she said, watching for his reaction in the mirror, "If I can find a little house to rent, will you come and live with me? As my lodger," she added hurriedly, in case he should think anything different. "This may be your lucky day, but it's not that lucky. All I'm offering is room and board. I won't try to reform you. If you want a chance in life, you'll have to make your own. But I'd like to know you have somewhere dry to sleep at night. What do you think?"

"I've no money," he pointed out, unnecessarily.

"I've got enough. Hell's bells," she snorted, "anyone who could afford to keep a budgie could feed you. All I ask is that you don't trash the place, you help me look after Patience, and you don't bring trouble to my door. I'm still a police officer. Any laws you're in the habit of breaking, you stop now."

"Doesn't Ash's wife—"

"Widow," Hazel said, correcting him.

"—want Patience?"

Hazel shook her head. "She doesn't like dogs."

She might have taken offense that he had to think about it. But then, he, too, was giving things up. His freedom to come and go unnoticed. His right to break any laws he could get away with. Any change carried the seeds of risk. He might have thought it better to stick to the life he knew.

But he didn't. "Okay," he said. As if she'd offered him ketchup on his burger. As if it was a thing of no great matter, to either of them, whether he said yes or no.

For a moment Hazel was taken aback. Then she understood that, to someone accustomed to disappointments, the best defense was not to put too much value on anything. "Okay, then," she said, and drove them home to Norbold.

The next morning she was waiting when the estate agents' opened.

M rs. Poliakov was sorry to see her go. Hazel thought she was even sorry to see Patience go. But then, she hadn't mentioned Saturday. She was pretty sure her landlady would have felt less sentimental about her departure if she'd said she was bringing a homeless youth to live with her.

At some point she was going to have to tell her father, too. Unflappable in many ways, he was still a conventional man. He might confine his comments to a raised eyebrow, but Hazel knew it would not so much disappear into his hairline, which had receded, as go clean over the top and fall down the back of his pullover.

But apart from the fact that no money would change hands—or if it did (Hazel was a realist) it would go the opposite way from usual—she was only doing what Mrs. Poliakov had done for the last thirty years: letting out a room in her house to someone who needed somewhere to stay. Saturday wasn't even a grown man, he was just a boy; and maybe people would talk, but Hazel had had worse things said about her. She wanted to help him, she could help him, and she was going to help him—whether he wanted helping or not.

The house was in a smoke-stained terrace close to the town center, five minutes from the park in one direction and the canal in the other. Studying the particulars, Hazel realized with a shock that she was putting the dog's requirements ahead of those of the humans involved. There was also a back garden. The daughter of a gardener, Hazel was suddenly struck by the fact that she'd missed having a bit of green space that was her own. It was overgrown—the house had been empty for a month; the estate agent was so keen to let it that he gave her a knockdown rent—but it's wonderful what you can achieve with a strimmer on the brush-cutter setting.

Some bits of furniture had been left behind by a previous tenant, including a Victorian bed in the main bedroom that was so big it must have been built up there, but there was still a list of basics she needed to buy. She made Saturday go with her, not so much for his design input as to help carry things.

She found him a cheap bed in a charity shop. Saturday was appalled at how much even a cheap bed cost. "You can't afford all this," he hissed at her, a little like Jiminy Cricket and a little like her mother.

"Yes, I can," she said.

"You're not working, either."

"I'm on invalidity. You get injured in the course of duty, they look after you." The fact that her injuries were mostly psychological, and at least in her own judgment had healed some time ago, had not inclined the assessors to deal more strictly with her. Hazel suspected they were paying her to stay off work because she was less trouble that way.

They carried what they could—the furniture would follow in a van—home to the little house in Railway Street. Patience had already appropriated the most comfortable chair, but she left it long enough to greet them at the door. She was carrying a ball.

Hazel vaguely recognized that it had been around for a while, but she hadn't had time to notice. "Where did that come from?" The lurcher had never really done toys.

"She found it," said Saturday, stacking paint cans. "Last week, while you were talking to the perv."

Hazel regarded him levelly. "You let her steal his children's ball?"

"She didn't steal anything," said Saturday dismissively. "They threw it away. It's got a hole in it the size of your finger. Only a dog would want it."

Even the lurcher didn't want it very much. In the back garden, after they'd spent most of Monday moving in, Hazel tried throwing it for her. Patience studiously ignored the thing; Hazel had to fetch it herself. It was blue, with a cartoon footballer embossed on it, and had no bounce left.

Knocking the house into shape took less time than she'd expected. With Saturday's help, which was neither very expert nor very dependable but was marginally better than nothing, she did most of what needed doing that first week. By the weekend the worst of the paintwork had been refreshed—however cheap the rent, she couldn't sleep in a Barbie pink bedroom—the kitchen and bathroom had been scrubbed clean, and new curtains, rugs, and throws had given the whole place a fresh look. Hazel was inordinately proud of it. This was the first time she'd had a house of her own. She'd lived with her parents, she'd lived in university accommodation, in flat shares with friends, in police station houses, and she'd lived with Mrs. Poliakov. She'd moved into the house in Highfield Road while Ash was in hospital. But she'd never been a householder before. Never been the one who'd have to fill in the census form. Suddenly, at the age of twenty-six, she felt quite grown-up.

Partly, she recognized, her enthusiasm stemmed from the fact that she'd finally found a way to move forward. Ash's death ten days ago had cast a pall over her soul—on top of which had come the Armitage fiasco. The little house in Railway Street seemed to represent a turning point. From now on things were going to get better. Better for Saturday, and also better for her.

After a little thought, she presented Saturday with his own front door key, together with the warning that she'd be running the bolt across before she went to bed and she got really grumpy if her sleep was disturbed.

He looked at it as if he didn't know what it was.

"You put it in the lock and turn it," she said helpfully, "then the door will open."

A little glitter of annoyance sparked in his eye. "I know what it does," he growled.

"Yes? Well, that one's a Yale key." She reached out and turned it in his hand. "It goes in that way up."

"Thank you," said Saturday.

Hazel smiled. "You're welcome. I know it's all a bit new. . . ."

"I didn't mean the key. At least, I didn't *just* mean the key. I meant"—his gaze circled the kitchen—"this. Thank you."

She nodded, returned to the cupboard she was stocking. "But I meant it," she added over her shoulder. "*Very* grumpy."

In spite of which, she was fully prepared for a testing of boundaries the first Friday night they were there. She was determined to keep her word and lock him out if he tried to roll home after midnight, drunk or high, or in the company of people her father and Mrs. Poliakov would have considered undesirable. She didn't expect to change him into a model citizen, overnight or probably at all; but neither did she intend to be a martyr to his lifestyle, and the sooner he realized it, the better.

In fact, he didn't go out at all, except to walk the dog. They sat together on the inherited sofa and watched television, which was more enjoyable than it should have been, simply because it was their television and their sofa and their home now. When Hazel was ready for bed, she found Saturday had succumbed some time earlier and was fast asleep, snoring softly, his head cushioned against the back of the chesterfield. She didn't wake him, just spread a throw over him against the early-morning chill and went to her bed smiling. She no longer had any reservations about taking the boy in. It had felt like the right thing to do because it was.

He brought her breakfast in bed, which was a nice thought, even though you could have varnished oceangoing yachts with the tea.

She just wished he'd be a bit more careful about locking the back door when he went out. Admittedly, she was a police officer and therefore probably neurotic about security; and Saturday wasn't used to having the kind of personal space you could lock, which didn't matter, because he also didn't own anything worth stealing. Hazel told herself he'd get the hang of locking up eventually, and in the meantime they could probably count on Patience to deter any prowlers. But it irritated her that the boy's immediate reaction to being reminded was to deny all responsibility. Again, in his old life, denying responsibility for anything and everything was a sound default position. But it wasn't unreasonable to expect him to start growing up a bit, now he was seventeen.

Then something happened that made her wonder if she'd been blaming him unfairly.

She was in the back garden with Patience. The dog brought

her the purloined ball. Hazel threw it down the garden, because that's what you're supposed to do; and instead of doing what she was supposed to do, which was fetch it, Patience gave a kind of lurcher shrug and wandered away.

Walking down the lawn after it, Hazel gave the dog a serious talking-to. "This is the very last time," she informed her sternly. "I'm not going to keep throwing it if you won't bring it back."

She retrieved the flattened thing out of the shrubbery. Patience was watching with interest to see what she'd do next.

"I mean it," said Hazel. "If you don't want to chase it, stop giving it to me."

Patience waved her long scimitar-shaped tail. She came and sat in front of Hazel, regarding the ball steadily.

"Last time," Hazel warned her again. "Last time *ever*, unless you bring it back." And she threw it toward the house.

Patience gave a gentle sigh and lay down in the grass.

Hazel stalked the length of the lawn and bent to lift the thing from the flower bed under the kitchen window. "That's it. That's absolutely it. I'm putting it away now, and you're not getting it back. You don't want to retrieve, fine. But don't ask me to throw what you don't want to fetch!"

Somewhere in the course of this one-sided argument, however, her attention shifted from the beat-up ball with its deflated cartoon footballer, and she finished the sentence on autopilot. She was looking at the flower bed, newly turned where she'd grubbed up four months' worth of weeds and planted some geraniums. The geraniums were fine, but between them—carefully between them, as if their owner hadn't wanted to leave any damage as evidence of his visit—there were footprints.

Sometime in the two days since she'd planted the bed, someone had stood looking in at the kitchen window.

Hazel was a pragmatist. She looked for simple explanations first. Had she left the marks herself when she was working there? Well, no. She'd heeled the plants in, but she hadn't stood among them with her face to the back window. She'd had no reason to do so. If she'd wanted to know what was going on in the kitchen, she'd have gone inside.

Saturday, then. Had he been out here with Patience and heard Hazel in the kitchen and looked in to see if there was any chance of a brew-up? He might well have done, thought Hazel, but he wouldn't have left footprints that big if he had. He was a seventeen-year-old boy the size of a fourteen-year-old girl, and those were the footprints of a man.

A shiver ran down her spine. She hadn't been in the habit of wandering around naked even before she shared her home with Saturday, but the idea of some stranger hiding in the dark and watching her was deeply unsettling. Her mind turning over the possibilities, Hazel headed back inside. "And you," she told Patience severely, "are about as good a guard dog as you are a retriever."

Two scenarios occurred to her. She didn't like the first, but the second was more worrying.

Hazel and her young lodger had moved into this house six days earlier. It was not impossible that one of the neighbors, curious about them, had taken the direct approach to nosiness and shinned over the back gate. The garden was sufficiently well enclosed to keep the dog in, but a determined Peeping Tom might have come equipped with a stepladder. Or just reached over and groped for the bolt. Hazel made a mental note to put a padlock on it before today was out.

The more worrying possibility was that the man watching from the garden knew exactly who she was, and also who Saturday was. That, far from being intimidated by her visit, Charles

Armitage had decided to return it. If so, he now knew things that she wouldn't have wanted him to.

She was more concerned for Saturday than for herself. Even on sick leave, a police officer isn't someone to take on lightly. If Armitage threatened her with violence, he'd quickly find colleagues from Norbold and farther afield lining up to deal with him. Not because they liked her, because most of them didn't, but because a police service that tolerates attacks on its members has lost its authority. Respect isn't just an aspiration: it's body armor.

The street kid, with no family, no status, almost no friends, would be a much easier target. If Armitage guessed that Saturday had seen what was hidden on his laptop, the situation could be salvaged easily enough. Street kids disappear all the time, and no one ever knows—or usually cares—if they've died or moved on or what. If the man or someone in his employ had stood in the back garden of the little house in Railway Street last night and seen the skinny youth in Hazel's kitchen, Saturday was now in danger.

A cold hand fingered her heart. What if Saturday was telling the truth and he hadn't left the back door open? What if the owner of the footprints had got a key or made one or found a way of doing without one, and had been inside the house? If he'd done it once, there was nothing to stop him from doing it again. That no one was hurt the first time was no guarantee that no one would be hurt in the future.

Hazel knew there were two things she ought to do. The first was easy: she could have the locks changed immediately, Sunday afternoon or no Sunday afternoon. The second, which seemed equally obvious at first glance, in fact presented considerable problems. She couldn't tell Detective Inspector Gorman that she'd had a visit from Charles Armitage without also telling him that Armitage had had one from her. And Gorman would hit the roof.

He'd be entitled to. She had interfered with an investigation that was his prerogative, even if other demands on his time had prevented him from proceeding as quickly as Hazel Best would have liked. He may even have been delaying his opening gambit deliberately, to give Armitage time to relax and grow incautious. When he learned that, far from being lulled into a sense of false security, Armitage had been warned that the police were still interested in him—pretty much what they knew and even how little of it they could prove—Dave Gorman would want her guts for garters.

The prospect of getting a right royal roasting should not have deterred her from taking whatever measures were necessary to protect Saturday and herself. But it's human nature to avoid a bollocking where we can, and Hazel at least wanted to be sure it was the best option before confessing to DI Gorman. She called the locksmith, deciding to defer any other action until it was clear that new locks wouldn't resolve the situation.

CHAPTER 17

THREE DAYS AFTER THE NEW LOCKS WERE FITTED, someone had been in the house again.

At first it was nothing much more than intuition telling Hazel that it was so. There was nothing to see: no broken glass, no jimmied woodwork. So far as she could determine, nothing had been taken; at first she wasn't even aware that anything had been moved. Was there an unfamiliar smell in here, then? But no; only the increasingly homely signatures of dog, which is rather engagingly the smell of broken biscuits, and—somewhat less beguiling—teenager's trainers.

She tried to tell herself she was imagining it. That the previous visitation had left her jumping at shadows. But somehow she knew better. "Absence of evidence," she murmured to herself, quoting from a distant lecture, "is not evidence of absence."

And finally she spotted something that supported what the short hairs on the back of her neck had been trying to tell her: something that shouldn't even have been in the sitting room, let alone displayed on the bookshelf as if it were a treasure. The ball Patience had brought home from the Clent Hills. The punctured, flattened blue ball with the cartoon footballer on it.

She called Saturday down from his room. (She'd bought him a junk-shop television. Now he could hardly be dragged away from it.) "I'm going to ask you something really stupid," Hazel said. "I know what the answer is. I just need to hear you say it, so there's no room for doubt. Did you put that up there?" She pointed.

The boy frowned, unsure what she was pointing at. "The candlestick? The photo of your mum and dad? One of the books? Whatever, the answer's no. . . ." Then he saw it. "What's the dog's ball doing there?"

"Thank you," said Hazel quietly. "So you didn't." Saturday shook his head. "And I didn't. And Patience can't reach that high. Our friend has been back."

"You mean . . ." Finally there was a hint of alarm in his voice.

"Yes."

"After you changed the locks."

"Yes."

"You think it was . . ."

"Oh yes."

Saturday thought about it. "You think he drove thirty miles and broke in so carefully that there's nothing to show for it, in order to put his kids' ball on your bookshelf? *Why?*"

"It's a message. He wants me to know that he can get at me anytime he wants. If I make trouble for him, he'll be back, and next time he won't settle for rearranging the ornaments."

Saturday was impressed. "All that from a dog's ball?"

"Before it was Patience's ball, it was his kids' ball. He knows I know that. He knew I'd know what bringing it in here meant."

Saturday sucked on his front teeth. "What are we going to do?"

A little bit of Hazel was grateful for that. Just because she'd tried to solve some of his problems didn't mean he had to return the favor, so it was nice that he wanted to. But the greater part of her was determined to keep him out of harm's way. She wanted to keep those thirty miles between Saul Desmond, known as Saturday, and Charles Armitage, with his interest in hurting children, for as long as she could.

"*We* are doing nothing," she said firmly. "*I* am going to have this out with Mr. Armitage, right now. I am damned if I'm having him threaten me in my own house."

"You'll be in a lot more trouble if he starts threatening you in *his* house."

"This is true," acknowledged Hazel. "Which is why you're going to sit by the phone. I'll call you when I get there. I'll call you again when I leave. If you haven't heard from me after half an hour, call DI Gorman"—she scribbled the number of his mobile—"and tell him what's going on. Tell him I may need help."

Somehow, the Clent Hills seemed closer this time. Too close. Hazel wasn't sure she should be rattling the cage of an unpredictable man who knew where she lived and could be there in under an hour. But the alternative was to let him think she was intimidated by his mind games. And maybe she was, but she was damned if she was letting him know that.

She wondered if he'd be expecting her. He must have known that one possible response to his invasion of her home was that she'd come back and make merry hell in his. But then, he hadn't left a message lipsticked to her mirror, something she would see as soon as she got home. It might have taken her a couple of days to notice the ball on her shelf and work out what it meant. So he wouldn't be waiting for her. But neither would he be surprised when she turned up.

In fact, he was on his way home from work. Hazel had her suspicions from half a mile back about the broad-breasted charcoal gray car she found herself following through the country lanes. It was just the kind of car she would expect a man like Charles Armitage to drive: just a little bit bigger, bolder, and more ostentatious than was strictly necessary.

And he realized it was her before he had the uncomfortable experience of turning into his own drive and seeing her turn in after him. Of course, if he knew her new address, he would certainly know what car she drove. In any event, realizing he was being followed, he pulled over beside the broad grass verge where Patience and Saturday had played with the ball, and climbed out.

"Miss Best," he rumbled by way of a greeting. "I'm surprised to see you again."

"Yeah, right," retorted Hazel. She got out of her car, too, discreetly checking the phone in her pocket.

Armitage frowned. "I thought I made it clear that I had nothing more to say to you."

"If you didn't want me coming back here, maybe you shouldn't have left an invitation at my house."

The frown deepened. "What?"

"The ball on my bookshelf? With the comedy footballer on it?"

He was looking at her as if she were mad and quite possibly dangerous. Which was fine with Hazel. She wanted him to be afraid of her. It might be the best protection either she or Saturday had against his malice.

She breathed heavily at him. "Mr. Armitage, I'm finding these games of yours increasingly tiresome. I thought we had some kind of an understanding. I thought you understood that I know what you've been up to, but in view of the difficulty of proving it now that you've disposed of the laptop, I was willing to give you a chance to mend your ways. I thought you understood that you're on our radar now, and there will be people watching you for a very long time. I'm only one of them. If you think that scaring me off is going to solve your problem, you don't understand at all how the police work. We're like the proverbial swan. Sometimes there seems to be nothing much happening. But if you look below the surface, the feet are going like the clappers to get us where we need to be."

Charles Armitage kept looking at her—as if, Hazel thought, she had the remains of her dinner on her chin. Of course, he wanted to make her think she might be mistaken. Know she was right but be afraid that she was wrong. Because in the face of outright denial, there was no more she could do this time than there had been before.

Policing isn't always about what you can do. Sometimes it's about what you can make people believe you can do. And sometimes that's a good thing and sometimes it's not, but today it was the only weapon left to her.

So she drew herself up to her full height and curled her lip at him. "Let's cut the crap here. We both know you've lied repeatedly since you lost your laptop, so there's no earthly reason I'd believe anything you say now. I'm not here for an explanation. I know why you broke into my house."

She raised a peremptory hand to forestall the protest he was obviously preparing. "Yes, I know—it wasn't you. But if you hire someone, the way you hired Martha Harris and now presumably you've hired someone else, you are responsible for their actions in every way that counts, legally and otherwise.

"So I'll say it again: I know why you broke into my house.

And when I talk to Detective Inspector Gorman, *he'll* know why you broke into my house. He already knows about the dirty pictures on your computer. When he hears you've been stalking me, he'll suspect you're more than just a consumer of child pornography, that you are in fact a purveyor. Someone responsible for ordering attacks on children, for making images of them, and for disseminating them via the Internet. Someone, in short, he'll want to get behind bars urgently enough to drop whatever else he's doing.

"Which probably wasn't your intention, was it? Well, welcome to the world of unintended consequences." She was a little taken aback at the venom she heard in her own voice.

"I didn't break into your house," said Charles Armitage. Behind the imperious calm she heard desperation. "I didn't send anyone to break into your house." Somewhere he found the gall to look down his nose at her. "And isn't that a rather pretentious way of describing two rooms with a Polish widow?"

Surprised, Hazel hesitated. Could he possibly not know she'd moved? "I'm not going to the expense of changing the locks again when you've obviously got some way of shimming them." She was well aware of the difficulties, even for an expert, of creating security that another expert couldn't breach. Ordinary household locks are meant to deter opportunistic housebreakers, not high-end professionals. Lock yourself out of your own house and you'll see how quickly your local locksmith can gain access—unless you're paying him by the hour. "What I'm going to do instead is warn you that the next time I see so much as a shadow on my window I'll be talking to Dave Gorman and so, in very short order, will you. If that isn't what you want, stay away from me."

"I didn't break into your house," said Armitage again. He paused, debating with himself whether to say more, decided he had little to lose. "And I find myself wondering why, if you're so convinced I did, you haven't spoken to Detective Inspector Gorman already."

It was, of course, the raised flagstone on which her shaky authority tripped and went sprawling. He must have realized that. But Hazel had hoped to have finished marking his card and be driving away before he could react.

The best she could do was bluster. "Detective Inspector Gorman doesn't need my help to deal with you. He'll search your house from rafters to cellar. He'll seize anything capable of storing digital images and question every member of your family. And he won't stop until he has the lot. All the grubby little pictures in your collection. How long you've been collecting them, where you got them. If you took any of them yourself, who helped you, and who your victims were. After he's finished, your reputation will be in tiny little pieces you could keep in an envelope."

Too late she heard what she was doing: warning him how a thorough investigation would proceed. Dave Gorman would have the battered, bloodied remnants of her warrant card for this.

But Charles Armitage seemed to have heard something that alarmed him. He took a step back and his face closed down, a shield to guard whatever it was he was most anxious to protect. For a third time, carefully now, he said, "I didn't break into your house. I haven't done any of the things you think I have. That's not quite true," he amended. "I did ask Ms. Harris to find out who you were, and that was foolish. I was . . . a little freaked by what had happened." He managed a wan smile. "It seemed like a good idea at the time."

Hazel had no sympathy for him. "An even better idea would have been *not* to fill up your computer with the kind of images that no self-respecting man would want to see once, let alone repeatedly. Would want to forget if he came across them by accident."

Armitage hesitated, thinking urgently. Without knowing it, he was twisting his fingers together as if wringing out a wet cloth. "Miss Best," he said finally, "I don't know what you thought you saw on that computer—"

"*Thought* I saw!" echoed Hazel indignantly, and in fact misleadingly.

"—but none of it was my doing," he continued with quiet obstinacy. "I am not particularly familiar with technology. I know how to use it for my work, I do the same things with it so often I could do them in my sleep, but there are whole areas that I know nothing about. That—what you're talking about—is one of them. I have never come across such images, even by accident. I have never downloaded them onto a computer. I have never wanted to.

"I'm a structural engineer. I'm interested in building things. Good, useful things that do a job for people, and make their days better and easier. I'm also a husband and father; I love my family and want to keep them safe. I haven't done what you think I've done. I'm no threat to you, and in fact you're no threat to me. You can't prove your accusation, partly because the laptop is no longer available but also because it isn't true. Please don't ruin my life trying to prove that it is."

Hazel knew she couldn't trust a word he said. But some treacherous corner of her heart wished she could—wanted it all to be a misunderstanding. But she believed absolutely that Saturday had seen what he said he'd seen.

"So you explain it," she said roughly. "Those images were on your laptop—we're not even going to discuss that. If you didn't put them there, who did?"

Armitage blinked. As if a chink had opened in the darkness and, just for a moment, daylight had streamed in. "Somebody playing a joke? Yes. I take it to building sites with me. I put it down while I go off to look at some I-beams. Maybe one of the laborers thought it was funny, to download some pictures that would blow the socks off that stuffy Mr. Armitage with his preoccupation with concrete mixes. . . ."

Hazel gave him a deeply skeptical look. "How would he have got past your password?"

"The same way you did—by knowing it's the one used by people with no imagination!"

She couldn't argue with that. "But if someone wanted you to find the pictures, why protect them with *another* password?"

"Because . . ." But he couldn't think of a reason, and the sentence petered out.

Hazel scowled at him. But it was a kind of double-edged scowl, facing both ways. She was missing something here. She'd known exactly who Charles Armitage was after Saturday told her what he'd seen on the man's computer. His attempts to frighten her had only confirmed it. She'd known exactly what she was dealing with when she first came here to confront him sixteen days ago.

Only somehow, this time she'd seen another side of him. The imagined laborer had a point: the man *was* stuffy. Middle-aged, middle-class, middle-income, middle-of-the-road. The kind of man who completed questionnaires with fives and sixes. Mr. Average. Hazel was inclined to believe him when he said he was a loving husband and father. Somehow, what she knew was now arguing with what she saw.

He said he hadn't sent anyone to break into her house. Well, he would, wouldn't he? Except, if his purpose was to show how far his reach extended, he wouldn't want her to actually believe that. And again, she more than halfway did.

So what did she know for sure? That the dog's ball was on her bookshelf. That before it was Patience's ball, it belonged to the Armitage children. Hopefully, they'd thrown it away after it got punctured, although possibly she'd sneaked in and stolen it off the front lawn, but either way, Hazel was meant to know where it had come from. Otherwise the message would have been meaningless and so would the threat. That ball was significant only if it was brought into her house and left where she would see it at the behest of Charles Armitage.

But Armitage denied it. And how could he not know that she'd moved—or if he knew, why pretend not to, when the effectiveness of his threats depended on Hazel's knowing who was threatening her?

Somewhere in the drive train of her mind, cogs were beginning to move and mesh. (With a degree in information technology under her belt, Hazel would have loved to compare her brain to a computer, connections lighting up the synapses faster than a Riverdancer's feet. But usually it felt much more twentieth century than that. Sometimes it felt like it was being powered by a turnspit dog.)

Sergeant Mole, who had talked at training college about the absence of evidence, had had other aphorisms as well. It isn't always necessary, he used to say, to see the chicken. If there are eggs in the kitchen, and chicken pellets in the shed, and chicken shit on your shoes, it is reasonable to infer the presence of a chicken, whether you can see one or not. And Hazel Best had seen signs of the chicken.

She took a long slow breath and let it out in a rueful sigh. She managed a smile. "Mr. Armitage, I don't think I'm achieving much here now, am I? It's just possible I owe you an apology. I thought I knew what was going on, but maybe I was wrong. Maybe I should go home, and we'll try not to bother each other again. What do you think?"

Charles Armitage thought it was an excellent idea. He tried, for the look of the thing, not to seem too eager, but still he jumped at it. "You *were* wrong about me. I promise you."

"Yes? Well, good. Just—you know—be careful. With the new computer."

"I will," said Armitage fervently. "Believe me."

She did. "What did you go for? A handy tablet, or something with some real wellie behind it?"

Armitage gave a wry smile. "I told you, I'm no expert. But for that price, I *hope* it's wearing wellies!"

"Lots of memory? Lots of speed?"

"Oh yes."

"Top-end graphics?"

"The best. So I'm reliably informed."

Hazel was nodding slowly. Sometimes you spend all day digging a trap, only to see the suspect tap-dance around the edge. But sometimes he jumps in with both feet. "Everyone needs a computer expert in the family these days. Who's yours?"

"My s—"

If Charles Armitage had finished the word, Hazel might have been left wondering if she'd jumped to the wrong conclusion. Again. But he didn't. He froze one letter in. The tentative smile fell off his face and his thick, soft body, which had been cautiously relaxing, jerked rigid. He knew he'd made a mistake. He knew *she* knew he'd made a mistake. It was too late to rectify it; all he could do now was wait to see how costly it would prove.

"I suppose we could keep this up for a while longer," said Hazel kindly. "Keep pretending the laptop was yours, that everything on it was yours, and that if you have a son at all, he isn't remotely interested in the Internet. But we're neither of us getting any younger, Mr. Armitage, and sooner or later we'll have to deal with the reality of what happened. Tell me about your son. Tell me about how you borrowed his laptop, and only found out what he kept on it after it was stolen from the petrol station."

CHAPTER 18

I F HE'D THOUGHT A LIE WOULD SERVE, he'd have lied. He'd done much worse trying to deal with the consequences of his carelessness. He'd hired a private detective. He'd tried to intimidate a police officer, for pity's sake!—him, Charles Armitage, who obeyed speed limits when there was no one about and halted at stop signs when there was nothing coming. He was one of nature's compliants. Show him a line in the sand and he'd die of thirst before crossing it.

None of which had prevented him from becoming a successful professional. If there was ever a trade in which slavish adherence to the rules was a virtue, it was structural engineering. (Creativity doesn't keep bridges from falling. Mathematics does.) Nor had it hindered him in his quest to be a husband and father. He'd found a girl who didn't like taking risks, either, and they'd built a happy life around obedience to the laws of God, man, and the parish council. They never put their bins out on the wrong day, and always sorted the recyclables first.

But there is literally no limit to what a man will do to protect his children. Even—perhaps especially—a man like Charles

Armitage. Lie? He'd have stripped to his underwear and claimed to be Superman if it would have done any good.

But he'd seen enough of this clear-eyed young policewoman to know that more lies wouldn't make her go away. He'd thought he'd got rid of her, but she'd come back. He still wasn't entirely sure why, but he knew now that she wasn't going to be fobbed off and she wasn't going to be frightened off. He'd have tried buying her off if he hadn't known with absolute certainty that it would make things ten times worse.

One possibility remained. It didn't offer much hope of rescue from the dreadful coils of deceit he'd managed to wind around himself, but in extremis any hope is better than none. It had always been his first choice, now it was his last resort. The truth.

"He's fourteen," he told Hazel quietly. They were leaning against a field gate. If anyone saw them, he'd say he was giving her directions. "I suppose it's the curious age. When I was fourteen, I was curious about girls, too, but there was no such thing as the Internet, so you had to pluck up the courage to meet them face-to-face. It was all horribly embarrassing, you just *knew* what was going through their minds while you were trying to strike up a conversation, but it had this in its favor: you never got the chance to see them as a commodity. Something to be used. *You* had to approach *them*, which was difficult, and they had only to turn up their noses at you to send you on your way a gibbering wreck. You *had* to show them some respect."

He sighed. "Teenagers today, they go on about all the friends they have, but what they mean is that someone found their photograph less than totally repulsive and hit a button on a computer. It doesn't *mean* anything. It's easy and undiscriminating, and in no way prepares them for proper relationships. They don't actually know how to make friends. They just sit in front of their screens, each in his own private space, and they barely understand the difference between what's real and what isn't. Because they're viewing the images in the same way, they don't really understand the difference between the fictional world of films and games and the real world, in which real people are being hurt. They know it, but they don't *feel* it."

Hazel didn't disagree with him. She didn't yet see how relevant this was, but he seemed to be trying to explain and she was willing to give him time.

"I don't know where he found those images." All the color had gone out of both his face and his voice; he seemed ten years older. "He says he stumbled across them at different times, and wouldn't know where to find them again. But that's a bit disingenuous. You might find something like that, but you wouldn't download it. Well—I wouldn't. And you wouldn't. I don't know about other fourteen-year-old boys. I kind of hope they would. The alternative is to think that my son is peculiarly perverted in his interests and instincts."

Armitage took a deep breath. "I knew nothing about any of this until the morning I was going to Norbold for a presentation to the council on the development at the Archway."

"Dirty Nellie's." Hazel nodded.

The engineer blinked. "Sorry?"

"Dirty Nellie's. I'm sorry to be the one to tell you, Mr. Armitage, but however impressive a design you come up with for it, and however trendy a name you give it, in Norbold it'll always be known as Dirty Nellie's."

"Really?" He took his glasses off and polished them. "How unfortunate. So I'm part of the team giving this presentation, and

I'm on my way out to the car when I trip over the next door's cat and drop my laptop. I switch it on to check it's all right, and it isn't. I can't seem to access any of the files I want.

"Which isn't the end of the world. I've got it all backed up on a memory stick—all I need is a laptop. My son was already at school, so I couldn't ask him, but I didn't think he'd mind if I borrowed his. Not really, not when it mattered so much. I picked it up and got on my way.

"I didn't really need petrol. But I thought it would look un-professional to go into the meeting and have to start fiddling with the memory stick, so I stopped at the service station, filled up, and spent a couple of minutes transferring my data onto my son's lap-top. I didn't hit any problems. Of course, I knew his password—we'd set it up together. I didn't know he had another level of security. I thought I'd managed to rescue the situation."

"Then somebody stole the laptop."

"Yes," said Armitage. The memory made him wince.

"You took it into the washroom with you?"

He looked surprised. "I wasn't going to leave it in the car, was I? That wouldn't be very safe."

Hazel forbore to comment. "What happened?"

He avoided her gaze. "I put it down while I washed my hands. And some . . . *toe-rag*"—it seemed to be the worst insult he knew—"snatched it up and legged it for the car park. By the time I reached the door, there was no sign of him."

Hazel sucked reflectively on the inside of her cheek. "Can you describe this toe-rag?"

Armitage shrugged. "Maybe my son's age. Maybe a bit older, though there wasn't much of him. Quick on his feet. Wearing a rugby shirt, I think, though I didn't recognize the club."

I bet I do, thought Hazel. The Saturday Irregulars. I'll give him *I found it in a washroom*! She said, "Why didn't you report the theft to the police?"

"I should have done. But I was already late for my presentation, and I still had the memory stick in my pocket, and I thought I could do all that later. I thought, What's the worst that can happen? I'll buy Bobby a new laptop. I'll have to anyway—we'll never get it back. I thought I'd get my meeting out of the way, go home, confess to my son, and then call the theft in to the Norbold police.

"Only of course, as soon as Bobby—that's my son—heard what I'd done, he freaked out. I mean *really* freaked out. Not 'I'm going to have to get everyone's e-mail addresses again, but at least I'll get a new laptop' freaking—complete and total panic. He was literally screaming at me. It took his mother an hour to calm him down enough to find out why."

Finally Charles Armitage met his visitor's gaze. "Miss Best, I don't want you to think we condone what he'd been doing. We were both of us deeply shocked and upset. We still are. Those aren't just pictures, they're pictures of young girls being exploited and humiliated. If I'd found out about it in any other circumstances, I'd—well, I'm not sure what I'd have done, but I'd have dealt with it like a responsible parent. We are responsible parents. We care about raising our children properly.

"But this wasn't something we could deal with in the privacy of our own home. The laptop had been stolen, and there weren't just those pictures on it, there was enough material to connect it to our family. It had my presentation on it, for heaven's sake! You found me through it. Someone could have used it to blackmail me. The best I could hope for, the very best, was that whoever stole it would keep it.

"So no, I didn't phone the police. I gave Bobby the bollocking of his life"—he blushed when he realized he'd said that to a strange young woman—"and I don't think any of us got any sleep that night. The next morning I made myself go in to work, as if nothing had happened. Every time a phone rang I wondered if it was somebody telling my employers what he'd found on my computer.

"Do you know, it almost came as a relief when Detective Inspector Gorman called? I knew what I was going to do. I was going to lie to him—say I'd downloaded the pictures. Bobby's fourteen years old. I honestly don't believe he meant any harm. I don't think he's a danger to anyone. I was willing to take the blame if it would save him from dragging a conviction for a sex offense through the rest of his life. Do you believe me?"

Hazel was shaking her head in despair. "Actually, I do believe you. It's just the sort of stupid thing that otherwise sensible people do when their children are involved. But it would have been easy enough to establish who downloaded the material. And as a juvenile, your son wouldn't have been in anything like the same trouble that you as a grown man would have been. Do you think we don't know what young boys are like? That we can't differentiate between a prurient teenager and a genuine pervert? Give us some credit!"

"Perhaps it was foolish," admitted Armitage. Telling the truth had obviously taken a weight off his shoulders. "But it's easy to see what needs doing when your emotions aren't involved. All I could think was that this was my son and somehow I had to protect him. I'd lay down my life for him. My reputation didn't seem too big a thing to give up.

"But Mr. Gorman didn't want to arrest me. He just wanted to return the laptop. No one had scrutinized it more deeply than was necessary to find out who owned it. I thought—I dared to think—we were off the hook."

"Why on earth did you send a private investigator to my flat?" Hazel was still indignant about that.

"Another bad decision," he said, squirming inside his clothes. "I just . . . I so badly wanted the business to be over! I didn't want someone coming around with a hand out after I thought we were safe. I asked Ms. Harris to find out if you were the kind of person who'd do that. If you'd made copies of Bobby's files with a view to doing exactly that."

"I am a police officer!" insisted Hazel, wide-eyed with outrage. "How dare you think that?"

"Yes," murmured Armitage. "I'm sorry."

She shook her head in a kind of wonderment. It was that simple? A teenage boy behaving as teenage boys have behaved since the year dot, only with the power of the Internet at his disposal, and a horror-stricken father doing what fathers do? But then . . . "And you really didn't send anyone to my house?"

"No," he said. "I really didn't." And Hazel believed him.

She put that aside for the moment. "All right. There are two things you can do. You can keep your head down, and wait to see if Mr. Gorman comes calling or not. I think he will, sooner or later, but you might get lucky. Or you can go and see him, and tell him everything you've just told me. If it was me, I'd want to get it out of the way, rather than jumping out of my skin every time the phone rings, but it's your call. I won't be doing anything more about it. If Mr. Gorman asks me a direct question, I'll have to answer it honestly, but otherwise you can forget about me. I'm satisfied that things happened as you say they did. I imagine you'll be taking steps to ensure that nothing similar happens again?"

Armitage nodded energetically. "He'll be using the new laptop in the living room from now on," he promised fervently. "And I'll be learning a bit more about the damn things, too."

*   *   *

Hazel called Saturday to say that all was well, then took her time driving home. At one point she deviated from the main road to take the scenic route, winding through the apple orchards that a few weeks earlier had been a froth of blossom. When she got home, she'd have to deal with Saturday, but before that she wanted some space to think.

On the whole her mission had been successful. She hadn't got anybody bang to rights (even Sergeant Mole hadn't actually used the term), but she was satisfied that the situation had been resolved. That Charles Armitage was not a predatory sex offender waiting to leap on her or anyone else, and that the author of the collection that had so shocked Saturday—no mean feat in itself—was an immature teenager with a man's urges and a boy's lack of self-control. She trusted Armitage when he said there would be no repetition. She suspected he'd be inspecting Bobby's computer every night until he turned thirty.

She hoped Armitage would find the courage to tell Dave Gorman what had happened. If he did, she thought the matter would go no further; if he didn't, she suspected that at some point it would come back to bite him. Either way, she felt no need to remain involved. She had achieved everything she'd needed to.

Which left the matter of the intruder at her house. Could she have imagined that? No. She'd seen the footprints; she'd seen the ball. Someone had gone to her new home and found a way in past her new locks. If not Armitage, then who? And why? She wandered around the orchards of ripening fruit, thinking until her brain ached, while the long evening turned into dusk.

Saturday had gone to bed by the time she got home. He was becoming a proper little suburbanite: a mug of cocoa and asleep by eleven, for all the world as if he had something to do the next morning. That could be her next project: finding him a job. But not tonight. Nor did she want to discuss the theft of Charles Armitage's laptop tonight, although there was absolutely no chance that she would let it pass. Tonight she had something else on her mind.

Patience looked up from the sofa when she came in. She waved her tail and Hazel stroked her ears. She made herself toast and coffee and took them back to the sitting room. "Do you want to go out?" she asked, but the dog declined, only turned around once and went back to sleep. Hazel ate her supper, then turned the light out, leaving the house in darkness.

She didn't sleep. She may have dozed; it was hard to be sure. Without turning the light back on, she could not have guessed to within an hour at what time of the night she became aware that she was no longer alone.

There had been no noise to alert her. But even before Patience stirred and sat up, a pale shape in the darkness, Hazel knew he'd come back. Their visitor, who'd stood in the flower bed, staring in at the kitchen window; who'd let himself into the house and moved things just enough to show he'd been there. Now, in the middle of the night, when decent people were asleep in their beds, here he was again.

She'd left the kitchen door ajar. On her left cheek she felt the whisper of air as he passed through it and behind her chair. Of course, the room was as dark for him as it was for her. He didn't know she was there, waiting in the high-backed wing chair, until she reached out and turned the reading lamp on.

"Hello, Gabriel," she said softly.

CHAPTER 19

HE MADE NO REPLY. He made no move. He was directly behind her chair, so Hazel couldn't see him without standing up and turning around. She felt no need to do either. She knew now who'd been coming into her house late at night when she and Saturday were dreaming—she about sorrow and loss, he almost certainly about television. She knew it before Patience got down from the sofa, stretched her long white body, and padded across the room, tail waving.

In the hearts of tumultuous events there are places, and moments, where nothing is happening. The eye of the storm. That was where Hazel was now. When what she felt caught up with what she knew, emotions from weak-kneed relief to volcanic fury would rip through her, and anyone in the fallout zone had better find something to stand behind. But it was too soon for that. Right now she was calm and in control, and enjoying the feeling of moral superiority that came from outwitting him.

Finally he managed: "How long have you known?"

"Only today," admitted Hazel. "The pieces finally fell into place a few hours ago."

"What . . . why . . . ?" He considered, tried again. "How?"

Now Hazel stood up and faced him. The last time she'd seen Gabriel Ash, she'd seen—or thought she'd seen—him shoot himself in the head. It seemed that death rather suited him. If anything, he looked tidier than usual—the thick black hair combed back, the collar of his shirt better ironed than when he'd done it himself. Hazel felt the smugness in her own smile and couldn't resist saying it anyway. "It was the curious incident of the dog in the night-time."

Gabriel Ash had read a lot of psychology and criminology; he'd read an unending stream of reports and reviews and articles sent to him in his capacity as a security analyst. Perhaps he hadn't read Sherlock Holmes. "What did the dog do in the night?"

"Absolutely nothing," Hazel said in quiet triumph.

Y ou first."

Ash demurred, glanced anxiously at his dog. "But . . ."

"You first," insisted Hazel. "Gabriel, I saw you blow your brains out! You said you were going to do it. I saw you do it and I thought you'd done it. What happened—did you miss?"

"You saw that?" He had the grace to sound appalled. "It never occurred to me that you'd be watching. . . ."

"It wasn't my idea." Her voice was hard. "But it was always meant for public consumption. You must have known that *somebody* who cared for you would see it."

Ash glanced at the lurcher. He didn't put the thought into words, but Hazel heard it just the same. He didn't think anybody cared about him except for Patience. Hazel felt a sudden, fierce impulse to slap him. The eye wall of the storm was spinning closer.

She gritted her teeth. "It was pretty convincing. How did you do it?"

Ash gave a self-deprecating little shrug. "Special effects. Popguns and blood packs. We ran through it six or seven times before we had all the angles right—before the camera was seeing everything it was supposed to and nothing more. Then we went live and did it for real."

"We—who?"

"Sorry." He wasn't trying to be secretive; there was just a lot of ground to cover and he was still reeling with the shock of discovery. "My department. My old boss set it up. Philip Welbeck—I've told you about him, haven't I?"

"He was the one who had you sectioned."

The least trace of a smile flickered across Ash's lips. "He was. To be fair, he was trying to stop me from getting Cathy killed."

But it made no sense. "Dave Gorman was on the scene within minutes. He told me he was too late. Are you telling me he was lying, too?"

Ash shook his head. "He was deceived, like everyone else. These people are professionals, Hazel—they dressed the set so no one would have suspected. They"—he swallowed, embarrassed—"got hold of a body. I don't mean they killed someone," he added hastily, as if the idea wasn't entirely preposterous. "I mean they brought a dead body from a morgue somewhere so they could be seen removing it afterward. Did Gorman tell you the Home Office arrived immediately after he did and took over?"

She nodded.

"We needed him to believe it as well. Everyone had to believe, except the smallest-possible inner circle. We couldn't take the risk of anyone having doubts and talking about them. Philip brought two sets of clothes, the same clothes, for me and the corpse. The moment the uplink was killed, his team yanked me out of that room and put the substitute in."

"Did he look like you? This corpse."

Ash passed a hand across his eyes. He whispered, "Not after they fired a gun inside his mouth."

So Gorman had seen what he was required to see, and was immediately hustled out of the back room of the Copper Kettle by the Home Office team. Soon after that he'd told Hazel what he honestly believed to be true. Because he believed it, she did, too.

Behind her eyes, the bridled rage was glowing incandescent.

Ash seemed unaware of it. He looked at Hazel hesitantly, as if about to ask something difficult. "Have you seen Cathy?"

Hazel clenched her fists until the nails dug into her palms, and the molten anger bubbled on the very lip of the crater. "Yes. I met them at the airport."

"How did she look?"

"She looked all right. A bit thin, and tired from the journey, but that's the least you'd expect. She'll have a lot of readjusting to do. But I think she'll be okay."

"They didn't hurt her?"

Hazel regarded him with exasperation. The angriest part of her wanted to tell him the truth: "Of course they hurt her! They hurt her, and went on hurting her, for four years. They made her do things she desperately didn't want to do. They kept her sons away from her. Of course they hurt her." Instead, she said distinctly, "Whatever physical injuries she had seem to have healed. The emotional ones will probably take longer."

"And the boys?"

"The boys are fine. I don't think anyone harmed them. It was how you always thought: they were held as a guarantee that you'd leave the pirates alone. When they thought you were no longer a threat, they sent them home. I met them off the plane and took them to Highfield Road." But he must know that. If he'd troubled to track Hazel to her new house, of course he'd been to his own.

Ash nodded, avoiding her gaze.

"Have you seen them?"

"They won't let me," he muttered miserably.

One of Hazel's eyebrows climbed. "Who won't?"

"Philip. The Home Office, SO15—the guys calling the shots. They don't want me ruining their operation by taking my sons for an ice cream."

Hazel could see their point. "Whose idea was it? Yours?" He nodded, shy as a child. She was unsurprised. "You thought the only way Cathy and the boys were coming home was if the pirates were convinced you were dead. So you approached your old boss, and he arranged it. Yes?"

"Yes."

"And you didn't see any need to tell me."

Ash knew she was angry. He spread an apologetic hand. "We couldn't tell anyone. It mattered too much. The first thing the pirates would do before accepting the evidence of their eyes was check how the people around me reacted. If you'd carried on as if nothing had happened, they'd have wondered if anything had."

Hazel hadn't expected that. "You think they sent someone from Somalia to spy on me—to make sure I was grieving appropriately?"

"Maybe they had to send someone, maybe they didn't," mumbled Ash. "But yes, I imagine someone was watching you, at least for a few days. If you'd known it was faked, you could have done something that didn't ring true. Just a suspicion would have been enough for them to hold on to my family. Then they'd have pulled up the tent pegs and disappeared into the undergrowth, where we'd never find them. We needed them to believe they were safe. It was our only chance of finding them and stopping them. That was the primary objective for the government guys. All I cared about was saving my family. But they were spending big money, public money, and they needed to be able to justify it. They needed to end the piracy once and for all."

"And have they?" asked Hazel coolly. "Found the pirates? Stopped them?"

Ash bit his lip. "Philip's working on it. It's a big undertaking. But this is an opportunity we never had before. The exchange at the border meant that we knew, for the first time ever, exactly where they were going to show up. They were under surveillance when they went back into Somalia, and they still are. When we're sure we've mapped the whole organization, it'll be expunged." He seemed to relish the sound of the word.

"Well, whoopee for our side."

He didn't understand her rancor. "This is important," he insisted. "Not just to me. Over the last five years, nearly thirty aircrew have disappeared, presumed murdered. Tons of munitions have gone missing, only to reappear in the hands of criminals and terrorists. It had to stop. I'm sorry if I upset you. . . ."

"*If?*" she echoed, her voice momentarily soaring.

"I couldn't think how else to handle it. I had to convince these men that Cathy and the boys were now surplus to requirements. The best way to make them believe was to make *everyone* believe. To make them think they'd seen it happen. If I could have stopped you from seeing it, I would have."

"You *could* have," cried Hazel. "You could have told me! You could have trusted me! I could have put on any act you needed me to, but you should have told me. You shouldn't have let me think I'd seen you die!"

"I'm sorry," he said again.

Hazel fought to bring her breathing under control. "So when are you going to tell Cathy that she's not a widow after all?"

Ash made an awkward shrug. "When Philip says I can. He's done so much for me, I can't risk jumping the gun. I'll see Cathy when it's safe." He looked at Hazel uncertainly from under heavy eyebrows. "My turn?"

Hazel was a long way from forgiving him. "What do you want to know?"

He encompassed the little sitting room with a jerky sweep of his arm. "You were waiting for me. How did you know?"

"Patience told me."

His head came up and his jaw dropped. Astonishment saucered his eyes. "You can hear her?"

Hazel closed her eyes for a moment, waited till the renewed urge to hit him passed. "Gabriel, don't be such a doofus! I mean, if anyone else—*anyone* else—had broken into the house, she'd have raised the roof. Even if she'd been here on her own, she'd have been anxious, unsettled when I got back. But I knew someone had been in here. How did you do that, by the way?"

"Philip got me a key. There's no end to the strings he can pull."

"Well, he can stop pulling mine!" snapped Hazel. "When I made myself think about it, it was the only thing that made sense. That you were still alive. That you wanted to see that Patience was all right. And while I was asleep upstairs, you were quietly playing ball with her down here. Only you made a mistake. When you finished, you put the ball somewhere I never would have put it."

He blinked. "The shelf? I thought . . ."

"Gabriel, who keeps their dog's ball on a bookshelf? Really," she added impatiently, "I think you're getting odder all the time!"

He said nothing. He felt there was nothing useful he could say.

"So now what? I'm supposed to go on pretending that you're dead?"

"Yes, please."

"For how long?"

Another of those awkward broken-winged shrugs. "I don't know. Until the matter's resolved."

"But what does that *mean*, Gabriel? Until a battalion of paratroopers drops into the pirates' camp? Until piracy stops being the chief export of Somalia? When?"

"Actually . . ."

Hazel knew that remote, internalized expression. It meant he was engaged in a debate inside his own head. "Actually *what*?"

Ash blinked, as if surprised to see she was still there. "Actually, to a large extent it already has. It isn't nearly as prevalent as it was a few years ago."

"Yes? Well—good. I still don't know what you expect me to do."

The hopeful look, together with the black hair that was getting long enough to curl around his ears, gave him the demeanor of a spaniel who thinks his owner might be good for one more throw of the stick. "Nothing. I need you to do nothing. Forget you saw me. Not forever—just till we've done everything we can to stop these people and make sure they never do it again. I can't say how long it'll take. Weeks rather than months—if we haven't succeeded by then, I don't think we will. Please, Hazel. Can you play dumb for another couple of weeks? In the interests of justice?"

Hazel regarded him levelly. But behind the mask of professional calm, like the makeup on a white-faced clown, her emotions were in turmoil. She was so glad to see him, so relieved to know he was all right, that she wanted to beat him senseless. "I expect so. But then, I expect I could have done it for the last three weeks, if you'd told me what you intended."

He only shook his head regretfully. "I couldn't."

"Fine," said Hazel, ending the conversation with her tone. "Then I think I'll go to bed and leave you with your dog. Let yourself out when you're finished. Oh yes—you always do, don't you?"

Ash bowed beneath her disdain as if it were blows.

With her hand on the hall door, Hazel paused, looking back at him over her shoulder. After a moment she said, "She knew. Patience. She knew you were coming back. Not just the last few days when you've been hanging around—since it happened. She knew you'd be back for her. It was almost the hardest thing, that I couldn't find a way of telling her you were dead. She didn't even seem to miss you. She moved in with me quite cheerfully because that's what she does: she fits in. You were away, so she came to stay with me for a bit, but she obviously expected you to come back and pick her up any day. And she went on expecting that, even as the days added up. You have no idea how awful it was, seeing her waiting for you when I knew—when I thought—she was never going to see you again."

Ash had no answer for her. Hazel went to bed.

When they were alone Ash sank, enervated, into the depths of the sofa, and Patience climbed up beside him. His arm went automatically around her shoulders. "I'm not surprised she's angry with me," he observed ruefully. "I keep hurting her. I don't mean to, but I keep doing it just the same."

Patience laid her head on his knee to get her long ears stroked.

"And another thing," said Ash, looking at her sharply, "what was all that with the ball? You said that was where it was kept!"

The lurcher raised one eyebrow at him. Her eyes were the color of caramel flecked with honey.

There was a man she suspected of doing bad things, explained the dog. She needed reminding that he had a son. What was I going to do, write her a memo?

CHAPTER 20

HAZEL DIDN'T HEAR HIM LEAVE, but not because she was
asleep. She didn't sleep. For the rest of the night she switched
between lying rigid between her sheets, her mind racing, staring
blindly at the dark ceiling, and tossing as miserably, as pointlessly,
as a stranded flounder. Her body ached for rest; her mind ached
for respite; but too much had happened.

And she was so *angry*. More than anything. More than surprised or delighted or relieved, she was unreasoningly angry with
Gabriel Ash for not being dead after all. She knew it wasn't an appropriate response. But she didn't know what was, and until she
worked it out, there was a vacuum there that rage was still pouring
into like a storm surge into a low-lying village. Until she found a
way to marshal her feelings about these events, sleep was a hope
too far. It came as a positive relief when the sun hauled itself
above the roofline opposite and twitched at her curtains, and she
could consign the night to the wastebin of lost opportunities and
start the next day.

It still wasn't much after six, and Patience cast her a jaundiced
look from the sofa, clearly thinking it far too early for civilized

people to be up and about. But Hazel wasn't prepared to apologize to a dog she obscurely felt had misled her.

"He'd been coming here for days, hadn't he?" she said accusingly. "And you said nothing!"

Only when the lurcher went on saying nothing did Hazel realize what she'd said. She gave a snort that hadn't too much laughter in it but still earned points for effort, and went to fill the kettle.

She must have disturbed Saturday, because he appeared a few minutes later, his hair even more like a haystack than usual, rubbing his eyes. "Kettle on?"

Hazel considered him irritably. She was aware that it was now some years since he'd had different clothes for sleeping and being awake in, but all the same, she didn't need to launch each bright new day with the sight of him in underwear that should have been washed days ago. To be fair, she couldn't picture him in striped pajamas. But he could pick up new T-shirts and shorts for a few pounds down at the market—she'd give him the money; it would be worth every penny—and like it or not, he was going to learn how the washing machine worked.

The boy had no idea what she was thinking. He tried a hopeful grin. "Any eggs?"

After the night she'd had, Hazel didn't give a toss for his feelings. "You lied to me."

At least he didn't deny it. "What about?"

"The laptop. You said you found it."

His eyes flickered warily. "I did."

"No, you didn't. The man put it down for a minute while he washed his hands. While he was still soapy, you were sprinting across the forecourt with the thing under your arm!"

Saturday considered his options. "He told you that?"

"That's what he told me."

"You know you can't believe a word he says. A man like that? A man with that kind of stuff on his computer?"

Hazel breathed heavily at him. But perhaps she owed him something of an explanation. "It was his son's computer. He'd borrowed it without knowing what was on it."

"You believe *that*? You don't believe me, but you believe that?"

"Yes, I do," said Hazel firmly. "The boy's fourteen years old. About the only age at which a normal human being can be forgiven for being curious about . . . that kind of stuff. Well, I'm pretty sure he won't have free Internet access again until he's old enough to know when to switch the computer off. Which just leaves you and your thieving."

Saturday braced himself. "Do you want me to leave?"

"No, I don't want you to leave," snapped Hazel. "I want you to stop stealing things!"

"I have."

Hazel rolled her eyes. "Yeah, right!"

But Saturday was quietly insistent. "I have. I told you I would when I moved in here, and I have. I can't change stuff that happened before."

It was certainly true that no one can change the past. "Really? You've gone cold turkey?"

He was a little scared of her in this mood, but he managed a chuckle at that. "Really."

"Well . . . good," said Hazel severely. "Now, for pity's sake go and get yourself cleaned up. After breakfast we're going shopping."

He stared at her. "Again?"

"Again."

* * *

While Saturday tried out his new sleep attire, Hazel sat up late with a book, waiting for the sound of a key in her lock. But Ash didn't come, and at two in the morning she gave up and went to bed.

He came the next night. Hazel had finished her book and moved on to a stack of magazines. Even so, she was struggling to keep her eyes open. Then Patience gave a soft whine and sat up, tail twitching, and Ash came in from the kitchen. He didn't look particularly surprised to see Hazel waiting for him. He didn't look particularly happy, either.

He was a tall man with a big frame, a frame designed to carry a lot more weight than it had in the time Hazel had known him. And like many big men who don't wish to appear intimidating, he'd developed a way of stooping slightly, like a bear caught with its head in a trash can. He was doing it now. "Are you still angry with me?"

Hazel put her magazine down and stood up. She shook her head. "No, Gabriel, I'm not angry with you. Not now. And I had no right to be angry before. The situation was none of your making, you were just trying to deal with it as best you could."

"I upset you," he said.

"I'll get over it. You had more to think about than my feelings."

He didn't deny it. "All the same, I'm sorry I didn't handle it better. I didn't expect . . ."

"What?" Her voice was a challenge. "That I'd take it to heart? Is that what you think? That we're just two ships passing in the night, whose actions have no effect on each other? Gabriel, you're my friend. I care what happens to you. I'll go on caring what happens to you. When this is all over and you're back with your wife and children, I don't expect I'll see much of you anymore. But I'm still going to care about you. I'd always be upset if I thought you'd been unhappy enough to do . . . what I thought you'd done."

Ash let out a slow, broken sigh and sat down beside his dog. "I don't deserve that kind of friendship."

"Yes, you do," insisted Hazel. "You are a good man. You are a good, kind, and clever man, and I don't want you ever to forget it. You deserve for good things to happen to you."

"In four years you were the best thing that happened to me," said Ash. "I'm never going to forget that."

It was, she thought, like seeing your teenager off to university: you knew it was the right thing for all concerned, but still everyone on the station platform wanted to bawl. She made an effort to change the mood. "So what was it that made you suspicious of Stephen Graves?"

If he hadn't already been sitting down, Ash would have staggered. He gaped at her until the burning of his eyes reminded him to blink. "I will *never*," he swore, "get the measure of what goes on in your head."

"About the same as goes on in yours, except perhaps a little slower." All the same, she was pleased. "So tell me: what first made you think he was more than just a victim in all this?"

He couldn't say, even to Hazel, "My dog remembered the taste of his trousers." He improvised. "A few things. The fact that piracy in Somalia had been dropping off considerably, except in this one sector. Arms shipments originating in Britain. Why? If they could bully Graves into cooperating, they could do the same to someone in France or Germany. But they didn't. They were interested only in shipments either from Bertrams or some other British company Graves was familiar with. That's a lot of eggs to keep in one basket, when at any time Graves could have decided he'd had enough and gone to the police.

"And the attack on us, which we blamed on Saul Sperrin until we found out there was no such person, came just a few days after I'd been to see him. I must have seemed like more of a threat to the operation than I realized."

"You think it was Graves who ran us off the road?"

Ash nodded. "A hired hit man would have done a better job and we wouldn't be here talking about it. It was amateurish. He ran us into a ditch and came to finish the job with a shotgun, but he got off only one shot before Patience took a chunk out of his backside and he ran. No one with a reputation to protect would have been put off that easily."

"So why not hire a hit man?"

"Because these things take time to arrange, and he thought he was running out of time. He thought he could salvage the situation if he moved quickly enough. I think, when I left his office, he followed us to your father's house. But it was a few days before he could get us in circumstances where he felt able to deal with us. Well, me really—you were just collateral damage."

"Gabriel"—she sighed—"you do say the sweetest things."

He gave a wry chuckle. "Yes. Sorry."

"And then"—if he wasn't going to bring it up, Hazel had to—"there was the massive coincidence of him and your wife."

Ash's eyes flared, but he said nothing. Hazel winced inwardly; she could have put that better. She hastened to explain. "What were the odds that the man you were questioning was the same man Cathy's abductors had chosen to put in contact with her? If we hadn't been so stunned, we'd have wondered the moment her face came up on his screen. The pirates took several shipments off Graves. If they'd wanted his assistance, why not keep one of the aircrew flying his cargo—someone he'd sent into danger? That was the way to pull *his* strings. Why assume he'd sacrifice his integrity for a woman he'd never met, someone he owed nothing to? He had to be part of the conspiracy. Gabriel, he wasn't just doing the pirates' bidding. He's one of them."

"You think . . ." It was odd that his voice should falter and fail like that. These were exactly the thoughts he'd been wrestling with, hammering out, for days. They were exactly the conclusions he'd reached. But somehow, hearing them on someone else's lips invested them with a reality they had not had until now. He swallowed and tried again. "You think Stephen Graves kidnapped my wife and sons?"

"I don't know." It was the honest truth; Hazel owed him that. "It may not have been his decision. But I'm guessing he was, or became, a party to it."

Ash took refuge from the burgeoning fury in the place where he always felt at home, the realm of pure reason. "Graves must have known that if I took up the case again, he'd be the first person I'd want to talk to. He had contingency plans ready to go as soon as I showed my face. He must have been on our trail before we got out of the goddamned car park!" He wasn't a man who swore routinely. But there are times when the Queen's English just doesn't cut the mustard.

Hazel ran the action across the editing screen of her mind's eye. "He followed us to Byrfield—he couldn't have known that was where we were going. But once we were there, he knew from the baggage that we were going to stay a few days. So he had time to pick up a shotgun, come back, and wait for a chance to ambush us where there'd be no witnesses. In the middle of the night, on a rural road miles from anywhere. It could have been days before anyone found us."

"But he failed. Thanks to Patience."

For the first time in a while, Hazel smiled. "Thanks to Patience, we got away with a fender bender and a few bits of lead shot in places you wouldn't show your maiden aunt. But he couldn't leave it at that. He had to deal with you, once and for all. Even better, he'd get you to deal with yourself. Kill yourself. It was pretty smart. He didn't need to take any more risks, he could do it all over the Internet—put you in contact with the pirates, let you see Cathy, tell you the price of her freedom. All it required was that you were a man who cared more for his wife and children than for his own life.

"It should have worked. His only mistake was to underestimate you. You *are* that man, but you're pretty smart, too. Well—on a good day. And you still have some useful contacts. You were able to make it look as if you were dead, without actually dying. Hell, Gabriel"—she still couldn't keep the occasional surge of bitterness out of her voice—"of course they were convinced. *I* was."

He couldn't keep apologizing. "You wanted to know when I first suspected that Graves was more than just another victim. I suspected when I sent him to meet Cathy. I thought, even if I was right—especially if I was right—he was the best man for the job. But I wasn't sure until now."

Hazel knew a compliment when she heard one. She felt her cheeks warm and her skin glow. She felt a sudden impulse to lean forward and kiss him.

And that came as a shock. They didn't have that kind of relationship. She'd started off feeling sorry for this strange, diffident, damaged man. Over a period of months that had mutated into a genuine friendship, deep and abiding, strong enough to survive all the other times she'd been angry with him.

But she had other friends, including other men friends. Pete Byrfield was one; another was the spiky archaeologist David Sperrin; until she'd turned their cozy little world upside down, she'd have counted a number of colleagues at Meadowvale Police Station. But she hadn't felt the same way about any of them as she'd come to feel about Ash.

But she wasn't falling in love with a married man: she could never have looked herself in the eye again. And feelings, she reminded herself sternly, are an unreliable informant. They wax and wane; sometimes they feel like they'll endure forever, only to peter out by the end of the week. No one is responsible for their feelings, but they are responsible for what they do about them, and Hazel Best was far too sensible to trade her self-respect for a feeling she hadn't had last time she checked and wouldn't have again at some point in the near future. It was a phantasm, born of shared dangers and shared triumphs. What she had with Gabriel Ash was precious, but it wasn't what he had with his wife and what Hazel would one day have with the father of her children.

She cleared her throat as nonchalantly as she could manage. "Okay. So Stephen Graves wasn't just the hapless tool of ruthless men somewhere in Africa: he's a co-conspirator. Except . . ."

Ash waited, then said, "What?"

"If he's criminally involved, and you gave him a good reason to go to a part of Africa where he has friends and resources, why did he come back? He should have vanished with the rest of the pirates into the wilds of Somalia, not come back to a grilling from Counter Terrorism and the distinct possibility of charges."

Ash frowned, scanning his internal hard drive for answers. But they wouldn't come. Perhaps he was too emotionally involved. Or perhaps they were wrong about Graves. But he didn't think so.

Hazel was saying, "I need to tell DI Gorman he should be talking to Mr. Graves."

"He may have worked it out for himself," said Ash. "On the other hand, he may not have all the information we have."

Hazel was puzzled. "I told him everything that happened."

Maybe, thought Ash, but I didn't. He said aloud, "It's not like being there. Something gets lost in the translation."

"Then I'd better talk to him tonight. And you'd better call your boss."

Hazel woke Dave Gorman, and got growled at for her pain. But she thought he understood the importance of what she was saying. Philip Welbeck answered Ash's call as calmly as if he'd been expecting it. As if he'd been toying with the same idea himself. It was three in the morning before they finished. Hazel regarded Ash pensively, unsure how to put this without causing offense. "Gabriel—where are you sleeping these nights?"

Ash smiled. "Not under the viaduct, if that's what you're wondering. Laura Fry has a room above her office. She's made me up a bed in there."

Hazel felt herself bristle all over again. "And how long has Laura been in on the secret?"

"A couple of days longer than you have, that's all. Philip Welbeck spirited me out of sight up a back corridor at Whitehall. But when Cathy and the boys came home . . ."

Hazel finished the sentence for him. "You wanted to be nearer to them. Have you been to see them?"

"No!" He said it so sharply, it had to be the truth.

"Even from a distance?"

Still the answer was no. "Too big a risk," he said regretfully. "To the investigation. And, just possibly, to them. I don't want someone taking potshots at them because I've been spotted lurking in the bushes behind Highfield Road."

It was a wise precaution. But Ash's sense of longing was palpable.

"Laura's office overlooks the park," said Hazel.

"Yes, it does." He didn't know where she was going this time.

"I'll find an excuse to take them there. I'll let Laura know when. It's not much, but I'll try to get you a glimpse of them. And I'll take some photographs."

Ash's dark eyes brightened so abruptly, it had to be tears. "Thank you."

CHAPTER 21

"YOU DID *WHAT?*"

A lot of things had changed in the last few months. One of them was Hazel Best. She would never have spoken like that to a senior officer when she first came to Meadowvale. Her parents had instilled good manners in her, and she'd reached her mid-twenties still believing that they cost nothing and improved everyone's day. She continued to believe that, but she'd reached a point in her life where, if the world kept throwing bricks at her, she wasn't going to keep replying with flowers. A soft word might turn away anger, but a baseball bat was more reliable.

Dave Gorman looked a little taken aback. "I sent him home," he said again. "I talked to him yesterday. He denied having any greater involvement than we already know about. I sent him home and told him to stay handy. What else was I going to do? Right now I wouldn't know what to charge him with even if I was sure we were going to charge him."

Hazel breathed heavily, and reminded herself that DI Gorman hadn't been there when she'd discussed Graves's role with Ash. What now seemed so obvious to her was news to him. "Stephen

Graves was not an innocent dupe in the kidnapping of Cathy Ash and her sons. He was involved. Maybe before the fact, maybe after it, but all the way up to his eyebrows. Get him back and charge him with conspiracy."

"Hazel—er—Constable—um—Miss Best . . ." He didn't even know what to call her. She *was* a probationary constable at Meadowvale, but not right now. Right now she was on sick leave. Right now she was here in her capacity as a concerned member of the public . . . wasn't she? As the late Gabriel Ash's friend, certainly. As someone who'd become involved in his family's tragedy. And, just possibly, as someone who'd worked out who'd done what while Gorman himself was still floundering. That wasn't his fault. Scotland Yard or Counter Terrorism Command or someone better qualified should be dealing with this. Dave Gorman was a small-town detective. He was a good small-town detective, but what he knew about Somali pirates you could put in your eye without rubbing. A month ago he'd thought such things happened in a world entirely disconnected from his world of burglars, drug dealers, teenagers armed with bread knives robbing corner shops, and the occasional, almost accidental murder, where one party was drunk enough to take a swing with a fire iron and the other was drunk enough to watch it come.

But it hadn't been Hazel Best's world, either. If she'd got up to speed in the time available, he should have done, too. He made a concerted effort to catch up. "Tell me again."

She told him again. Honesty compelled her to add, "I can't prove any of this. Not yet. But it's the only thing that makes sense."

Gorman was seeing her in a whole new light. "And you figured this out all by yourself?" He heard how patronizing that sounded, and had the grace to blush. "Sorry, that didn't come out quite how I meant. I mean, that's pretty impressive thinking, Hazel."

"If it's right."

"Whether it's right or not. If it is, we'll find the evidence once we look for it. But you need the theory first, and you got it, and I didn't."

The man was clearly discomfited. But there was no way Hazel could tell him she'd had help. She believed Ash's secret would be safe with DI Gorman, who might not be one of CID's greatest thinkers but was honest and reliable and to whose hands she would entrust any confidence that was hers. But this wasn't, and she wasn't free to share it. Nor would it have served any useful purpose. All she would achieve by telling him Ash was alive was to confuse him further.

She shrugged. "You've had other things to worry about. I've been thinking about nothing else, all day and most of the night, for three weeks."

"Yes. Well, that isn't great, either," said Gorman. "For you, I mean. Leave it to me now, Hazel. I'll haul Graves back in and we'll find out how dirty he is. But you need to step back. Chill out. Go sit in the park or something."

That reminded her. She gave him her most winning smile. "There's something you can do for me, Dave. Call Cathy Ash and . . ."

Cathy had spent Monday morning at the shops. Of course she had, thought Hazel. For four years the only clothes she'd owned had been those she'd been kidnapped in and whatever her abductors had provided her with. Of course the first thing she'd want to do, after emerging from the exhaustion that followed the thrill of release, was hit the shops with a well-charged credit card.

She'd paid a visit to a hairdresser's as well. They'd worked wonders with the ragged, sun-bleached crop she'd kept trimmed with a blunt pair of scissors and a scrap of mirror. All in all, she was barely recognizable as the woman Hazel had met off the plane from Addis Ababa.

Except perhaps in her eyes, which retained the look of a captive: self-contained, cautious, acutely aware, and giving nothing away; reflecting still the traits that had kept her alive through an experience that would have destroyed many people. What she'd been through couldn't be cast off with her much-mended clothes; her soul wouldn't be repaired by expert reshaping followed by a shampoo and a sachet of brightener. Only time, and plenty of it, would make inroads against the hurts and memories stacked behind her eyes.

But she greeted Hazel rather more warmly than the last time they'd met, so perhaps she was coming to terms with what had happened, no longer saw in every new face a fresh enemy.

"Come in," she said, holding the front door wide, "let me make you a coffee. But I can't be long. Mr. Gorman asked me to call at the police station again."

"Yes, I know," said Hazel, "he sent me to pick you up. I'll look after the boys so you and the DI can talk in peace. We could go for a coffee afterward, if you like."

"Oh—yes," said Cathy, a shade uncertainly. But then, she'd rather lost the knack of social occasions as well. "Yes, that would be nice."

As she drove them to Meadowvale, Ash's sons arguing on the backseat over a plastic toy, Hazel said quietly, "There must be lots of things you want to know. Ask Dave Gorman. What he knows, he'll tell you; what he doesn't, he'll try to find out. He's a good guy. You can trust him."

"I don't want to be a nuisance," Cathy said carefully.

"Don't even think that way. It's our job—the job of the police—to make things easier for you, not the other way around. If there's anything worrying you . . ." That was stupid; kicking herself, she tried rephrasing it. "If there are particular things that are troubling you, that you need help or advice dealing with, Dave Gorman will want to know. If he can't help you himself, he'll find someone who can."

"Everyone's being very kind," murmured Cathy. Then, after a longish pause: "There is one thing."

"Tell me."

"When will we be able to have a funeral? It's nearly a month, and I don't know what the delay is. It's not like we don't know how Gabriel died. But until we can lay him to rest, it's as if we're not really dealing with what happened. Not really acknowledging what he did for us. I suppose he's in a chill cabinet somewhere. But it's not dignified, and he's been there long enough. We owe him a decent burial now."

This the most Hazel had heard her speak. Cathy, too, seemed surprised by her passion: behind the fading tan, her color rose. "I'm sorry. I'm not doing this very well. I've spent four years too afraid to ask for anything I wasn't given. But I don't think Detective Inspector Gorman is going to beat me up for asking when I can bury my husband, is he?"

Hazel managed a little smile, though it was a close-run thing, because her heart was twisting inside her. She ached to do the one thing she absolutely must not do. "No, he isn't. He'll understand absolutely. I don't know what the delay is, either," she lied, "but he can make some phone calls and find out. I imagine it's just that there are so many different agencies involved—police, Home Office, Foreign Office, the Ethiopian embassy. . . . But it has to be sorted out. You need to be able to move on with your life."

"I'm not sure I want to move on with it," said Cathy softly.

"No. But you need to."

Hazel led the way to DI Gorman's office, but she didn't go in. She took each boy by a hand—the older one plainly resented it—and said, "I think we'll wander over to the park while you're busy. Ice creams all around?" The resentment mellowed a little. To Cathy she said, "Perhaps the inspector would get someone to bring you over when you're finished."

Dave Gorman nodded. Cathy, though, looked ready to object.

"I'll look after them," Hazel promised, and Gorman ushered Ash's wife into his office.

Hazel parked beside the wrought-iron gates. The ice-cream van was already on-site, though it was barely midmorning. The boys demanded all the trimmings; Hazel threw caution to the wind and did the same. With sprinkles and flakes and chocolate sauce, it wasn't so much an ice cream she came away with as a heart attack in a wafer cone.

They were already on the same side of the park as Laura Fry's office. Hazel picked the house out from the long terrace of identical three-story buildings, looking for a face or movement at the top-floor window. She saw nothing. She knew better than to wonder if that meant he'd forgotten.

Feigning tiredness, she dropped onto a convenient bench. One facing the road, not into the park. Little Guy sat down obediently beside her, half hidden by his ice cream. The older boy,

Gilbert, made a point of sitting down on the grass instead, half turned away from her. Hazel had no issues with that. It wasn't her view of him that mattered.

Hazel looked for a neutral topic of conversation. "So how does it feel to be back home?"

"This isn't our home," Gilbert replied sternly. "We're Londoners."

Of course they were. They had both been born in Covent Garden; you couldn't be more of a Londoner than that. "That's right—I'd forgotten. But your dad was born in the house where you're living now. He played in this park when he was a little boy."

"We aren't *living* here," Gilbert said distinctly over his shoulder. "We're *staying* here."

"Well, I'm glad you are," said Hazel gamely. "I've been wanting to meet you for a long time."

"We've been to Africa," piped up Guy, his face already a bandit's mask of chocolate sauce.

Anyone with children of her own would have automatically attacked him with a handkerchief. Hazel, with no offspring and no siblings, had only her training to guide her, and Sergeant Mole had been strong on child protection and interviewing child witnesses but had had nothing to say on the subject of chocolate sauce.

"I know you have." Hazel nodded encouragingly. "Did you see any lions?"

"Don't be silly," said Gilbert dismissively.

"I saw a lion once," volunteered Guy.

"No, you didn't," said his brother.

"Yes I did," insisted the younger boy. "It was in a cage."

"Don't listen to him," snorted Gilbert, "he's stupid."

"*You're* stupid!"

"Neither of you is stupid," said Hazel pacifyingly. "A lion in a cage is still a lion."

"It wasn't *just* in a cage," grumbled Gilbert in an undertone, "it was on the TV."

Hazel glanced at her watch and wondered if DI Gorman would keep Cathy occupied for the full half hour he'd promised. She passed some time taking the photographs she had promised Ash.

In fact it was forty minutes before the area car dropped Cathy Ash at the park gates. Hazel rose immediately and waved her hand. "We're over here."

Cathy whipped out a tissue as Guy, spotting her, jumped down from the bench and trundled toward her with stump-legged determination. "Down the throat," she reminded him mildly. "The ice cream's meant to go down the throat, not all over the face." His little round face emerged, grinning and unchastened, from the mop-up.

"What have you been talking about?" asked Cathy.

"Lions," Hazel replied, "and whether seeing one on TV counts. Football, and whether you're allowed to support Manchester United when you've never been to Manchester. Oh yes, and whether Superman could take Godzilla in a fair fight."

Cathy laughed. "That's my boys. That one in particular"—she indicated Gilbert with mock indignation—"will argue that black's white rather than agree with anything anybody else says!"

"In that case," countered Guy smugly, "I'm going to argue that white is black."

"Sit down," said Hazel, indicating the bench she'd risen from, "get your breath back. Had Mr. Gorman anything new to say?"

The women sat together. Cathy looked puzzled. "I'm not sure

why he wanted to see me. He asked about Stephen Graves—how well did I know him, how much did I know about him, how and when did we meet." Her voice hardened. "I'd have thought he'd be more interested in the men who abducted me and held me at gunpoint for four years."

"That's probably someone else's job," Hazel suggested. "What did you tell him?"

Cathy looked at her oddly. "Everything. Everything I could remember. Several months ago the pirates stuck a laptop in front of me and told me to talk to him. We've probably talked five or six times in total. I don't know him. I didn't know his full name until he came to meet me at the Ethiopian border four weeks ago."

"How many of them?" Hazel heard herself interrogating the woman and stopped abruptly. "I'm sorry. I don't suppose you want to talk about this any more than you have to."

Cathy shrugged. "It doesn't bother me. Not now. I'm not sure how many of them there were. I probably saw half a dozen at different times. But I was locked up in a room with no windows. I've no way of knowing how many there were who never got the job of bringing me food or taking me to the latrine."

Hazel bit her lip. She knew she was prying where she had no right, where the memories were still too fresh and too painful. And then, she had only to be patient. When Ash was free to return to his family, he'd hear everything that had happened in all the detail his wife could furnish, and Hazel would get a digest then. If Ash had time for their friendship now that his family had returned home.

CHAPTER 22

WHEN DI GORMAN SENT FOR STEPHEN GRAVES AGAIN, the man had disappeared. He'd left his Grantham office to go home on Monday afternoon but he never got there, and his wife was bewildered and increasingly anxious. She'd been about to call the police when they arrived at her door.

"I take it somebody checked the flat in Cambridge," Ash said to Hazel that night.

Of course they had. The porter had used his passkey, but no one had been in the flat since the scenes of crime officer wound up and left. Not Stephen Graves, and not the flat's mystery tenant, Miss Carole Anderson.

"Has anyone ever actually met Miss Anderson?" Hazel asked, querulous with disappointment. "Or was she Stephen Graves in a dress and sun hat, setting up a bolt-hole under an assumed name?"

"I don't know about the dress and the sun hat," said Ash, pausing just long enough to picture it and smile. "There was certainly a woman living there until recently. But the paper trail doesn't lead to anyone real. The ID documents she provided were forged."

"When did she leave the flat?"

"About a month ago. At least, that's when the porter saw her last. She didn't say she was leaving, so he assumed she was on holiday or a business trip or something. But all her personal belongings were gone. Except the computer that Graves used to talk to the Somalis, and there was nothing on that to identify her, either."

"Graves said she'd been abroad for months. That he was keeping an eye on the place for her."

"He lied," Ash said simply.

"I don't suppose it was Mrs. Graves?" Her tone was more of hope than expectation. If Graves's wife had been involved in the conspiracy, she might lead them to him. But Hazel wasn't surprised when Ash shook his head.

"The porter looked at a photograph—he said they could hardly be more different. Mrs. Graves is older, shorter, and plumper."

"Clever makeup and a cushion up her jumper?"

Ash grinned. "I'd like to think our highly trained professional police investigators would have noticed the cushion."

"Who is she, then?"

Ash shrugged. "An associate? A girlfriend? Without even her real name to go on, she'll probably be harder to find than Graves."

"And he's on his way back to Somalia by now. He'll be safer there than anywhere else on earth. I still don't know why he risked coming back to England when he could have just given Cathy her tickets and left her at the airport." She drew a deep breath. "Gabriel—how long are you going to wait before you decide that he's gone where you can't follow and let Cathy know you're still alive?"

Ash flicked her a haunted look. He was back on the sofa, the white dog's long body draped across his knees. "I don't know."

"Somebody needs to make a decision on that, and sooner rather than later. If you went around there tonight and told her—don't worry, I'm not suggesting you should—she'd be stunned, and then she'd be thrilled, and then she'd be angry with you for deceiving her." Hazel knew this for a fact. "But if it drags on for another month, she may be so angry she'll never forgive you. Don't wait until she's come to terms with your death and is making plans for the rest of her life."

He swallowed. "I can't make that decision. I owe everyone too much. My family are safe in England instead of hostages in Somalia. I couldn't have done that on my own. I can't just grab my trophy and run, and leave everyone else to cope with the fallout."

"Talk to Philip Welbeck," advised Hazel. "Get him to put a sell-by date on the operation. I don't . . ." She bit her lip. "I don't want you, or Cathy, to have gone through so much only to lose what you did it for. To come so close to happily ever after but end up alone again."

Ash understood what she was saying. He knew she was right. He just didn't know what to do about it. "I'll talk to Philip," he promised. "Hazel . . ."

She raised an inquiring eyebrow.

"I haven't thanked you. For this morning. Well, for everything you've done, but especially for this morning."

Hazel smiled. "You were there, then. I couldn't see you. But I didn't think you'd have forgotten."

"No."

He seemed to be struggling with something. Hazel frowned. "Gabriel? What is it?"

It was guilt. "I didn't recognize them," he admitted. "If you hadn't been there, if I hadn't been expecting to see them, I wouldn't have known them. My sons. But they could have been anybody's. Any two boys playing in the park. I thought I'd know them a mile away, but I didn't."

"Hell, Gabriel," said Hazel impatiently, "it's been four years! Of course they've changed. Gilbert's twice the age he was the last time you saw him. Guy's gone from being a toddler to a six-year-old. A schoolboy. At least he will be when you have time to arrange it."

Ash hadn't thought of that. "We'll have to get them some help. I don't imagine they've had any education. They'll need to learn to read. Even Gilbert was only just starting—he'll hardly remember anything he learned four years ago."

"There'll be time," Hazel reassured him. "All the time in the world now. Let them catch their breath first. The important thing is for you all to get used to one another again. If they didn't look familiar to you, how do you suppose you'll look to them? Guy may not remember that he ever *had* a father."

She saw the shock cross his face and hastened to soften the blow. "You'll deal with it. You'll spend time together and you'll deal with all the problems you meet. But it won't happen overnight. You're setting yourself up for grief if you think it will."

"You were with them. You talked to them." She could hear the envy in his voice. "How did they seem?"

He was asking the wrong person. Hazel was no connoisseur of children. "They seemed fine."

"But they can't be, can they?" said Ash fretfully. "Almost all the life they've known has been as captives among murderers. They were kept away from Cathy for a lot of the time. God knows who was looking after them. God knows what they've seen, what's happened to them. I don't know if they'll ever fully recover, but they certainly can't be *fine* this soon after!"

"All right!" Hazel spread her hands to ward off his anger. "Poor choice of words. But I don't know what to tell you. I didn't know them before, and I don't know any children their age to compare them to, but to me they seemed pretty normal. Maybe Gilbert seemed a bit . . . unsettled. Anxious, and looking for someone to take it out on.

"I think that's pretty normal, too, in the circumstances. Not just the way they've been living, but the way they came home. Cathy must have given them some reason why you weren't at the airport to meet them. If she told them what she believes to be the truth, they think you're dead; and if she told them some fairy story she thought would make things easier, they must be afraid you don't want to see them. Either way, that's a tough thing to deal with before you're ten.

"But listen, they're out of danger now, and you have all the time it's going to take to put things right. You and Cathy will need to get to know each other again, and you'll have to start afresh with the boys—tell them who you are, learn who they are. You're going to need patience."

At the sound of her name, Ash's dog looked up and smiled. He stroked her head and she settled down again.

"And Cathy. How did Cathy seem?" It was as if he was snatching love letters from the flames. Every fragment he could get his hands on was a treasure.

"I thought she was coping pretty well. I don't think you need to worry, Gabriel. I think they've all come through remarkably well. You'll have a better idea when you're able to talk to Cathy in person, but in the meantime, don't torture yourself. The worst is over, for them and for you. Of course you won't just slot back into how things were four years ago. But you've got what you wanted. Soon you'll have everything you wanted."

"Not quite everything." Hazel was surprised at the steel vibrating in his voice. "I wanted to rip their kidnappers' hearts out. I wanted to see them burn."

"That's someone else's job," she reminded him. "And just because they haven't been found yet, that doesn't mean they won't be. They aren't faceless anymore. Even in Africa, Graves may find it harder to evade justice than he imagines."

"What about his office? There could be some evidence there. . . ."

"A specialist team has gone into Bertram Castings and locked it down," said Hazel. "They're picking the computers apart for every scrap of information that might be helpful. They know what they're doing, Gabriel. You can't help—truly you can't."

"I'm going mad, doing nothing! Venturing out only in the middle of the night, talking only to you and Laura, knowing my family are less than a mile from here and I can't—I absolutely can't—go and see them. It's driving me crazy."

Hazel understood his frustration, but she was running out of sympathy. This was the bed he'd made; he had no right to complain to her that it was uncomfortable. The events he'd set in motion had to play out to the finale, and both of them had to stay in their seats until someone played the national anthem and set them free.

"So no change there," she muttered irritably; and was rewarded by the startled look of a man who, bending to sniff a flower, has got a noseful of hornet.

CHAPTER 23

L ACK OF SLEEP WAS BEGINNING TO TAKE ITS TOLL, making Hazel not just irritable but stupid as well. It was all right for Ash, she reflected sourly as she dragged herself into Tuesday a little before eight; he could sleep all day in his secret attic while Laura Fry dispensed equal measures of sympathy, wisdom, and waspishness to her clients downstairs. But Hazel had to carry on as if nothing was disturbing her routine except occasional moments of grief.

She hauled herself into the shower, tolerated its assault for a few minutes, then dragged herself out again. Lacking the energy to lather, she wasn't confident she'd come out much cleaner than she'd gone in, but it was at least a gesture. She found her way into a fresh shirt and jeans and stumbled downstairs.

She was astonished to find the little table in the kitchen set for breakfast, the electric kettle steaming, the toaster toasting, and Saturday—wearing one of his new, unslept-in T-shirts—as attentive as a creepy waiter in a low-budget horror film, ready to fry her egg to order.

She peered myopically at his bright scrubbed face, his amazingly tidy hair, and the cogs of comprehension ground inch by inch toward a conclusion. "You going somewhere?"

"I've got a job interview."

They were words Hazel had never expected to hear from him. More important, they were words Saturday had never expected to speak. They chimed like a carillon of bells, thrilled like the first notes of a fanfare. They fluttered like flags for the launch of a new life.

It wasn't, in all conscience, the kind of job interview that most people would get excited about. The petrol station where he had acquired the Armitage laptop had put a postcard in the window for someone to stack shelves in the shop and keep the jet-wash machine charged with shampoo. It was a job for someone leaving school with no qualifications, unless you counted an instinct for locating the cheapest bottle of cider in any part of town.

But then, that was pretty much who Saturday was. He hadn't much to offer, only a certain wiry strength and—it seemed—the desire to do the job.

He hadn't even—and this immediately struck Hazel as an obstacle—the one qualification his prospective employers would insist on, a track record for honesty. Over her egg she inquired, with as much tact as she could muster, how he intended to deal with the inevitable interest in his probity.

"That's easy." He beamed. "I'll tell them about the laptop."

Hazel froze mid-chew. "The laptop that was stolen from their washroom?"

Saturday nodded enthusiastically. "I'll tell them I was going to keep it but I didn't."

"Well—good luck with that," said Hazel, doubtful but entirely sincere.

After he'd gone off, first raiding her side of the linen closet for—dear God!—a clean handkerchief, she slumped back into the armchair, alone with the white dog, and fell to thinking about families. About Saturday's family, and whether they'd be pleased or appalled to see his keenness to interview for a dead-end job he probably wouldn't even get. About Charles Armitage, who was willing to go to prison rather than let his fourteen-year-old son pay the price of his Internet obsession. About Gabriel Ash's family, who thought he'd died to save them and were in for—putting it mildly—a shock.

About Stephen Graves's family, on whom he turned his back without hesitation when that became the price of his freedom. Who were sitting in their nice house outside Grantham, waiting for the phone to ring, knowing by now that it probably wouldn't and that even if it did, the call would be taken by one of the quiet, watchful, entirely serious police officers who had moved in with them. The plump middle-aged wife who couldn't match for glamour the resident of the Cambridge flat, and the children who'd always thought their dad—with his gray suits and his business trips and his conversation full of government regulations and double-entry bookkeeping—was a bit boring, and now would give anything for him to be boring once again.

"He'd already left them," she said aloud.

Patience lifted one ear, inviting her to elaborate.

"Stephen Graves's family," Hazel explained. "I don't think he'd really been with them for some time. He was still putting food on their table, but the future he saw for himself was with someone who mattered more to him. The woman at the flat wasn't a casual friend who let him use the place for his secret computer. She's his mistress."

The white lurcher yawned, showing teeth that went right back to her ears. Hazel almost heard the words *You could be right.* She blinked.

"That's where he's gone. That's why he came back to England instead of staying in Somalia—to be with her. Miss Carole Anderson—or at least the woman who uses that name. After Gabriel showed up again, he warned her to leave the flat. So she went somewhere safe till he could join her. When Dave Gorman let him go, he didn't go home, because everything he wanted was somewhere else."

Hazel paused in her soliloquy. The theory was perfectly feasible; nothing she knew contradicted it. And she was pleased to find she could do this on her own, not just in partnership with Gabriel Ash. But right or wrong, it didn't take her anywhere. There was no trail of bread crumbs to follow.

If she was right, Graves had gone to ground here in England rather than trust his luck to the airports, with their observant staff and their WATCH OUT FOR THIS MAN flyers. But that wouldn't make him easier to find. He could be anywhere, living with any one of thousands of women the police had no reason to know about. The only thing they knew about this one was that her name wasn't Carole Anderson. When she left Cambridge she presumably took a flat somewhere else, making a new life that Graves would slip into. They would make new friends, who would have no reason to question whatever account they gave of themselves. He'd got false papers for her; he could get some for himself. To all intents and purposes, they would disappear.

The mistake people make when they're trying to vanish is to go back when they should be going forward. To return somewhere familiar rather than start from scratch in a place that means nothing to them. If Stephen Graves was the man he increasingly appeared to be—not the pawn of criminals but their partner—he probably wouldn't make that mistake. But what about his girlfriend?

Perhaps she had no experience of this sort of thing. Perhaps the only reprehensible thing she'd ever done was love a bad man. If so, she might have fallen into the trap of escaping her present life by returning to a former one.

All her personal belongings had gone from the Cambridge flat, Ash had said. But it takes more than a couple of suitcases to pack away a woman's life, and if she'd rolled up with a removal van, the porter would have noticed. So she'd taken everything with her name on it, and the clothes she'd need, and anything that was both portable and valuable, like jewelry, which she could turn into cash if she had to. But she must have left many things behind. Perhaps among them she'd left a clue. A clue to where she'd come from and where she might return.

If Stephen Graves's love nest had been in Norbold, so that DI Gorman would have overseen the search, Hazel would have asked him what had turned up. Would have offered to help him conduct a second search on the basis that, in a woman's flat, another woman might spot something that a man might miss. But Cambridge CID owed her nothing, and nothing was what she confidently expected to get out of them.

Which left what Sergeant Mole at the training college had liked to describe as "the old-fashioned way."

Hazel was on her way to the front door when a disembodied sense of disappointment made her hesitate and look back. "Fancy a drive?"

Patience bounded onto the backseat as soon as the car door was open, and waited for Hazel to fasten her seat belt. Ash said she didn't like wearing it, but Hazel didn't care if she liked it or not, and it seemed the dog recognized that pouting worked better on men than on other women.

I t was a big apartment block: the job of porter was shared by a
pair of brothers, as was the ground-floor flat sandwiched between the boiler room and the laundry. Both incumbents had
been interviewed by the police. Neither had remembered anything terribly helpful about the woman who had lived under their
roof.

If Hazel had been a man, they'd have declined to go through
it all again. But she wasn't. She was an attractive young woman
with a lot of curly fair hair wrestled into a rough bunch behind her
neck, and she had bright green eyes flecked with copper and an
open, engaging smile; and the older brother ushered her to the
best chair while the younger put the kettle on.

They talked for a while, Patience curled up quietly on the rug.
Neither of the brothers liked dogs, but it was too hot to leave her
in the car, and they tolerated her because Hazel Best had a talent
for making people enjoy talking to her. Then they went upstairs
to the Anderson apartment.

The scenes of crime officer had finally finished, taking his tools
and his tape with him, leaving behind the furniture and the pow-
dery residue of his fingerprinting.

Hazel had been here before, the day she and Ash followed
Graves to the flat where he talked to the pirates. It hadn't struck
her at the time—there had been other things to think about—but
she realized now that Graves's girlfriend, ostensibly abroad on business, had already moved out. Though furnished, the place hadn't
felt lived in. Since then that impression had been compounded by
the work of serious professionals stripping it down for whatever secrets it might be hiding, so that now the apartment was like a hotel

room, equipped with all the necessities for the next person to come through the door and nothing to make them feel they were entering someone else's space.

"*Did* she actually live here?" asked Hazel. "I understand she was abroad a lot."

"No, she lived here all right," said the older of the two brothers. "It didn't always look like this. I was up here a few times—problems with the central heating—and it looked like anybody's flat then. Magazines on the coffee table, coats in the hall cupboard, kids' toys, everything."

"How long was she here?"

"Three and a half years." He'd had to look it up for the police.

"I don't suppose she told you where she was going?" Hazel knew what the answer had to be.

"Didn't even tell us *that* she was going. First we knew was when the police turned up, and all her stuff was gone."

Hazel nodded. "So when was the last time you saw her?"

"A month ago, or maybe a little more. The boyfriend came by sometimes, said he was keeping an eye on the place for her. We just thought she was on holiday again. She did like her foreign holidays. Always topping up her tan somewhere."

Hazel heard an echo of something that had been said before. "Kids' toys? Miss Anderson had children?"

The older brother leered at her. "Now, miss, don't be so old-fashioned. Lots of single ladies have kids. None of our business, as long as they don't disturb the other residents."

"And did they?"

"Quiet as mice," said the younger brother. "Almost *too* quiet. You expect little boys to make a *bit* of noise, it's only natural. All those guns, and not so much as a pop out of them."

Hazel's eyebrows rocketed. "All *what* guns?"

The younger of the brothers grinned. "Don't be silly, miss—*toy* guns, not real ones. They had a real collection. It's funny, that. People don't like their kids playing with guns so much these days."

"No, they don't," agreed Hazel. "But the man who used to come here was in the arms business. It probably seemed quite natural to him."

The older brother looked sidelong at her. "Were they his children?"

"I don't know. Maybe." That was one possibility: that, unsuspected by his wife, Graves had been living a second life for years. That he'd had children with his mistress, and kept them all in comfort in Cambridge and took them abroad for holidays in the sun. She wondered how she could check if the business trips he'd made on behalf of Bertrams corresponded to Miss Anderson's holidays.

But it wasn't the only possibility. "I hope so," she heard herself say.

Something occurred to her. She rooted through her bag, finally found her phone. Trepidation delayed her only a moment longer; then she held it out. "Have a look at this. . . ."

CHAPTER 24

HAZEL KNEW IN THE MOMENT of waking that the day ahead was going to be a long and difficult one. It was going to be difficult if she couldn't get the answers she needed to the questions plaguing her, and even more difficult if she did.

She began by phoning her father's employer.

Peregrine, Lord Byrfield—known almost universally as Pete—was delighted to hear from her. Until they'd renewed their acquaintance a few weeks earlier, it had been years since they'd done much more than wave to each other across a field, and Byrfield had somehow never updated his memory of the handyman's daughter from when he knew her as an outdoorsy twelve-year-old exercising his sisters' outgrown ponies.

Hazel wasn't twelve anymore—Byrfield had also forgotten that when she was, he was only sixteen himself—and though she still seemed entirely at home amid the woods and meadows of his estate, he had to admit that she'd changed. The corn-colored hair had turned a shade of rosy gold; the frank, open gaze had acquired depth and understanding without losing its impish good humor; and the tomboy's freckled face had changed in the myriad tiny ways that happen when girls become women, and at the same time had hardly changed at all. Quite apart from her support at an unsettling time in his life, Byrfield had enjoyed her company and looked forward to her next visit.

She was quick to disappoint him. "It's not actually you I'm looking for," she admitted honestly. "Is David still at Byrfield?"

Pete's half brother—they'd agreed on that as a viable description, though the reality was in fact more complicated—was an archaeologist. "Sorry, no," said Byrfield. "He's on his way to Carnac."

"Karnak in Egypt?"

"Carnac in France. Something to do with standing stones."

Hazel had a pen ready. "Can I have his number?"

Byrfield read it out to her. "If it's urgent, you might catch him in London before he leaves."

"I don't need to see him. I only want to pick his brains."

Pete Byrfield felt a quiver of satisfaction that he would not have acknowledged—not to her, not to anyone.

David Sperrin's phone rang for so long that Hazel was ready to give up. Then he answered with a characteristically graceless "Now what?"

She didn't know what questions to ask him, only the answers she wanted him to give. She vaguely remembered something he'd said—she couldn't help it, but when he held forth on archaeological method, part of her brain shut down in self-defense—about science's being able not only to date ancient human remains but to reveal details of people's lives that seemed impossible to know thousands of years later.

"Uh-huh." She seemed to hear him nod. "Stable isotope analysis."

Hazel waited for him to explain. Sperrin waited to be prompted. Hazel breathed heavily at her phone. "Which is what?"

He gave her the abridged version. When she still didn't understand, he gave her what he thought of as the version for idiots and small children. Taking notes, she had him spell some of the words. "Enamel hypoplasias," he said a second time. "H-Y-P-O-P-L-A-S-I-A-S."

"-A-S-I-A-S," repeated Hazel, scribbling furiously.

And: "Mass spectrometry," said David Sperrin. "S-P-E-C-T-R-O-M-E-T-R-Y."

"-M-E-T-R-Y," echoed Hazel.

And: "The ratio of strontium-87 to S-86."

And: "In the case of deciduous teeth, you can even say at what age nursing ceased."

When she'd worked out what he was saying, Hazel held the phone away from her, glaring at it as if he were there in person. "And what *possible* excuse," she demanded incredulously, "could I offer for asking someone to pull one of her children's teeth out?"

Now she heard Sperrin shrug. Interpersonal relationships had never been his strong point. "How about hair?"

"How *about* hair?"

The explanations were getting shorter. Hazel could almost see him checking his watch. "Look, Hazel, it's great that you're finally taking an interest in archaeology, but could we talk about this some other time?"

"No," she said firmly. "Tell me about hair."

When she used that tone of voice, usually she got what she wanted. This time she got David Sperrin to tell her about hair. About stable isotopic ratios of strontium and oxygen. About how water percolating through rocks picked up their mineral signature.

About hair fixing the relative proportions of minerals present in the drinking water.

"Okay?" said Sperrin. "Hazel, I really have to go now. If you need any more"—she thought he was going to tell her to call again—"Google it. Bye." And the phone went dead, leaving her to wonder what kind of urgency could attend the study of ancient artifacts.

H azel didn't like lying. She'd been brought up to tell the truth and shame the devil; and in her professional life, too, while there might occasionally be some merit in the little white lie that salved feelings and persuaded the lethally offended to believe they might have misheard, on the whole she had found honesty to be the best policy. Lying required too much imagination and too good a memory.

This wouldn't be a little white lie. She had a horrible suspicion growing at the back of her mind, and she was looking for the evidence that would either prove it or dismiss it entirely. If she could have seen a way to obtain it legitimately, that's what she'd have done. But she had no authority to demand what she wanted, and though she could have asked DI Gorman to make the request, she'd have had to tell him why. And she really didn't want to do that. If she was wrong, she didn't want anyone to know that the notion had even crossed her mind.

And if she was right, she wanted to talk to Ash before she spoke to anyone else.

Cathy opened the front door on to a hall filled with suitcases. For a moment Hazel didn't know what to say. "Going somewhere nice?"

"To visit my mother," said Cathy, folding T-shirts. "She hasn't seen the boys for four years, and she's not well enough to travel herself. So we're going up to Chester for a week or two."

"Cheshire's lovely at this time of year," Hazel mumbled weakly. "Er . . . before you go . . ."

"Hmm?"

"I have a favor to ask."

Cathy looked surprised. They weren't exactly friends. But she understood that Hazel had been kind to her husband and didn't want to seem churlish. "What do you need?"

"I'm putting together a token bag. It's a kind of tradition in my part of the country. When somebody dies, you collect tokens from the people who cared about him. A photograph, a poem, a holiday souvenir, a bit of jewelry. Then you bury the bag with him."

Cathy was looking at her as if she was mad. "Gabriel will be cremated."

"That works, too." Hazel nodded desperately. "It's just a way of seeing someone off. Like a wake, only you don't have to get the carpets cleaned afterward."

Cathy shook her head bemusedly. "And you want me to contribute something to this . . . token bag? What?"

"I was hoping you would. Anything. A wedding photo? Something he bought for you? A favorite CD—anything."

It wasn't worth arguing about. "All right. I'm sure I can find something. Does it have to be now? As you see, I'm rather busy."

That was the bit Hazel hadn't anticipated. It required some tap dancing. "Would you mind? Only, once it's made up, it has to go around to his friends for everyone to raise a glass to it." Oh God—did that sound even *remotely* credible?

Cathy blinked. "I didn't know Gabriel *had* that many friends."

Hazel worked at keeping the amiable smile in place. "He made a lot of friends in the last few months. My father, for one. And the family my father works for. I need to take it down to Cambridgeshire for them to toast it."

Was it her imagination, or did that cause a flicker of concern to cross Cathy Ash's face? "That's where you're from?"

"It's where I grew up. My father was in the army. When he left, he took a job on a small country estate. He still lives there."

If it had ever been there, the concern was gone now. "All right. Fine. I'll go and get something." Cathy headed for the stairs.

"Thanks," said Hazel. "And, er . . ."

Cathy turned back. "Yes?"

"I was hoping you'd snip a lock of hair off each of the boys."

By now all Cathy Ash wanted was to get rid of her late husband's weird young friend with her bizarre country rituals. "Yes, sure. They're in their room. Give me a minute." She vanished around the turn of the stairs.

Even so, Hazel didn't entirely believe she'd succeeded until Cathy returned with an envelope. Since it was unsealed, Hazel opened it enough to see inside. There were two photographs: an old one of Cathy and Ash, and a much more recent one of the two boys, taken since their return. There were also two snippets of hair, one mid-brown, the other almost black.

"Thank you," said Hazel, and she sealed the envelope.

CHAPTER 25

S HE DIDN'T WANT TO SEE ASH UNTIL SHE KNEW, one way or the other. He was too good at reading her expression, plucking secrets from behind her eyes as if they were books on a library shelf, titles printed on their spines for all to see. She'd talk to him when she knew what she had to say. To share her suspicions and then make him wait for proof would be cruel. So she went to bed early, turned out her light, and stopped her ears to the only sign of his arrival, which was the soft, happy thump of his dog's tail against the back of the sofa in the sitting room downstairs.

Saturday made breakfast again in the morning. He had news of his own. "I got the job!"

Hazel had dismissed the possibility so completely that she struggled now to recall the details. "The one at . . ."

"Whorley Cross," he reminded her impatiently, "the filling station. I got it. And before you ask," he added pointedly, "I was not the only applicant."

"Well, that's . . . great," said Hazel, mustering enthusiasm for the boy's sake. "The interview went okay, then."

"Wicked," said Saturday.

"You did tell them about . . ."

"The laptop? Yeah."

Hazel was genuinely impressed. "What did they say?"

"That asking them for a job showed chutzpah," Saturday declared smugly.

Hazel frowned. "They speak Yiddish?"

Thus pressed, the boy passed on their exact words. " 'Some nerve,' " he said happily. "It means the same thing."

Hazel wasn't entirely convinced, but if he'd got the job, he'd got the job. "Well, well done. Welcome to the world of money in your pocket and responsibilities on your plate."

In truth, Saturday's job didn't seem to offer a great deal of either. But this was a boy who'd got by week after week, season after season, on small change and things he found lying around. Even a part-time job at minimum wage promised unfamiliar plenty.

"When do you start?"

"Eight o'clock tonight. Finish at midnight."

Which meant she either had to warn Ash or leave him a note. If she left a note, he'd know she was avoiding him, and think he'd done something to upset her. She'd have to hope that sheer amazement at Saturday's news would keep him from wondering what else was occupying her mind.

In the event, Ash didn't come that night. Hazel was watching late-night television with Patience when Saturday came in at half past midnight.

He assumed she'd stayed up until he got home. Hazel was about to put him right, but stopped herself when she realized there were two good reasons to hold her tongue. One was that she couldn't tell him why she'd stayed up. The other was that it was years since anybody had cared enough about this boy to stay up until he was safely home. It was something only families did, and he hadn't had a family for a while; and if a bit of him dared to think that maybe he'd got something like a family again, Hazel wasn't going to tell him he was wrong.

"So how did it go? Any problems? What's the boss like?"

But another thing Saturday wasn't used to was protracted physical effort. Generally, when he'd had enough of doing something, he stopped doing it and put his feet up. But for four hours this evening he'd been constantly lifting, carrying, serving, helping, and cleaning, and he was exhausted. His eyes were bleary with tiredness. "Can I tell you in the morning? I'm knackered."

Hazel sat up a little longer, but still Ash didn't come. Then she went to bed.

S he paid for the analysis herself. She had no doubt that if she'd taken her suspicions to DI Gorman, he'd have signed for it on the CID account. But then the results would have gone to him instead of coming to her, and she would have no say in what followed. By footing the bill herself—and it wouldn't be easy, since lab work is never cheap—she retained control over who would know what when.

It wasn't that she had any intention of keeping the results from the police. Almost whatever they showed, they would be helpful to the inquiry, and Hazel was as keen as Gorman to see justice done. What she was buying with the contents of her piggy bank was time. Not enough to allow the guilty parties to scuttle out of reach of the law. Just enough that if there were things Gabriel Ash had to be told, he could hear them from her.

The downside of receiving the results directly was that she had no one to help her understand them when they arrived on Monday. She read them through again and again, making notes of the questions they raised; then she phoned the laboratory for further clarification; and even after that, she spent the afternoon on the Internet, cross-checking that the information in front of her did indeed mean what she thought it meant. And it did. Whichever way she came at it, it checked out, all the way down to the geology. She experienced a brief surge of hope when limestone turned up in the bedrock under both Somalia and the east of England, but they were different kinds of limestone, and they occurred in conjunction with different minerals. By the time she'd made her last phone call and turned her computer off, there was no longer any doubt in her mind.

She looked at Patience. "Now we wait."

Patience, of course, said nothing. But it didn't take a great deal of imagination to sense an impulse of sympathy in the golden-toffee eyes.

Ash spent five days in London. A black van with darkened windows had collected him from the rear of Laura Fry's office a little after midnight on Thursday; now it returned him to a Norbold whose streets were silent and empty under a sky whose stars were paling with the first promise of dawn.

He nodded to the driver—they hadn't exchanged names in all the hours it took to drive from Norbold to London and back again—climbed down into the dark alleyway, and let himself in at Laura's back door. There was no one else in the house, but he didn't turn the lights on. He made his way upstairs by the narrow beam of a penlight, unlocked the door at the top of the second flight, and sat on the makeshift bed in the dark. His body ached for sleep, but he was too tired to undress or even just pull the covers over him. Instead, he sat hunched about his weariness and reflected on the developments of the last few days.

He hadn't known what to expect when he'd got the message to pack a bag—although everything of his own that he currently had access to wouldn't have filled a bag—and wait to be collected. If the driver knew any more than he did, he had been specially selected for his disinclination to converse. Only when the van arrived in the familiar streets around Whitehall did Ash guess that his appointment was with his old boss, Philip Welbeck.

In the days when he worked in an office, Ash had mostly worked office hours. But there had been times when he'd burned the midnight oil in response to some developing situation, and the department still carried a skeleton staff around the clock to deal with whatever occurred. So there were lights on in some of the offices, and a handful of people wandering around in loosened ties and cardigans. Since none of them blanched or held up their paper knives in the shape of a cross, Ash inferred that everyone here knew his suicide had been faked. Indeed, staging it must have involved some of them.

Welbeck ushered him into his own office and poured coffee from the big percolator in the corner. All security operations run on three things: information, mental acuity, and coffee. The coffee is the easy part.

"You're looking better," observed Welbeck.

"The last time you saw me, I had a hole in my head and fake brains on my shirt."

Welbeck laughed. "I meant generally. You're looking more like your old self."

Ash nodded. "I'm a lot better, thanks. Especially . . ." He hesitated on the cusp of an indiscretion. But both of these men guarded too many secrets to keep secrets from each other. "I've seen them. The boys. And Cathy. I've seen them."

Alarm flickered in Welbeck's eyes like a tiny flare going up. That hadn't been part of the deal. "You've been home?" All their carefully laid plans, all their costly machinations, brought to nothing by something as human as a lonely man wanting to see his family . . .

"No," Ash reassured him quickly. "No, they haven't seen me. Hazel Best laid it on. She took them to the park. I could see them from the window over Laura's office."

Welbeck was only slightly mollified. "So the Best girl knows."

Ash nodded. "I . . . made a mistake. I went to check on my dog. I thought I could get in and out without anyone knowing." His eyes dipped. "I was wrong."

"Can we trust her not to talk?"

"Absolutely," swore Ash. "I'd trust her with my life."

"You're trusting her with something much more important than that," murmured Welbeck. "My operation."

"You can trust her, too."

Welbeck nodded slowly. He was a smaller man than Ash, shorter and lighter in build, and though he wasn't much older, the stresses of his job, or perhaps just adverse genes, were already playing havoc with his hairline. "Anything else I should know? Anyone else who might have seen you?"

"Just Laura Fry. And my dog."

"Ms. Fry works for me. And I don't imagine your dog will shoot its mouth off after one too many in the Rose and Crown."

Ash shook his head. "She's careful that way." He almost

added, "Most people don't even know she can talk." But he wasn't sure how Welbeck would react. If he thought Ash was being flippant, well and good. But he might send the black van away and whistle up a white one. Again.

Ash spent most of the following days and nights working in a tiny room behind Welbeck's office, going through his old files for any clues, hidden in the mass of material and not recognized when he was originally collating it, to where Stephen Graves might have gone to ground.

"Four years ago," said Welbeck, looking over his shoulder, "as a result of your work on these files, the pirates decided you were getting too close and arranged for Cathy and your boys to be abducted. Then they felt safe—until you went to see Graves six weeks ago. You didn't know he'd thrown his hand in with them, but he wasn't willing to take the chance that you'd work it out."

Ash didn't look up from the computer. "How deep do you suppose Graves's involvement goes?"

Welbeck watched him, head cocked to one side like a bird's. "You're the security analyst. What do you think?"

Ash considered. "I think—I *think*—he may be in it as deep as any of them. It's possible the whole bloody business was his idea."

"Have you any evidence for that?"

"Not yet." Ash nodded at the screen. "Maybe it's in these files. That's why you brought me here, isn't it?"

Welbeck nodded, a tiny smile playing around his lips. "The same thought occurred to me. It may all be organized from Somalia, which is what we always thought. But it would be easier to run it from England, where the shipments originate. And it would explain why they concentrated on cargoes from British manufacturers.

We know that Graves was in contact with the pirates, and we don't know of anyone else who was.

"Maybe it's that simple," he mused. "Graves isn't helping them under duress, he's running the operation. He sells his armaments, he insures them for transport, then he steals them back and sells them again, under the counter. Sometimes he steals someone else's shipment—they share information within the industry precisely to combat this sort of thing—to avoid arousing suspicion. We didn't get to the truth of it four years ago because we were looking at it the wrong way around. Graves doesn't answer to the pirates. They answer to him."

"Everything that's happened could have been done by Stephen Graves," Ash said slowly. "Including . . ."

"Yes."

"If I find Graves abducted my wife and sons," Gabriel Ash said carefully, "I will tear his heart out."

"Prove it," said Philip Welbeck, "and I'll let you. Work the files with this alternative scenario in mind. If we're right, there may be material in there that can tell us how it was done and by whom. Go through it all again, see what you can turn up."

Ash was scrolling steadily, his attention split between the screen and this conversation with his boss. "There's no sign of him surfacing?"

"Not yet. He may have got past us, but I think he's still in the country. It would be the smart thing to do—lie low and wait till the flyers we sent out have had beards and mustaches doodled on them. Then he can hire a boat or a light aircraft to slip him across the Channel. Perhaps there's someone in the files he could be hiding out with."

The pages were scrolling past too quickly to read, just slow enough to scan. Ash knew that if there was anything in there that he wanted, he'd spot it. "If we don't find him, how long do I have to stay dead?"

It was a legitimate question. Welbeck didn't resent his asking it; he just didn't know the answer. "Be patient. I know you want to go home, but we're only going to get one shot at this. You're my best analyst, and Graves—assuming we're right about him—knows that. It's why your family was targeted, rather than mine or someone else's. While he thinks you're dead, he knows the police are looking for him, but he probably thinks he's a low priority—wanted for weakness and making some bad decisions, but not much more. He thinks that if he's careful, he'll be able to slip under the radar and pick up again pretty much where he left off.

"If he knew you were alive, he'd shut the whole operation down, get out of England, and disappear for good. We'd never find him; and if we don't find Graves, it could all start up again. Everything you've been through, everything your wife and sons have been through, will have been for nothing."

Heading back to his own desk, Welbeck paused in the doorway. "One more thing to consider. If he learns that you tricked him, he may want revenge enough to risk breaking cover. He got at Cathy once. We'll do all we can to protect her, but I can't guarantee he won't get at her again. For all the money we spend on witness protection, still sometimes people are found. Be patient, Gabriel. You've waited four years. Wait a little longer."

So Ash sat in the room behind Philip Welbeck's office, and he worked through his old files, and he tried to remember what had been going through his mind as he made these records four and five years ago. What thoughts had occurred to him and been long-fingered to await corroboration; what notions he had dismissed as implausible. From where he was sitting now, almost nothing seemed entirely implausible.

But too much had happened in the intervening time. He couldn't put himself back in the place where he was, mentally, professionally, when he was building these files. Looking at it now, he barely recognized the work as his. If there were any coded messages in there, he was unable to read them.

After five days he confessed himself beaten. Welbeck had the black van drive him back to Norbold.

CHAPTER 26

H E WASN'T SURE HOW SENSIBLE it was to keep going around to Hazel's house, but he meant to go just the same, as soon as the streets were empty. Norbold wasn't London or Brighton, cashing in on an around-the-clock economy; even the drunks liked to be tucked up in their beds by one in the morning. Ash had found that if he waited until half past, then left by Laura's back door and slipped from one dark alley to the next, he could make it all the way to the back of Hazel's house without seeing—or, more important, being seen by—anyone except cats. And once an urban fox, and even the fox didn't notice him.

He made himself coffee and toast, more to pass the time than because he was hungry. He was looking forward to seeing Patience again, but what he really needed was to talk to Hazel. Tell her where he'd been, what he'd been doing. Not because he was desperate for human contact. This week he'd spoken to more people, old friends and new faces, than in the whole of the previous four years. He was exhausted by the casual chatter. But Hazel Best filled a special role for him. She was his sounding board, as he was hers. They could talk together about things too crazy to discuss with anyone else.

Ash wanted to talk to Hazel about Stephen Graves. His conversations with Welbeck had, potentially, cast new light on the man's activities; Ash thought Hazel might help him organize the half-formed thoughts that had sleeted past while he was doing battle with the files. He hoped he wouldn't find her asleep. But after a week without contact, she was hardly still waiting up for him. Of course he could wake her. But if he ventured upstairs, he risked waking her young lodger as well, and while he was happy to entrust his family's safety to Hazel's care, he didn't feel the same way about Saturday.

The witching hour approached. As he got up to wash his face, he heard the unmistakable sound—clear as a chime in the silent house, the silent street—of a key in the lock downstairs.

His whole body froze. By now he knew Laura Fry's routine too well to suppose she'd returned to catch up on some late-night paperwork. But no one else had a key.

Ash was not such an innocent as to assume that doors could be opened only with the key that came with the lock. There's the clever way, which is to have the right tools and the right skills to pick it, and the direct approach, which is to corner the locksmith who fitted it and ask for a duplicate. That was how Welbeck had got him a key to Hazel's new house.

But the seminal point, the only point that mattered right now, was that if it wasn't Laura, it was someone who had no legitimate business here. If Ash was discovered, alive and well and living in an attic in Norbold, the best chance of bringing to justice the men behind a conspiracy that had cost so many lives was going over Niagara in a barrel.

His options were limited. If someone had come here looking for him, it was because he was known to be here. He could try killing the torch, hiding under the bed, and holding his breath, but he doubted the intruder would go away without searching the attic. If he tried to leave, they would meet on the stairs.

Attack is often said to be the best means of defense, and when discussing the matter like sensible human beings or running like stink aren't going to work, very often it is. The shock of the cornered rat suddenly flying at its tormentor's throat may be enough to put even a hardened aggressor momentarily on the back foot, and if you're desperate enough, a moment may be all you need. Ash was a big man, and no longer as cadaverous as he'd been six months ago, and it was possible that if he jumped on someone who wasn't expecting it, in the dark, he might conceivably win.

But then what? Even if he could subdue the man with one hand, he couldn't use the other to dial 999. The Norbold police thought he was dead. He might eventually persuade them otherwise, he might still have his captive when they arrived, but his secret would be out and Welbeck's operation as thoroughly blown as if the intruder had completed his task. Ash could call Welbeck, but Whitehall was a long way away and the basic mathematics of the situation remained. Whatever he did—whether he fought or not, whether he won or lost, even if he died in the attempt—whoever had sent this spy was going to know that Ash had faked his suicide and the jaws of a trap were poised to snap shut. They would know sooner if the man downstairs was allowed to do what he'd come here for, but just as surely as if the local police stormed in here with tear gas and Tasers. There was nothing Ash could do to keep the secret.

There was one thing. The thought of it hit Ash like a steel toe cap in the belly. He'd considered fighting. He'd considered dying. Now he considered killing.

Gabriel Ash had worked in national security for seven years, not including the four he'd been on sick leave. He had never been licensed to kill. He'd never been licensed to shout loudly or carry a pointed stick. He was a desk jockey—always had been, always would have been until he took his pension and the CBE that went with it. By nature he was meticulous, analytical, occasionally intuitive, but never aggressive or confrontational. He was the kind of man who apologized to people who bumped into him in shop doorways.

Rats aren't aggressive by nature, either. Their first choice is always to run away. They attack only when they're backed into a corner and have nowhere left to go. That was where Ash was now. He'd backed away until he could retreat no farther; and if he was discovered now, it wasn't just his life at stake. His family were back in England, but were they safe? Philip Welbeck, who hadn't spent his entire career at a computer console, couldn't guarantee it. There weren't many things that would induce Ash to consider launching a murderous attack on someone. No principles, no causes, no amount of money or status or honor. But the safety of his wife and children?

After everything they'd been through? He'd have taken a flamethrower to anyone who threatened them again.

And that was how it had to be. No warning, no quarter, no chance for the intruder to put his hands up and come quietly. Gabriel Ash was no street fighter: the element of surprise was the only weapon he could field. If he gave it away in the interests of good sportsmanship, he would lose. He would lose, he would quite possibly die, and if he didn't, there was a chance that his wife and sons would. The notion of himself as an ambush killer filled him with horror, but he was a rat with its back to a wall. He had to do this, if he could, and try to forget what it was he was doing and remember instead why he was doing it.

The element of surprise would not be enough; he needed to arm himself. He didn't know any karate or the pressure points that would make a man's brain shut down, and he'd been in his twenties before he realized ikebana was not a martial art. The decision was easier than it might have been because his choices were so limited: the torch (tiny and inoffensive), the laptop (his homework: Welbeck had loaded his files onto it so he could put his time in purdah to some use), and two liters of bottled water. If bottles were still made of glass, as they had been in his youth, it would have been the ideal impromptu weapon—a blackjack with deniability. But a plastic bottle would either bounce or split, inflicting not so much lethal injury as bloody annoyance. It would have to be the laptop. At least it was tolerably heavy, its corners hard; swung with enough conviction, it should floor his opponent, giving him time to—

What? Heel-grind his larynx, suffocating him? Break his neck by sheer brute force? What, then?

Ash couldn't afford to think that way. All he could do—all he had time to do—was one thing after another, deal with each problem as it presented. The first was to incapacitate his visitor with a scything blow from a ballistic laptop to the side of the head. Only if that worked would he have to figure out what to do next.

The moment of truth was approaching. He could hear steps on the uncarpeted top flight of stairs. At the last possible moment Ash leaned forward and turned the key, whisper-quiet, in the lock. He needed the door to open when the intruder tried it so that he would walk in, feeling for the light switch, and Ash would have room to swing his weapon.

The footsteps stopped, only the thickness of the door away. Ash held his breath. A glimmer of moonlight from the window showed the tarnished brass handle starting to move. Ash held the laptop in both hands, higher than his head, ready to swing with all the power and determination he could muster as soon as the deeper blackness of a figure appeared in the doorway.

The door opened. Against the dark landing, the shape of a human figure appeared in the frame.

"Forgive me," whispered Gabriel Ash.

The light came on, throwing the dusty room and the two figures into sharp relief.

"Good grief, Gabriel," said Hazel Best, staring, "put that down before you hurt someone!"

CHAPTER 27

ASH PUT THE LAPTOP DOWN ON THE BED. A moment later he thumped down beside it, anticlimax releasing a tremor behind his knees that threatened to drop him to the floor. He'd been ready to kill someone. He'd psyched himself up until he was ready to kill someone—anyone, someone he didn't know but who posed a threat to him and his family. If he'd done a slightly better job of it, if he hadn't delayed just that few seconds longer, he could have killed Hazel.

He was panting for breath, as if he'd been running. "I was going to come and see you."

"Yes? I wanted to see you, too."

"How did you get in? Lockpick, skeleton keys?"

Hazel looked at him as if he'd been sniffing the bleach again. "I asked Laura for the key."

"Ah," said Ash, feeling foolish. In the world of national security, sometimes it was easy to overlook the simple charms of the blindingly obvious.

"Where have you been?"

Ash gave her the abridged edition. He had nothing to report

that was either helpful enough or interesting enough to be worth elaborating on.

"It was a good idea," Hazel conceded. "You might have spotted something that, first time around, you had no reason to notice."

"That's what Philip said. But I didn't." Ash forcibly unclenched his fingers from around the laptop. "How was your week?"

"I've been busy, too." For half a minute she said nothing more. She closed the door and leaned against it, hands clasped in the hollow of her back, one knee bent and the foot flat against the dusty wood. This is something you really can't do in high heels, but Hazel lived in jeans and trainers these days and this was her yogic thinking position.

Eventually she continued. "I've some things to tell you, Gabriel. Things you'll struggle to understand, and then struggle harder to believe. But you need to hear them, and you have the right to hear them before anyone else. All right?"

They'd switched the attic light off again. Probably no one would have noticed, but there was no point advertising the fact that the top of the building was still occupied after its owner had gone home. The little torch, which gave a good light where it was pointed and a faint glow everywhere else, was ideal for Hazel's purposes. This was going to be hard enough without Ash's eyes raking her like claws.

"All right."

Perhaps because the light was so low, she adopted instinctively the rhythmical tone of someone telling a bedtime story. It wasn't very appropriate, but nothing else would have been, either.

"I want to talk about hair. Ordinary human hair. It grows at a rate of about six inches a year, and each hair has a natural life span—typically two to four years, although in some individuals it's longer—after which it falls out. Unless you're unwell or a man of a certain age, the loss is barely noticeable—a few strands in the brush every morning—because the hair is constantly replaced."

In the half-light Ash's lips formed the shape of the word *hair* and his heavy brows were puzzled. But Hazel didn't allow herself to be distracted.

"People say you are what you eat, and it's certainly true in the case of hair, which reflects our diet, and particularly the water we drink. Water picks up minerals from the local geology, and the growing hair fixes them in the same proportions. So you can chart someone's travels over a period of a few years by comparing the minerals in their hair to those in various geographical locations. It's called stable isotope analysis.

"The ratios, specifically of strontium and oxygen, are like a fingerprint—you get enough points of comparison and you can say that this person was drinking water in Lancashire, for instance, and not on the Isle of Wight. Even where the same minerals are present, the proportions of one to another vary significantly. It's a comparatively new technique, but they've reached a level of accuracy where the analysis is accepted as forensic evidence. In the case of suspected terrorists, for instance. They can swear blind that they've been on holiday in Margate, but if their hair shows they were in Pakistan, a jury may think they were actually at a jihadist training camp." She looked at Ash, sitting bewildered on his borrowed bed. "Are you with me so far?"

"I understand the principle," he said. "I'm not sure how it helps. Are we still talking about Stephen Graves? Because the nature of his work at Bertrams must involve a lot of travel. He's probably drunk the water in places where it isn't supposed to be drunk."

Hazel chewed unhappily on the inside of her cheek. But she had only two alternatives: to get it said or to let him find out some other way. She took a deep breath. "I'm not talking about Graves. Gabriel, I had samples of your sons' hair analyzed. They haven't been in Somalia; or rather, they have, but it was only a flying visit. For most of the time they were missing, they were living in southeast England. The best geological match is Cambridgeshire."

There, it was said. She waited for Ash to react. To absorb the implications of what he was hearing and gasp. But he said nothing. She'd expected an argument; she'd been ready for him to accuse her of something—stupidity, misunderstanding what she'd been told, even lying. But not this terrible silence. "Gabriel?"

"You think . . ." Even when he found a voice, it wasn't capable of doing his bidding; it cracked and ran out, and he had to start again. "You're saying they were here all along? In England? Not Somalia? When they were taken away from Cathy, they weren't kept in another part of the camp—they were sent back to England? *Why?*"

Hazel could do tact. It had always been one of her professional strengths, the reason she'd been called on to deal with difficult situations that were beyond her level of training and, arguably, her competence. She had a feel for how to break bad news in a way that was not shockingly abrupt but didn't prolong the agony, either. It was a product of her genuine interest in people and sympathy for their misfortunes.

But she didn't think tact was called for now. Gabriel Ash was her friend, and if she thought about his misfortunes the tears could still spring to her eyes, but actually that wasn't what he needed from her right now. Right now he needed to understand. He needed to know what she knew, everything that she knew, and grope his way toward an understanding of what it meant; and no amount of hearts and flowers would help him do that.

"That's one possibility," she said carefully. "I thought about it but, like you, I couldn't imagine why. If the reason for separating them was to make Cathy more compliant, the boys needed to be close enough to be produced if the pirates wanted to reward her or needed to threaten her. And why risk sending them back to England, where even people who didn't know them would want to help them?"

There wasn't light enough to read his expression, but Hazel saw Ash's head move as he looked up at her. "My God." The bottom had fallen out of his voice. "You think . . . you think they were *all* in England, all along? For four years? That they were held somewhere near Cambridge, and Graves only *told* Cathy they were in Somalia? Is that even possible? Could he have maintained the deception that long?"

His thoughts were racing like a river in spate, tumbling over one another in their urgency, bouncing off the sides in a welter of foam. It was theoretically possible. If she'd been kept in a closed room, with minimal access to the outside, it might have been possible to exclude any clues that what she'd been told wasn't right. Guards who could pass for Somalis. A basic block-built structure with no view to anything green. Four years' captivity would have involved three English winters—to keep the illusion going, the electricity bill would have been horrendous. . . .

"What about the computer?" he asked breathlessly. "Why didn't we realize the transmission was coming not from four thousand miles away, but from just around the corner?"

Hazel sighed. "Because we saw what we'd been told we were going to see: a frightened woman in a pirate camp in Somalia.

Actually, we saw almost nothing—a bare room. But there was nothing to tell us it *couldn't* be Somalia, and at that point we didn't know Graves was an unreliable witness. We thought that, however questionable his actions, he was telling the truth. Plus, you can route computer communications through different hubs to make it hard even for experts to trace their origins. Just from looking at the screen for a few minutes, nobody would have known."

"They were here all along? In England? A couple of hours away?"

"I think so, yes."

"She was never more than a few minutes from help, and she didn't know?" Ash's voice cracked again on the tragedy of it.

Hazel steeled herself. It was now or never. "Unless she *did* know."

The silence stretched till it groaned. Hazel could feel it like static on her skin. *Say something,* she begged in the haven of her own skull. *Say something, say something, say something . . .*

Ash didn't ask her to say it again, because he'd heard the first time. He didn't ask her to explain, because her meaning was clear. He said nothing, because, until he knew what was going to come out when he opened his mouth, it wasn't safe to. Instead he reached for the torch and, still without a word, turned it on Hazel's face.

She went to raise a hand in front of her eyes. But she stopped herself, let him see her blinking in the beam. The gentle glow that had made this conversation easier for her had deprived him of information he needed. How her interpretation of these events was reflected in her expression. If she believed it. If she knew how much she was hurting him.

For a long moment Hazel let him take in whatever it was he needed to see. Then she said quietly, "I'm not making this up. When you're ready for the science bit, you can study the report." She took the sheets out of her pocket, unfolded them, and put them beside him on the bed. "You can talk to the laboratory that did the analysis. I have. I asked how sure they were. They said there's always a margin for error in any analytical process. I asked how big, they said not very big at all. I asked if they could mean Somalia when they said Cambridgeshire, and when they stopped laughing they said no, an error that big wouldn't be in the margin, it would be all over the page.

"They were sure, Gabriel. They're sure enough about the procedure that the prospect of someone going to prison on the strength of it doesn't give them sleepless nights. Almost all the time your sons were missing, they were in England.

"And it makes no sense that they would be in England while Cathy was in Somalia. So either the pirates managed to deceive her for four years—*and* smuggle her out there in time to be met by Graves and the British consul, still without her realizing—or she was lying."

From behind the torch Ash's voice rasped like fingernails on a comb. "If people were pointing guns at you, you'd say anything they wanted, too."

"I probably would," Hazel agreed. "Until I was where they couldn't hurt me anymore, at which point I'd want to put the record straight. Because nobody, not even my husband, would have a better motive for seeing the bastards found. Any information that I had, that I thought I had or that I even thought I might have, I'd want to put in the hands of someone who could use it.

"Cathy's had that chance several times over. She's been here in Norbold for a month. Her sons are safe. She's talked to your boss, the guys from CTC, and Dave Gorman. If she'd said something under duress that might be misleading them, she's had every opportunity to put it right. She hasn't taken it."

"Then she didn't know." Ash's voice was so thick it was almost incomprehensible.

"That's one explanation," said Hazel levelly.

He didn't want to ask. He didn't want to say it, and he didn't want to hear her answer. But in the end he had to. "What other explanation is there?"

She pitied the man with all her heart. She'd have given anything to save him this. But some quirk of intuition had set her on a train of thought that no one else had thought to travel, with the result that she'd seen things that more experienced investigators hadn't. If there had been any doubt in her mind, she'd have been talking to those investigators now, not to Ash. But there wasn't. She didn't like the answer she'd come up with. She didn't expect him to like it, either; probably his first instinct would be to shoot the messenger. It didn't have to matter. Unless she'd gone horribly astray, this was something they had to deal with.

"That she was part of the conspiracy."

CHAPTER 28

SOMETIMES HAZEL ACTED ON IMPULSE, seizing the surge of the tide and trusting that intuition and goodwill would see her through. At other times, though, she planned her moves meticulously, working through all the possible combinations—of what might happen, how people might react, what she should do and say next—in the hope of being able to respond effectively whatever turn events should take.

Before coming here she'd considered all the ways this moment might play out. The arguments Ash might marshal to confound her. The clever, tortuous ways he might find to avoid the unbearable fact that the wife whose loss he had mourned to the brink of madness had betrayed him. That she'd been living comfortably in a smart Cambridge apartment paid for by her lover while Ash crucified himself.

Hazel had thought he would hear her out until he realized what it was she was actually suggesting. But then all her calculations failed, like the math of physicists trying to map the Big Bang. The closer she got to the moment of truth, the more her predictions broke down, the wilder the extremes to which small variations on the theme might fling her. He might listen in silence, allowing the professional part of his brain to work the problem and come, however reluctantly, to the same conclusion. He might shout and throw things. There was every chance, Hazel thought, that his fragile recovery might implode, leaving him weeping uncontrollably while she hunted desperately for Laura Fry's home number.

There was also the possibility that he might hit her.

There was nothing delicate about Hazel Best. Much of her childhood had been spent in the country, helping to move bullocks and falling off ponies. She had embarked on her career as a police officer knowing that intermittent acts of violence came with the badge. You didn't go looking for fights, but sometimes they were unavoidable. You watched your back, and those of your colleagues, and they watched out for you, but still sometimes a situation got out of hand.

Hazel had been struck before and expected to be struck again—by drunks, by thugs, and by otherwise decent people in the throes of hysterics. She had been hit with fists, with weapons—she'd done a short posting in a district of Liverpool famous for its sales of baseball bats despite its having no baseball team—and once with an artificial leg. It was inevitable, and if you couldn't deal with it you couldn't do the job. But she also knew that if Gabriel Ash struck her now, their friendship would be over.

Not because she wouldn't forgive him. She understood how much he'd been through, and how much more she'd just dumped on top of him. If he couldn't handle it without momentarily losing control, she could understand that, too. Ash was the one who would never forgive. Hitting her would put him on the wrong side of a Rubicon there would be no returning over, regardless of whether her theory was ultimately proved right or wrong. The last four years hadn't left him with much in the way of pride. But whatever the provocation, raising his hand to a young woman who was trying to help him would leave him with none.

If the room had been bigger she'd have stepped out of reach. But her back was already against the door, and she was damned if she was going to open it and retreat to the landing as if she was afraid of him. She'd seen things that he hadn't because her emotions were not involved in the same way. She'd told him because he needed to know. Whatever he did next, this dim attic, in the quiet of the night, with only the two of them present, was the best place to deal with it.

He didn't hit her. It was impossible to tell, from what she could see of his expression, whether he had mastered the urge or never felt it. But his eyes burned like coals in the backwash of the torch, and the August night seemed to grow hotter with the fever in his skin.

Finally he said, in a voice that was more breath than sound, "Perhaps you should leave now."

Hazel shook a stubborn head. Some of the corn-colored hair, escaping from the bunch she gathered it in, danced around her face. "No, Gabriel. Tell me I'm wrong. Tell me you know Cathy better than I do and there has to be another explanation. Or tell me you don't care who did what, you don't want to know who did what, all that matters is that your family is safe. But don't tell me to go away and stop bothering you. You don't owe me much, my friend, but you owe me better than that."

Some things command respect. The hunted animal, too tired to run any farther, that turns at bay in order to go down fighting. The mother defending her young with a ferocity she could not muster to defend herself. And Hazel Best, who didn't need to be here, who could have turned over her findings to her friends in CID, secure in the knowledge that, whatever they discovered about Cathy Ash's involvement, her husband would never have to know where the suspicion had originated.

Though Ash was appalled by what she was proposing, a fragment of his mind that had managed to remain objective was able to admire that. The way she would always do what she thought was right rather than what she knew was easy. In the short time he'd known her, it had got her into endless trouble. She'd been proved right more often than not, but even that wasn't the point. The point was, it took guts to do the unpopular thing, and he'd never known anyone with more.

But what she was saying was untenable. He literally could not entertain the idea that, in a war against criminals who put a cash value on people's lives, his wife had taken their side, not his. It couldn't be true. He knew it in his heart, in his bones. Whatever she'd done had been forced on her.

What had she done?

He swallowed. "You're wrong. You have to be wrong."

Hazel kept her voice steady. "I may be wrong about some of it. But there are things that I'm sure of, facts I can prove, and other things that I can't explain any other way."

That stirred him to a little last-ditch passion. Anger was a curd on his tongue. "You're infallible now? There's always another explanation. Have you put any of this to Cathy?" Hazel shook her head. "Of course not. If you had—if you'd talked to her instead of pestering me with your fantasies—you'd know how utterly, stupidly wrong you are. Cathy is an innocent victim. She was kidnapped and held prisoner for four years. For four years she thought every day could be her last."

Hazel didn't flinch from his machine-gun fury. "I don't think she did. I think she helped Graves to keep you out of commission. I don't know why she did it, but I think that's what she did." There were, Hazel knew, only three possible reasons—fear, love, and money—but she didn't need to tell Ash that right now. Not when she'd already dismissed the first.

"But it's absurd!" He was saved from a complete loss of control, and things he might have said that would have brought this conversation crashing to a halt, by the genuine belief that she had misread the situation. "How would Cathy even know Graves, much less know he was involved? I didn't. None of us did."

"But *he* did," said Hazel. She could feel herself shaking inside now, wondered if Ash could hear it in her voice. "You'd interviewed him a couple of times by then. He knew you were closer to the truth than you did. He made inquiries about you, and they took him to Cathy."

"And he kidnapped her," insisted Ash.

"It's possible he did." Hazel nodded. "In the first instance. But then he made her an offer she didn't feel she could refuse: Join us, or you and your boys will be in Somalia by the end of the week."

"She'd have said yes," conceded Ash, his voice low. "Anybody would."

"Yes." She said nothing more, waited.

"And then," Ash said slowly, "as soon as she was free to, she'd have called me, and I'd have got her and the boys to safety before going after Graves with a chain saw."

Which was where the defense of duress fell down, and both of them knew it. If the woman really had been living pleasantly in Cambridge, what could have stopped her from contacting Ash or Ash's office or the police for four years?

"She'd have done anything to protect the boys." Even in his

own ears it sounded like an excuse. But it was true. Presented with a straight choice between their well-being and his, Ash knew Cathy would have chosen her sons. It's what mothers do. She would fight like a tigress to protect them all, but if she couldn't, the children would come first.

"Yes," Hazel said again.

His head came up pugnaciously. In the half-light she couldn't see his face, only the burning of his eyes. "You're determined to think the worst of her!"

"Gabriel, I'm not!" But she bridled her tongue. In his pain he was striking out at the nearest target; it was a miracle that he wasn't doing it physically. "Truly. I'm sorry. I'm sorry it's me saying this stuff. I'll be sorry if I'm wrong, and even more sorry if I'm right. But believing what I do, I had to tell you. You think this is a figment of my imagination? If you can look at the facts honestly and come to another conclusion, no one will be more relieved than me."

Ash sucked in one deep breath after another, like someone preparing for a dive. "All right, tell me. All these *facts* you've discovered." He managed to make it sound like the kind of *f* word usually represented by a row of stars. "Tell me what gives you the right to say these things about my wife."

Hazel was deeply impressed that he was managing to remain logical. It didn't have to matter that he was talking as if he hated her. This was more important than the feelings of either of them. People had died. At least, people had disappeared, and it was too much to hope that the crews of several aircraft were *all* living under assumed names in Cambridge.

She kept her manner cool, forensic. "The hair samples show that the boys were in England, probably close to Cambridge, most of the time they were supposed to be in Somalia. Graves told us he was keeping an eye on the Cambridge flat for a woman who was working abroad. But the porters told me she was there for three and a half years, until sometime in June."

"So?"

"It was mid-June when you interviewed Graves on our way down to visit my father. At the time you thought he was just one of the manufacturers who'd lost arms shipments. But if he is in cahoots with the pirates, you turning up again must have alarmed the hell out of him. He'd thought you were an ex-problem. But you were back in business and you'd got as far as his door. He had to do two things as a matter of urgency. One was to shut you up for good, hence the ambush on our way back from the horse fair. The other was to warn his co-conspirators."

"Cathy is *not* a co-conspirator!"

There was nothing to be gained by arguing. Hazel pressed on. "At which point, Miss Anderson suddenly left her flat in Cambridge, without telling the porters where she was going or how long she'd be away. But she never meant to return. All their personal belongings were removed—hers and the children's. All she left behind were the furniture and that computer, set up to handle video calls."

That hit Ash like a fist. "Children?" he said faintly.

Hazel nodded. Again she waited.

Eventually he whispered, "Boys? Girls?"

"Two boys. Gabriel, they were your sons. It's straining credulity to think anything else. When she learned you were back on the job, she packed up and left. I presume she went to Africa then. To be safe if you couldn't be stopped, to be brought back if you could." She didn't spell it out—"if they succeeded in accomplishing your death"—but Ash knew what she meant.

"Graves set up the video call," Hazel went on. "All they needed was a bare room somewhere and enough know-how to re-route the transmissions. We thought we were following Graves to Cambridge, but actually he was leading us. He wanted to show you that your family were still alive but also still in danger. And we fell for it like a couple of amateurs," she added bitterly. "I thought it was as real as you did."

"Then . . ." A ghost of a voice in the half darkness. "Their offer. My family's lives for mine. If you're right . . . Cathy wanted me dead as much as Graves did."

Hazel winced. It had been necessary to convince him. It seemed she'd succeeded. She wished she could feel happier about it. "She may have thought she was in too deep to object to anything he proposed." It wasn't much of an argument, but it was all she could manage to smooth a little balm on Ash's excoriated soul.

He shook his head, almost in wonder. "There was only one way she could come home—if I wasn't there waiting for her. If she'd come back to me, sooner or later one of the boys would have said something that blew her story apart. She could drill them in what they could and couldn't say, and protect them from interrogation, but she couldn't keep them from talking to their father. Sooner or later, one of those little boys was going to say something that proved his mother a liar."

Hazel had nothing to say that would make this any easier for him, and saw no need to pile more evidence on what he had already accepted. Maybe tomorrow she'd tell him that she'd shown the Cambridge porters the photographs she'd taken of Ash's sons, and they'd recognized them immediately.

He gave it one last try. "Could he have . . . compelled her? Threatened her? Threatened the boys?"

"It's possible."

But Ash had never seen any point in fooling himself. "If she'd needed help dealing with him, it was all around her. As close as the nearest police station. She lived in Cambridge for three and a half years? If she'd felt threatened by Graves, she'd have done something about it."

"You realize," Hazel said after a decent pause, "I have to go to the police with this."

He hesitated, but not for long. "Yes."

"And it'll be out of our hands what happens next."

Still buffeted by the inner turmoil, Ash was slow to realize that what had sounded like a statement was in fact a question. "I suppose so. . . ."

Hazel sighed. If they'd been discussing anyone's situation other than his own, he'd have realized at once that, while there could be no question about what she had to do with her information, there might be some flexibility as to when she had to do it. But he was too shocked, too deeply hurt. He needed her to guide him through the maze of what was possible.

She said patiently, "If you wanted to, you could talk to her first. I can hold off for a few hours, if you want to see her before she's arrested."

He tried to think about it rationally. "I said I'd stay away from her. I promised."

But the situation had changed since that promise was made, and Hazel knew things that Philip Welbeck didn't. "I'm not saying it's a good idea. Just that, if you want to, this will be the last chance."

Even then Ash didn't realize what it was she wasn't saying. That if, in spite of everything, he'd sooner see his wife disappear than face prison, this would be his last opportunity to help her. Once Hazel had talked to DI Gorman, no one would care what either she or Ash wanted. Cathy would be arrested, tried, and convicted for her part in a murderous conspiracy. She would be an old woman before she was free.

But there was a limit to what Hazel was prepared to do, even for her friend, and telling him how to subvert the course of justice was beyond it.

"I suppose," Ash said slowly, "I could give her the chance to explain."

That's one explanation that'd be worth hearing, thought Hazel.

He made his mind up. "I'll go around there now, while the boys are asleep. They don't need to hear the things I'm going to need to say."

But of course, that wouldn't work, either. "They're not at Highfield Road, Gabriel. They went up to Chester a week ago, to see her mother."

Almost more than anything Hazel had said, that seemed finally to put the thing beyond doubt. To a man desperate to believe in his wife, everything else could have been the result of threats, misunderstandings, poor judgment. But that was a lie, and there was only one reason Cathy Ash might lie to Hazel Best. So far as Cathy could know, no one harbored any suspicions about her involvement, so it wasn't her own whereabouts she was anxious to keep secret.

Ash's voice came out dead flat. "Her mother's been dead for years."

Hazel had thought she knew everything that mattered. She was startled to find she didn't. "Then we've no idea where she went when she left Norbold."

236

Ash sucked in a long, slow breath, considering. Looking for alternatives. Finding none. "Of course we have," he said at last. "She's gone to him. To Graves. She's taken my sons and gone to meet the man she betrayed me for."

CHAPTER 29

FIRST THING IN THE MORNING, Hazel talked to DI Gorman. She couldn't be sure if he accepted her theory as gospel, but before she'd even finished he was on the phone to Philip Welbeck in the quieter part of Whitehall. Soon after that Welbeck called Laura Fry, and Laura went up to her attic to tell Ash he was a free man.

But he wasn't there.

Dave Gorman was famously even-tempered, for a detective inspector. He wasn't exactly an intellectual—he still played rugby when he could, and he had the lowest hairline of anyone Hazel had ever seen not eating a banana—but he wasn't a bully. He didn't believe that suspects confessed sooner or constables worked better for being shouted at, and he was better at listening, and at thinking about what he'd heard, than many of his rank.

So the sound of his voice coming through two closed doors and down the stairwell raised eyebrows at the coffee machine in the ground-floor corridor. Then someone mouthed the words *Hazel Best*, and everyone else nodded their understanding.

238

"For an intelligent woman," Gorman thundered, "you do a damn good impression of a bimbo sometimes!"

Hazel winced. But she hardly felt able to argue. Once again, despite her good intentions, she'd made misjudgments you wouldn't expect from someone on their first week out of police college, allowing a situation to develop that would have been prevented by one phone call to the right person at the right time. She might have thought she was helping her friend, but in reality she'd created an opportunity for a distressed and vulnerable man to cut himself off from all sources of help and go alone in pursuit of two dangerous people.

"I'm sorry," she said in a low voice. "It was stupid. I didn't expect . . ."

"*What* didn't you expect?" demanded Gorman. "That Ash would be angry enough to do something crazy? *Why* wouldn't you expect that? The man's unhinged at the best of times! Did you think he'd behave *more* rationally when you told him his wife had only been pretending for the four years he'd thought she was dead?"

"Of course not." She didn't dare raise her eyes yet. "I just didn't expect him to do anything about it. I didn't think there was anything he *could* do. He said he didn't know where she'd gone."

"And you believed him?"

"Yes! He was upset and hurt, and if Cathy had still been at Highfield Road, I'd have—I don't know—sat on his head till he calmed down. But she wasn't. She'd taken the boys and gone away, and she'd lied about where she'd gone to. And yes, I believed Gabriel when he said he didn't know where she would go, except that she'd probably gone to Graves." She risked a covert glance at the DI. "Well, CTC have been looking for him for a week and not found him. Why would Gabriel Ash know where to look?"

"You think he's just wandering about on spec, hoping to get lucky? Posting pictures in post office windows like his wife was a lost cat?"

Hazel shook her head. "I'm guessing that after I left him, he sat up the rest of the night thinking about it, and finally he thought of something worth checking out. That doesn't necessarily mean he was right," she added hopefully. "If he checks it out and it was wrong, he'll come home."

"And if he checks it out and it was right," snarled Gorman, "he's going toe-to-toe with a man who gets people killed. You'd better hope Ash is on a wild-goose chase. If he isn't, the next time you'll see him is on a slab."

G abriel Ash drove north in his mother's car. Hazel had made him tax and insure it and send it for a service after they got back from Byrfield. He suspected she was making the point that if she'd wanted to be a taxi driver, she wouldn't have joined the police. At the time he'd thought it a waste of money: a man who'd hardly left his house for four years didn't need a car. Now he was glad she'd insisted. The more reputable hire firms object to dealing with dead men, and if he'd tried to steal one, doubtless he'd have been caught. He had no talent for lawbreaking.

Fortunately, the senior Mrs. Ash had believed in putting her money into things that would last. So while the Volvo was of pensionable age, the freshly tuned engine was as keen as a retired racehorse gone hunting. Ash got onto the motorway, followed the arrows for the North—it would be hours before the signs got more specific—and let the old girl have her head.

Even this early in the morning the motorway wasn't empty.

It was never empty. But it was much quieter than it would have been if he'd agonized just an hour longer about what he should do, and he slipped into a comfortable gap between a soft furnisher's panel van and a big refrigerated trailer, and let them bear him along like surfing a tarmac wave. Decision making cut to a minimum, he was free to consider the situation in which he found himself: the things he had to do, the things he had already done.

Of the latter, he felt worst about the way he'd treated Hazel. He hadn't been lying when he said he didn't know where Cathy had gone; knowing had come later, stealing up by degrees along with the daylight as he sat alone in the attic room overlooking the park, hunched over, hugging himself like someone in pain. But he could have called her. Perhaps he shouldn't have told her where he was going, but he could at least have told her not to worry, that he knew what he was doing. Although that *would* have been a lie.

Briefly, before common sense intervened, he'd been tempted to ask her along. Her companionship would have shortened the miles, but he owed her better. In the months they'd known each other she'd made a massive difference to his life. Ash knew he'd made a massive difference to hers, too, but in a less positive way. She'd had a good career ahead of her before she met him. Conceivably she might have one again, but not if she was made once more an adjunct to mayhem. He had very little idea how matters would resolve once he reached the Lake District, but however many times he fed the available data into the computer between his ears, he couldn't get an answer that didn't involve bloodshed.

The other reason he'd been tempted to ask Hazel to come was that he missed his dog. But he hadn't succumbed to the whimperings of loneliness. He cared too much for both of them to knowingly take them into danger.

As for the danger to himself, rather to his surprise—he had never counted himself a brave man—it barely figured in his thinking. He was aware that he was on his way to confront two people who would be dismayed to see him alive and could not be relied on to swallow their disappointment gracefully. Graves certainly owned a shotgun, and it seemed likely that a man in the arms business could access other weapons, too. Ash thought he had a Swiss army penknife under his dashboard somewhere.

But then, what was between himself and Stephen Graves was never going to be settled by firepower; or if it was, Ash would lose. In a way, the outcome of the confrontation was less important to him than the fact that it should take place. He was in that desperate position where things could hardly get any worse. If he found them at the boat, Graves would certainly be armed, and regardless of what Ash brought to the party, he wouldn't be going home when the clock struck midnight. Then again, if that was what he found, he didn't much care about going home.

And if, somehow, he found Cathy alone, any kind of weaponry would be superfluous. He wasn't going to hurt his wife. He loved his wife—even now, even knowing what she'd done to him, Gabriel Ash was stuck like a flawed record on the fact that he loved his wife. He had loved her, he did love her, he would always love her. The woman who had put him through hell was somehow apart from that. Some other Cathy, existing in a parallel universe, whose actions produced ripples in the space-time fabric that were capable of being felt in Ash's world but not of affecting his feelings. Perhaps the woman he loved existed now only inside his own head. But that was real enough for Ash, and meant she would be forever safe from him.

This wasn't about vengeance. He wanted to know what had

happened to make her behave as she had. To know, first, if she'd done what Hazel thought she'd done, and then why. He wanted to know what he'd done wrong.

Even as he drove, Ash knew he might be wasting his time. Cathy might not be at the houseboat. It hadn't been obvious, even to him, that she would go there. The idea had come to him only with the dawn, and the memory—there had been so many that night—of joyous weekends the couple had spent there in the first years of their marriage. It had belonged to an uncle of hers and had been used throughout his extended family. By now the uncle might be dead and the boat sold, and Cathy somewhere else entirely. He might be making this long drive for nothing. But he couldn't think where else she might go. And the tenuous connection—the accommodating uncle not only didn't share her married name but he didn't even share her maiden name—might have added to the boat's attractions as somewhere to evade attention for a while. Ash knew about it, but Cathy believed Ash to be dead. Possibly no one else in the world might think to look for her there.

But if he was right, and that was where she had gone—and if Hazel was right, too, and Graves was there with her—what then? What was he expecting to happen? Graves had tried to kill him once: was there anything to stop him from trying again? Would Cathy want to stop him from trying again? Ash genuinely didn't know. He still hoped—fiercely, if forlornly—that there was a reason for everything she'd done. But what if the reason was that she'd grown to hate him?

He drove north, and the day grew bright, but Ash's soul remained deep in shadow.

* * *

Gorman had calmed down by now. That didn't mean Hazel was off the hook.

"He *must* have said something," insisted the DI. "Not necessarily last night. But you've known this man for four months. You know him better than his therapist. Think, Hazel. Think about all those casual conversations there was no particular reason to remember. Those 'We went there on holiday once and it rained all week' conversations. Think of places he's mentioned. If he's thought of somewhere Cathy might go, it's because it meant something to him once; and if it meant something, he may have spoken about it. Maybe only in passing. A place name, an occasion—something. Think, girl!"

"I *am* thinking!" protested Hazel. And she was; her brain felt like he'd put it through a wringer. "There's nothing there. He never talked about things he and Cathy had done. Well, hardly ever. He thought she was dead, remember. He wouldn't want to share his memories of her with me."

"Maybe not," allowed Gorman, "but that doesn't mean nothing ever slipped out. Where did they meet? Where did they go on honeymoon?"

"They met at the University Boat Race." Hazel sounded surprised that she knew that. "I don't know where they went on honeymoon. I know they had a flat in Covent Garden, and that Cathy liked London better than Gabriel did."

"We know about the flat," said Gorman dismissively. "She won't go there. And if she's gone to lose herself in London, we'll never find her—but then, neither would Ash. He's thought of somewhere she might go that he *might* find her. Our only chance of finding either of them is if he said something to you, about someplace that only the two of them knew about, and you can remember. Hazel—*try* to remember!"

"I *am* trying," she wailed. "There's nothing there!"

"All right." Gorman knew he'd get nowhere by bullying her, that a change of subject was more likely to yield results. "Then tell me this. If he finds her, what do you think he'll do?"

Hazel felt as if she was being asked to reveal things about Ash that she'd been told in confidence. But she was not a private citizen; she was a police officer. Even more important, Ash's life was at risk. If he found his wife with Stephen Graves, it was hard to imagine that all three of them were going to walk away unscathed.

She took a deep breath, started at the sharp end. "He won't be armed. To the best of my knowledge he doesn't own a gun, has never owned a gun, wouldn't know where to get a gun, and wouldn't know how to use it if he did. Even at the peak of his career, he was no James Bond. He was an analyst—most of the time he worked at a desk, collating data.

"And then, I'm not sure how much of what I was telling him he actually believed. I know he understood enough to resent it; and I think he accepted the logic behind it. Emotionally, though, I'm not sure he believed it. He felt there had to be another explanation. I think maybe that's what he's doing now—looking for an explanation from the only person who can give him one."

"Do you think he's right? That Cathy Ash had a good reason for playing dead?"

"No," said Hazel. "But maybe I'm not the best one to ask. I like Gabriel, and I can't say I felt the same way about his wife."

Gorman gave a somber smile. "Does that make her a villain?"

"Of course not," said Hazel briskly. "Taking their sons and disappearing with them, and letting him think they were all dead while she was living it up in Cambridge—that's what makes her a villain."

They returned to the question of where Cathy Ash might be

now. Still Hazel had no insights to share. "I could go to Gabriel's house, have a root around, see if anything rings a bell."

"I have people conducting a search there right now." Gorman sounded faintly displeased, as if she was suggesting he might have overlooked this obvious line of inquiry.

"That'll help if Cathy's left a map marked with a big red *X*," said Hazel a shade tartly. "It won't help jog my memory."

"No," agreed Gorman. "All right. DS Presley's in charge. Tell him I sent you."

CHAPTER 30

HOW LONG DOES IT TAKE TO SEARCH A HOUSE? That depends on who's doing the searching. If it's a man, he'll devote ten minutes to the job before deciding that (a) he's had burglars and the item he's looking for is no longer on the premises, or (b) women are constitutionally better equipped for the task, so he should leave it to his wife. If it's a woman doing the searching, it'll take as long as it takes until she finds what she's looking for.

But if it's a police team looking for evidence, as a rule of thumb it takes three days to thoroughly search a house. Detective Sergeant Tom Presley was two hours into the job of searching the Ash house at Highfield Road, and already he was mentally penning his resignation. Or possibly a suicide note.

There was something desperately sad and depressing about the big old house. It had been a prestigious property once, but the glory days were long gone. Ash's mother, widowed young, had lived here alone after he left for university, and she'd never had much incentive to keep it up-to-date. As she grew old, even necessary repairs had been skimped on.

Then his world had fallen apart, and he'd come back here like a wounded animal seeking somewhere familiar to die. He'd done nothing to the place, either. There was no central heating, only a couple of open grates, seldom lit, and some two-bar electric fires. Cold radiated out of the walls, even in summer. The heavy plush curtains, designed to keep the drafts out, kept the sun out, too, and the variations-on-a-brown-theme wallpaper had been unfashionable when it went up twenty years ago. He'd brought nothing with him, made do with what his mother had left behind. Except for the wicker dog basket, squeezed into a tight space in the kitchen and never, as far as DS Presley could see, actually used. There was dog hair on the sofa, the rug, and upstairs on the single bed in the back room Ash had used—his wife had commandeered the front two bedrooms for the three and a half weeks she and her sons had stayed there—but none in the dog basket.

"If anybody ever catches me living like this," he observed, only half in jest, "will they please put me out of my misery?"

The embarrassed silence was the only warning he got that Hazel Best was standing behind him. "Ah, Hazel . . ."

She fixed him with a look that was closer to dislike than she could usually maintain for long. Then she said, with the kind of restraint that is the next best thing to hitting someone with an iron bar, "I'm going to say this just once more, and after that I expect everyone to remember it. Gabriel Ash is not an idiot. He isn't deranged or mentally retarded. He is not a sandwich short of a picnic and his elevator serves all floors. He's a highly intelligent man who's endured more stress than any of us can comprehend, and if we found ourselves dealing with what he's had to deal with, I don't imagine any of us would make a better job of it. Some of us"—her glance flicked Tom Presley like a whip—"might make a worse one. So yes, maybe he's let the decor slide a bit. That does not entitle any of you to treat him or speak of him or think of him with anything less than respect."

She walked past Presley and the rest of them and entered the drawing room with a degree of dignity that could almost be called hauteur, and the shocked silence lasted until after she'd shut the door.

Then Detective Constable Rodgers observed cautiously, "Didn't she used to be a teacher?"

Presley cleared his throat. "I believe so, yes."

Rodgers nodded. "It shows."

Hazel Best didn't just surprise her colleagues sometimes: sometimes she surprised herself. Everyone in the house had more experience and more seniority than she had, and none of them had said anything very terrible. She just got so tired of it. Of people who should know better treating Ash like a joke rather than a victim. If he'd been knocked down in the street by an inattentive driver, every one of them would have rushed to help. Instead he'd been run down by an emotional express train, and left broken and bleeding by the track, and rather than gathering around with splints and oxygen and hot, sweet tea, they made fun of him. They called him Rambles With Dogs. She was angry with them and ashamed of them; and maybe she'd spoken out of turn, but what she'd said had needed saying.

She sat in Ash's mother's best armchair, getting her breath back. At least she'd found a way of getting the front room to herself. The search would continue along the hall and up the stairs, but it wouldn't come in here until there was no alternative. Even then Presley's team would draw straws for who was going to disturb her.

Hazel looked around curiously. In all the times she'd been in this house, she'd never explored this room. The reason was the same reason so many people don't use the biggest room in their house: because their mothers said you had to have one room where things stayed looking nice, and the only way to achieve that was by excluding people. So the best china, which was never used, and the best chairs, which were never sat on, and the best rugs, which people had to walk around, were all concentrated in the front room and seen only after family funerals or by the person doing the spring cleaning.

The other thing that people kept in the front room was the family album. These days most people keep photographs on their phone or their computer, but Mrs. Ash would certainly have had a family album, and Hazel thought Ash would have continued sending contributions for it while she was alive.

If there was somewhere that Ash had guessed Cathy would go, it was probably somewhere they had been together, in happier days. And maybe they'd immortalized it in photographs.

Hazel found a stack of albums in the bottom of the sideboard. Some of them were clearly ancient, showing women in long skirts and men in buttoned-up jackets; the prints were stuck in with little adhesive corners, and someone had written names, places, and dates below many of them. "Mother and Mrs. Kitchen, Blackpool, 1932" was one such legend. Another read, "Father atop the General, Marmbury Stumps, 1949"—which might have been a bit ripe for most people's family album, except that the General was a horse.

Toward the end of the century, as photography became easier, less care had been taken in cataloguing the prints. Important ones were still labeled—"Henry and Elizabeth, married Norbold Parish Church, May 2, 1971"; "Gabriel's christening, Norbold

Parish Church, February 15, 1975"; "Gabriel's graduation, Oxford, 1997"—but most were just tacked loosely in place, nameless faces in unknown places on occasions long forgotten.

What was she expecting, Hazel asked herself sourly, a photograph labeled "Gabriel and Cathy at their favorite hideaway," with a sign in the background to identify the location? Nothing she knew of detective work suggested it was ever *that* easy. Quite often it proved impossible: you *never* found the *X* that marked the spot. Promising lines of inquiry petered out because a victim with other things on his mind failed to leave a trail of crumbs leading to his murderer's front door—or if he did, a conscientious street cleaner swept it away. The success of a criminal investigation is less dependent, usually, on inspiration and more on a scrupulous chain of evidence connecting the *who* with the *what*.

So it was going to take time, effort, and a degree of concentration she'd struggle to maintain here, with Presley's team tiptoeing around her from time to time. She found a cardboard box in the kitchen and packed the albums into it.

"Where do you think you're going with those?" demanded DS Presley.

It was a reasonable question, and Hazel tried to answer it reasonably. "I'm going to work on them at my house. There's too much going on here for me to think."

"You can't do that! That's evidence."

"Of what?" asked Hazel. And that, too, was a good question, as well as being irritatingly grammatical.

"Er . . ."

Hazel took pity on him. "Ask Mr. Gorman. He wants me to work on this stuff—he thinks I might spot something nobody else would. Look"—she showed him—"it's a box of old photographs. It *can't* be evidence of any crime you're interested in."

The sergeant was unconvinced. But he called DI Gorman; then he stood back from the doorway to let her pass. "Still seems pretty irregular to me," he grumbled.

"We're on the same side here, Sergeant," she reminded him. "We're all just trying to find out where these people have disappeared to and stop them from doing any more harm to one another. I don't know if I can do anything useful with these"—she hefted the albums—"but I have to try."

That made sense. Mollified, Presley nodded. "Try."

Saturday offered to help for a couple of hours before work. (Before work! It pleased Hazel's heart, how quickly he'd slipped into the thought processes of the gainfully employed.) But though the offer was kindly meant, this was something she needed to do alone. If it was her memory the pictures needed to jog, it was her eyes that needed to see them.

The youth nodded, shrugging off the rejection as he'd shrugged off so many in the past, and pivoted on the bottom step, heading back to his room. On impulse Hazel left the photo albums she was laying out on the coffee table and crossed the room quickly enough to catch his wrist. He turned back to her, startled, eyes saucering—and she astonished both of them by leaning up and kissing him.

She felt the need to explain. "That was a sisterly kiss, not to be confused with anything more promising. But I want you to know how proud I am of you. Of how you've got your life together. You told me you'd turn over a new leaf, and you have. You've stayed out of trouble, you've got yourself a job, you're turning into a model citizen. When I offered you a room, I had no idea if you'd be able to make a go of it, or if you'd slip back to your street friends and your street ways. I knew you were worth taking a chance on. I didn't know if you'd be able to do anything with that chance.

"Saturday, it pleases me more than I can say that you've made me feel pretty silly for worrying. I don't need to worry about you—you're going to be fine. You're a smart, decent young man, and you make your old landlady very proud!"

Saturday went on staring at her for a minute. Then he blinked, nodded, and continued on up the stairs. Hazel smiled to herself. She'd seen what it was he was blinking away.

She headed back to the coffee table and began leafing through the albums, randomly, seeing nothing that meant anything to her. Then she took the photographs out and spread them on the sitting room carpet. Not all of them, just those from the last forty years—even a favorite haunt from Ash's childhood might have drawn him back decades later with his wife. There were still dozens and dozens of them. Hazel had no idea how she'd get them back in the right albums when she'd finished.

She spread them out and let her eyes slide over them. She arranged them into a rough chronology, with the little shock-haired boy to the left and the grown man with his wife and sons to the right. There was, of course, nothing from the last four years. There was hardly a moment of those four years Ash would have wanted recorded for posterity; and after his mother died there was no one to send them to.

Hazel then discarded those that had nothing to say beyond *Here we are, still alive and breathing.* She needed information, not smiles and a cross section of knitwear. She was looking behind the people in the photographs to the backgrounds, watching for recurring themes.

There were three photographs, taken over twenty years, against the backdrop of Blackpool Tower. But then, most English families would have taken occasional holidays in Blackpool; and when she found the group posing dutifully on the steps of a large terrace house, with "Back at Mrs. Sidgewick's again!" penciled on the reverse, Hazel put them aside. No one in his right mind would have taken Cathy Ash to a Blackpool B and B.

What else? Views of the Lake District. Every family in Britain had also holidayed in the Lake District. Lake Windermere, the bridge at Ambleside, Castlerigg Stone Circle, Ullswater, Derwentwater. Wonderful vistas of purple mountains with wonderful names—Haystacks and Catbells and Striding Edge—and azure lakes, and no hint of all the rain that kept the lakes brimful.

A surprise then: Gabriel Ash showing a degree of sporting prowess. He'd never said anything about archery. But here he was, about twelve years of age, with a bow almost as tall as he was and a silver trophy. There was so much she didn't know about him. He'd done forty years' living before they'd even met. The place he'd thought of, where Cathy might go, could be hidden anywhere in any one of those years.

Gabriel the archer, Gabriel the student, Gabriel the graduate. Gabriel the bridegroom. Gabriel the father of sons. Family snaps, nothing more. Important to him, important no doubt to his mother, but no help now. Hazel wanted scenery, landscapes, something behind the familial cheeriness that might be identifiable; buildings or hills or a river that would appear on a map if she could figure out where to look. Like that one—where was it?—on the boat with the big house in the background. The boat might be long gone, but the house would still be there. Maybe that was somewhere Cathy might think of hiding and Ash might think of looking.

It wasn't a eureka moment: Hazel didn't suppose she'd cracked the case with that twitch of intuition. But if they'd had somewhere special, they would have taken photographs there. Cathy would have photographed Ash, and Ash would have photographed Cathy; then they'd have flagged down a passing rambler to photograph them both. They'd have sent a copy to Ash's mother and she'd have put it in her album. So it should now be on Hazel's sitting room carpet.

But if it was, she wasn't seeing it. She wasn't even seeing the one with the boat anymore. There were, however, lots of lakes, or possibly the same lake from different angles; and surely—yes, this one—another shot with the big house in the background. From farther away this time, with the tree-clad slope climbing steeply behind it. She turned it over, but there was nothing written on the back. But it had to be the Lake District, didn't it? Unless it was Scotland. Lots of lakes—lochs—and hills there, and a fair number of trees. Was there anything Scottish about the house—pepperpot turrets, crow-stepped gables, men in kilts playing bagpipes on the front lawn? The house was too distant in this shot to be sure. Where was the other one?

She frowned. What had she done with it? Puzzled, she bent and leafed through the prints. She knew—from the ages of the subjects—approximately when it was taken and therefore where it should have been. Still she couldn't find it.

The temptation is always to believe that the missing item must be there, that we're just not seeing it. But Hazel had been taught observation as a professional skill, and to trust the evidence of her eyes. She didn't start searching through the whole collection again. Instead she sat back on her heels and thought. Then she got up and went to her bedroom.

She found it in her handbag. Because it hadn't come from the Ash family albums. It was the one Cathy had given her along with the locks of the boys' hair.

It showed what she remembered it showing: Ash looking happier than Hazel had ever seen him, his arm about his wife and the wind in his thick hair, on the deck of a small houseboat moored to a jetty. A stony lane ran up the hillside and, high above the lake, the house occupied the top right-hand corner of the shot. It still didn't look particularly Scottish.

Hazel called Laura Fry at home. "Did Gabriel ever mention a boat to you? I have a photo of him and Cathy on what looks like a houseboat."

As a therapist, Laura had been accustomed to peculiar questions coming without much warning even before she knew Ash and Hazel. She didn't ask why Hazel wanted to know; she concentrated on trying to answer. "He talked about a few holidays they had together. Tunisia was one; Thailand was another."

Hazel was shaking her head. "This looks very like England. Maybe the Lake District."

That rang a bell. "Oh—yes, they did that a few times. The boat belonged to a relative of Cathy's. They'd go up for the weekend sometimes."

Hazel felt her senses quicken. "Do you know where it was?"

"I don't think he ever told me. Is it important?"

"Probably not. Just an idea I had." Hazel was trying to hide her disappointment. There was a chance that Cathy had thought of that boat as a secret refuge, and that Ash had thought of it, too. But she hadn't enough information to find them.

She couldn't bring herself to move on. She was on the right track: she knew it in her bones. She went back to the photographs, separated out those that might have been taken in the Lake District, scrutinizing each in turn until her eyes itched. Then she went back to the picture Cathy had given her. The boat might be gone, but the house would still be there and so would the jetty. Someone familiar with the area would recognize them. If she showed that photograph to a Lake District postman, for instance . . .

She could head up there now, tonight, and do exactly that. She might find the house. She might even find the boat. Then what? If Ash hadn't found Cathy there, she could bring him home. But if Cathy had gone to the boat, Graves might be there, too.

Hazel was going to need help. She couldn't ask Dave Gorman to go with her on what might so easily prove a wild-goose chase. She could ask for backup from the local constabulary, but the request would have to come from Gorman.

So the DI was her next call. By now, she was pretty sure, his heart must sink at the sound of her voice.

CHAPTER 31

DI GORMAN LOOKED AT THE PICTURES. He listened to what Hazel had to say. Finally he said, doubtfully, "So these photos were taken anything up to ten years ago. Is there any reason to suppose the boat's still there?"

"Well, no," admitted Hazel. "But the house will be."

"But the Ashes have no connection with the house."

"No. But the boat may still be there. Even if it isn't, whoever owns the house may know where it went. If Gabriel could find it, I'm sure we can."

"But you're not sure Ash has gone there. That any of them have gone there."

Hazel had to concede that she wasn't. "I know it's a long shot. But even long shots pay off sometimes. You told me to think of somewhere they might have gone. Well, this is it."

He had said that. And she could be right. But it wasn't grounds to mobilize a task force. "Tell you what, Hazel. It's too late to do much tonight. First thing tomorrow I'll fax a copy of your picture to Cumbria, see if any of the local lads recognize this house. If they do, they can go and see if the boat's still there, and if anybody's on it. Good enough?"

Hazel stared at him as if he were mad. "Of course it isn't good enough! You want to send a couple of local plods to bring in a man who's wanted for hijacking airplanes? Stephen Graves will eat them alive!"

"He's a businessman. . . ."

"He's in the *arms* business! He came after Gabriel and me with a shotgun!" Hazel took a moment to curb her temper. "All right. But Gabriel's been missing for twelve hours, maybe longer: he could be in a lot of trouble by now. Send the fax tonight, ask Cumbria to get on it at first light. And warn them what they might be walking into." She turned to go, taking the photographs with her, leaving Gorman the photocopies.

"Hazel?"

She stopped, turned back. "What?"

"Don't even think of going up there alone. If there's anything to find, we'll find it."

She nodded, managed a smile. "I know."

"And?"

"And I won't even think of going up there alone."

Gorman grinned. He'd lost a tooth playing rugby, wore the gap as a badge of honor. "Good girl."

But then he didn't hear her murmur as she headed down the stairs, "You're never alone with a lurcher."

Before she embarked on the long drive north, Hazel was clear in her own mind about what she *didn't* hope to achieve. She thought she could find the jetty where the houseboat had been moored; though that didn't mean that Ash or his wife or his wife's lover was there now or ever had been. But she wasn't going to arrest anyone. She had no intentions of putting herself in danger.

Even when she was troubled, she wasn't stupid. If she could find the boat, the local constabulary could detail firearms officers to deal with Graves.

That was the point at which Hazel thought she could do some good. If Graves was there, he would be arrested; if Cathy was there, she, too, would be arrested; and that would leave Ash—if he'd found them—stunned, bereft, unable to begin the process of getting himself and his sons home. Hazel wanted to be at his side, to help him do what needed doing and then to bring him home.

For the same reason, she collected Patience before hitting the motorway. She knew Ash well enough to suspect that, if she found him in a state of fugue, he might take more comfort in his dog's presence than in hers. Plus it meant that, at least technically, Hazel hadn't lied to DI Gorman.

It was a good road but still a long way. At least most of the traffic was heading south by now, a ribbon of headlights streaming toward her through the night, a trail of taillights in her mirror. It was gone midnight before road signs directing her to the North had given way to more specific destinations like Kendal, Windermere, and Keswick. And she still didn't know where she was going.

Help came, a little before dawn, in the shape of a fat man with a straw in his mouth, carrying a pitchfork, with the words emblazoned across his ample belly: THE LITTLE FARMER—ALL DAY BREAKFASTS, ALL NIGHT SNACKS. Hazel swung off the motorway where the pitchfork pointed and pulled up in front of the diner. There were three big trucks in the parking lot but no customers at the tables inside.

She climbed out stiffly, easing her cramped limbs while Patience disappeared discreetly around the back of the car. When she returned, Hazel settled her on the backseat. "I'll get you something to eat, okay?" The dog blinked, almost as if she were nodding.

The Little Farmer was true to its advertising: it was still open, though the chef was asleep over the counter and the bell tinkling over his door didn't wake him. Hazel cleared her throat robustly and he looked up in momentary alarm. Then he remembered where he was and yawned. "What can I get you?"

"Sausage, bacon, and egg," said Hazel. "Twice—once in a bowl for my dog. Another bowl of water, and a pot of tea."

The chef didn't even look surprised. The food arrived promptly. Patience disposed of hers, and Hazel went back inside to spend a little longer over her own meal. She ate at the counter, keeping the lonely chef company. Over her second cup of tea she produced the photographs. "Any idea where that is?"

He'd nothing better to do, wouldn't have for another hour or more. He studied the pictures. "Looks vaguely familiar." He groped under the counter, came up with a handful of guidebooks. "Hang on, hang on. . . . No, that's not the one. . . . Windermere, Coniston Water . . . Ullswater. There we are." He turned the book so she could see. "Isn't that it, up on the hill? Sedgemere House."

He was right. It was. The angle was different, the photograph taken from farther along the lake, but the house was recognizably the same, even to the jetty below it. And at the time that the photograph was taken—Hazel checked the copyright date, which was only two years earlier—the little houseboat was still moored there. Her heart quickened. Maybe it was still there today. Maybe the goose she'd been chasing wasn't so wild after all.

She bought the guidebook from him. It seemed the least she could do. At the back she found maps to all the tourist attractions. Sedgemere House was marked as open for prearranged tours only, but that didn't matter. All she needed was its location, on the hillside above the long finger of Ullswater, the roads that would take her there, and the lane—a mere scratch on the map—that would take her down to the jetty.

Now Hazel had a dilemma. She wanted to call DI Gorman, tell him she'd found the house in the picture, and ask him to send the cavalry. But if she did that, he'd know she'd gone against . . . not his orders—he probably wasn't in a position to give her orders—but his express wishes. He had her mobile number; she thought he'd call when he got an answer to his fax, and the circumspect thing might be to wait for that call. But Ash could be in trouble now, needing her now, and even Dave Gorman wasn't likely to be in his office before seven in the morning. So either she wasted two hours doing nothing but keeping on his good side or she made her way to Ullswater and found the road to Sedgemere House and the lane—track, rather—down to the jetty, and then . . .

Well, one of only two things, actually. She could proceed with caution down to the lakeside, see if the houseboat was still there, and if it was, who, if anyone, was on it. But that would put her in danger and anger DI Gorman. The alternative was to wait, handy but out of sight, for Gorman's call. That would be the sensible thing to do, and Hazel had always prided herself on her common sense.

The rising sun found her driving west into the northern Lakes, wilder and less fashionable than their southern cousins. Since leaving the motorway, she found the roads oddly quiet for the Lake District in summer. But of course it was barely six o'clock. All the tourists were still in their beds and the first of the day's Cumberland sausages had yet to hit the frying pan. She followed the map, looking first for the road that would take her down the southern shore of Ullswater, then for the laneway to Sedgemere House. Somewhere along that lane, the jetty should come into view. She guessed wrong at the first attempt and ended up in someone's farmyard, with his dairy herd coming the other way, but her second guess was better. The lake, which had been playing hide-and-seek with her for the last mile, reappeared in front of her. A moment later, she glimpsed the side of the house through a screen of conifers, then the end of the jetty, finally the little houseboat snugged in close to the shore.

Somehow it managed to come as a surprise. As if she'd never really expected to find it; as if there was some doubt in her mind that it even existed. But there it was, a small, squarish white boat with touches of blue about it, tied fore and aft to the old black timbers of the jetty. There was no one in sight, either at the boat or anywhere around, but there was a car parked halfway down the track. A big gray car in the style of an earlier decade.

"He's here," whispered Hazel.

Patience thought so, too. The dog tugged excitedly at her seat belt, whining under her breath.

Despite her sense of urgency, Hazel forced herself to be cautious. She quietly backed away, until the jetty disappeared once more from sight. Then she got out and walked forward in order to study the scene without being noticed.

There was just the one car, Ash's mother's Volvo, and nowhere another could have been concealed. Either Ash had found the boat deserted or whoever had got here first had already left. Hazel let out her pent-up breath in real relief. She knew she couldn't deal with Stephen Graves, but she'd have died of anxiety waiting for those who could.

But surely Ash's car meant he was the only one there now. It was probably safe to approach. Even so, Hazel saw no reason not to cover her back. She called DI Gorman's mobile number.

The man might not have gone off duty before midnight. This might be his wake-up call. It couldn't be helped. She had to tell him that she'd found Ash and where they were. Once he'd finished shouting, he'd send someone from the local constabulary to meet them.

Gorman answered eventually. He didn't sound as if she'd disturbed his sleep. He sounded as if she'd disturbed him while he was brushing his teeth.

He listened more than he talked; even so, he couldn't contain the occasional exclamation—of surprise, of dismay, of downright disbelief. He took down the directions she gave him. Finally he said darkly, "We'll talk about this later. For now, stay put and wait for backup."

"I'm going down to the boat," she said. "There's no danger. Gabriel's on his own."

"Wait for the area car! You don't know what you'll find down there." But she was already gone.

It wasn't there now, but there had been another car. Beside the jetty was an area of flattened grass with tire treads and the distinctive marks of a woman's shoes pressed into the damp earth. Even in summer, the ground never dries out for long in the Lake District.

Hazel had walked down the grassy slope, at a tangent to the stony track that curved around to the jetty. Arriving at the water's edge, she sidestepped the parking area to preserve the evidence, but then she hesitated. Gorman was right: she didn't know what she'd find on the boat. She was assuming that Ash was here alone. But that, she now realized, could be a bad mistake. If Graves had finally managed to kill him, he might have taken the body away for disposal where some canoeist wasn't going to snag it with his paddle, and have every intention of returning when he had. Perhaps she should wait. . . .

The decision was taken out of her hands. She'd left Patience in her car, tethered by the seat belt, with the window open for ventilation. But somehow the dog had freed herself, and now she trotted past Hazel with her nose high, scenting the air. Hazel called her name sotto voce, but the lurcher ignored her, continued out onto the jetty. When she reached the boat, she let out a single high-pitched bark.

And since that put paid to the option of covert surveillance, Hazel followed. With the element of surprise gone, it was important to take control of the situation before anyone had time to react.

Of course, it shouldn't have been a solitary probationary constable on sick leave attempting to take control. Hazel knew that well enough. But she was the one here. Help was on its way, but it hadn't come yet, the dog had given away her presence, and there was still the chance that Ash was in the kind of trouble that couldn't wait. On balance, therefore, Hazel thought it better to board the boat immediately and establish who was there and what they were doing, and hope that when the area car from the nearest police station turned into the lane, it would have its siren wailing for all to hear.

She fixed Patience with a steely eye. "You and I are going to have words when this is over."

The dog didn't move. Her hackles were up, and a low growl was purring in her throat. Hazel reached for a stanchion and swung herself onto the deck.

By now she could smell it, too: the sickly sweet scent of blood. The smell of something very wrong. Her heart sank. She'd half expected the thing to end in anticlimax—Ash here alone, any others who had been here long gone, leaving her to make complicated explanations to the local lads currently speeding through the country lanes with their blues-and-twos going. But it wasn't going to be like that. A lot of blood has to have been spilled before you can smell it, enough that whoever lost it needs help. At least it removed the last argument for doing nothing. She reached for the companionway and stepped inside.

What greeted her made her jaw drop and her eyes widen in shock. She stayed frozen on the steep wooden steps, her vision adjusting to the dimness of the cabin, knowing she made an easy target for anyone in the mood for more violence but momentarily quite unable to move.

When the tightness in her chest reminded her to breathe, she sucked in a great lungful of air that loosened the stricture in her throat. Even so, her voice didn't sound remotely like her own. "God in heaven, Gabriel," she gasped, "what have you *done?*"

CHAPTER 32

IT WAS AFTERNOON BEFORE ASH LEFT THE MOTORWAY. The traffic had been horrendous; it wasn't much lighter now, and the road was less capable of dealing with it. But speed wasn't an issue. No one was waiting for him at the houseboat. Perhaps no one was there at all.

He hadn't thought to bring a map, was relying on memory alone to find the place. He'd done the journey four or five times, most recently some six years ago, and each time Cathy had been beside him, guiding him. She'd been coming here since childhood, had learned to swim in the cold waters of the lake, knew every sheep trod within a five-mile radius.

Bringing him here for the first time had been like giving him a present wrapped in rainbows. She had loved him then. When had she stopped? When he took her to London? But she loved London, too, quickly surrounded herself with a network of interesting and attentive friends. She loved the fact that if the days weren't long enough to see what the capital had to offer, it all went on into the night as well. That couldn't be what he'd done wrong. He hadn't forced her to relocate to London, and by the time they'd been there a month, it fitted Cathy like a second skin. London wasn't the reason she'd come to hate him.

Ash made a couple of false turns and had to retrace his route. Every time he turned off a major road onto a minor one, the traffic thinned abruptly, so that he had the last length of laneway to himself. The lake, which had sat at his shoulder for several miles, had slipped from sight before he made the final turn; now he breasted a little rise in the lane and the sapphire length of it was spread out to the right and left of him, brilliant in the sunshine. He remembered that heart-stopping moment from every time he'd been here. The beauty of it never faded.

When the jetty came into sight, he stopped the car and parked in a gateway. It seemed wiser to go the rest of the way on foot. That may have been a mistake. Nothing that anyone on the houseboat could do in the few moments between hearing a car and its arrival was as important as having the means of a speedy departure close at hand.

But he chose to walk down the last few hundred meters of track, and the decision earned him a prize he would not otherwise have had: the sight of his sons playing unawares beside the lake. Ash caught his breath. Then he sank slowly onto his knees to watch them unobserved.

With the water so close, Cathy had made them wear life jackets. Gilbert was old enough to resent being treated like a baby; sullenness radiated from him like heat from a smoldering fire. He sat on the landward end of the jetty, bare legs dangling over the grass, casting indignant glances toward the boat to see if his mother was feeling silly yet.

Two years younger, and with a sunnier disposition, Guy didn't care if the life jackets were necessary. The sun was shining, the water was sparkling, they were living on a boat, and he'd found a bird's skull polished white by the weather. What radiated from him was the sheer joy of being six years old and without a care in the world.

Ash knelt in the grass, with the afternoon sun beating down on his back and tears winking like crystal on his cheeks, and had no idea what to do next. They believed he was dead. Two months ago he'd believed *they* were dead. If he called to them, they wouldn't know him. They hadn't seen him for four years. They couldn't have picked him out of a police lineup if two of the other men had been black and one had been a dwarf. If he approached them, they'd yell for their mother. If he tried to grab them and drag them to his car, they'd scream blue murder and fear him forever.

And he still wouldn't have achieved what he'd come here for. Failure should have been a price worth paying for the safe return of his sons, but he wanted more. Needed more. Needed to hold them and take them home with him, but also to talk to Cathy and find out what had happened. Hazel's theory didn't explain everything. Ash was desperate to hear his wife say something that would make sense of what she'd done. That would justify letting him think he'd brought about the destruction of his family. Even hearing that she was in love with Stephen Graves would be something. No one is entirely responsible for the things they do for love. If she could tell him that she'd been overwhelmed by the strength of her feelings, that she'd wanted Graves to the exclusion of honor, decency, or any regard for the man with whom she'd spent the previous eight years, he could begin to forgive her. He would have killed for her; perhaps that was how she felt about Graves.

But she'd loved him once, Ash was sure of it. He needed to hear her say it; and then say that how she'd felt for him once, now she felt for someone else. Then he would take his sons and go home; and tomorrow he would tell the police everything he knew that might help bring Stephen Graves to justice. If Cathy, too, found herself gathered in by the long arm of the law, he would feel a twinge of regret, but his primary concern was to ensure the boys were safe and happy. It had taken him four years, but his job was done. A criminal enterprise that had hijacked millions of pounds' worth of armaments and cost dozens of lives was broken. It was a major achievement. One day, perhaps, it would feel like it.

Down at the jetty, Gilbert grew bored with waiting to be noticed, still perfectly safe, meters from the water. He stood up and, with a last accusing glance at the boat, hands in pockets, walked up the grassy bank, scuffing his shoes.

Guy looked up as he passed. "Do you want to play zombies?"

"No."

"Okay." Untroubled, Guy went on playing with his bird's skull, while Gilbert went on being displeased.

When he was perhaps fifty meters from the shore, he turned back and called out rebelliously but not quite loud enough to be heard from the boat, "Is this far enough from the water?" He took off his life jacket and threw it down on the grass.

Which is when he saw Ash.

One of the defining achievements of Western society in recent decades has been to make its children afraid of half the human race. The vast majority of children who come to harm do so at the hands of those they live with; but the notion of the strange man stalking the streets in search of children to carry off is one that every cherished girl and boy will be familiar with. In large parts of the civilized world it stops them from playing outside with friends until they're almost old enough to marry and drive a car.

So the first emotion that Gabriel Ash saw flicker across his elder son's face after four years—he'd been too far away at the park—was fear. He felt his heart breaking within him. He wanted to leap to his feet, reach for the boy, and clasp him tight against his chest—and he knew that if he tried, Gilbert would scream in terror and run from him. So he stayed where he was, kneeling in the grass, and a kind of desperate smile diverted the tears into the corners of his mouth.

When he didn't move, the alarm in Gilbert's eyes turned by degrees to puzzlement. The fine, dark brows gathered. He looked at Ash, then uncertainly back at the boat, and then at Ash again. He said, "I've seen you before."

Ash nodded. "I used to know your mother. Years ago, when you were little."

"Did you know my father, too?"

"Yes, I did."

"He died," said the boy, watching for the effect of this revelation. "While we were on holiday."

"I heard that," said Ash. He couldn't think what else to say.

"We had to come back. We'd only just got there."

"That must have been . . . difficult."

"He was clever," Gilbert said, waiting as if he expected to be contradicted. "My dad was."

"Yes?"

"Clever, but not smart," explained Gilbert. "That's what my mum says."

Ash bit his lip. "That sounds about right."

"She's down at the boat. My mum. Shall I call her?"

"In a minute." He'd driven two hundred miles to see her, to ask her what had happened; now it turned out he didn't want to talk to her at all, didn't need to know. All he wanted was his sons, and they were right here, and if only he'd brought Hazel with him, she could have stayed with them while he told their mother he was assuming custody. He could just have taken them, of course, and left her to wonder in increasing panic what had become of them, but he wouldn't have done that. He remembered too well how it felt.

Slowly, careful not to scare the boy, he climbed to his feet. "Will you do something for me, Gilbert? Will you keep an eye on Guy while I have a word with your mother?"

Gilbert Ash was at an age when his default position for any-thing asked of him was refusal. If Cathy had asked him to finish the last of the chocolate ice cream from the freezer, he'd have said no before realizing in horror what it was he was saying no to. For some reason, though, when the tall, stooping man he vaguely re-membered asked him to look after his younger brother, he under-stood that it was important and he nodded. "All right."

"Thank you." Ash walked down the grassy bank and out onto the jetty. After a moment's hesitation he stepped over the fenders onto the deck of the houseboat.

CHAPTER 33

CATHY WASN'T EXPECTING HIM. Of course she wasn't: she thought he was dead. She thought she'd seen him die. She wasn't expecting anyone else, either, so she assumed the footsteps on the deck overhead meant the boys had finished playing and were hungry again. She raised her voice to carry up the companionway. "Supper's in the oven. It'll be ready in half an hour."

There was no reply, but she heard the narrow double doors at the top of the steps fold back, and turned with the smile already on her face. "I told you, half an—"

That was when she saw him, sitting on the top step, his long legs bent, his arms folded on his knees, watching her.

The words turned to cinders in her mouth, the blood in her veins to ice. She couldn't remember the sequence of muscular movements that would close her mouth. Her legs went weak under her, so that she had to clutch the edge of the table. All the color drained from her face.

For long moments she seriously entertained the possibility that he was an illusion. Possibly a ghost; possibly a phantasm dreamed up by a guilty portion of her brain to punish her. Cathy

Ash was a rational woman, but it still seemed marginally less improbable than the actual physical presence of her late husband on her uncle Ernie's boat.

Her bloodless lips moved. Breath came out, but still nothing recognizable as words.

"Hello, Cathy," Ash said quietly.

Finally she managed to say, "You're not dead."

Ash barked an ironic little laugh. "Try to sound a bit more thrilled."

"You shot yourself! So that the boys and I could come home. It was live on the Internet. I saw it!"

He shook his head. "Special effects. You remember Philip Welbeck? He always did have a taste for the dramatic."

She couldn't tear her eyes off his face. "You're all right."

Ash considered. "I wouldn't go that far. I don't think my therapist would go that far. Let's say I'm better than I was. Sometimes I sleep."

The initial shock was beginning to fade. Cathy felt her brain lurch with the effort to catch up. And, having caught up, to map her way out. She needed to know what he was going to do. And for that, she needed to know what he knew. Maybe little enough. It meant nothing that he'd found her here, only that he guessed this was where she would come. "You've seen the boys?"

"Yes."

"They're alive because of you. They're here because of you. We all are."

Ash breathed steadily for a moment. "Cathy—I know you haven't been in Somalia. Or at least, only for long enough to be brought back."

The quick clutch and declutch of gears as Cathy adjusted her strategy. "I'm not entirely sure where we've been."

"No? I am. It was a nice apartment. No wonder you didn't want to stay in my house."

She could lie. She didn't think she could lie well enough to convince him. Or she could tell him the truth. What would he do if she told him the truth? She wasn't afraid that he'd hurt her. Would a half-truth serve?

"He threatened me. Stephen Graves. He was the brains behind the whole piracy business. You didn't know that, did you, when you asked for his help? He used us as human shields. He threatened me, and he threatened the boys. I knew what you must be going through. I couldn't find a way out."

"Threatened you." Impossible to tell if he believed her or not.

"You thought he was one of the pirates' victims? No. That may be how he came in contact with them, but after that he was part of the organization. I think, to all intents and purposes, he ran it from his factory in Grantham. He fed them information about arms shipments they could hijack and what security measures had been taken. After you went to see him—the first time, five years ago—he knew you were smarter than the other people who'd questioned him. He realized you'd work it out, that he needed a hold over you. He picked us up off the street between home and the corner shop."

"Picked you up. Kidnapped you?"

"*Yes!* What did you think, we met at a tea dance? I went out for milk, bread, and broccoli, and found myself in the back of a van with duct tape over my mouth!"

"Where did he take you?"

"I don't know. The van drove for a couple of hours, then stopped. We were in a builder's yard, something like that. They kept the boys in the van, took me into a kind of warehouse. That was when I met Graves."

"What did he say?"

"That you were putting a profitable enterprise at risk. That I was going to help him get a bridle on you."

"How?"

Cathy swallowed. She looked older than he remembered, and thinner, and there was a hardness that Ash didn't recall, but she was still a beautiful woman. "He gave me a choice. He intended to keep the boys. They were his guarantee that you'd leave him alone. I could stay with them or go back to you. I'm sorry, Gabriel. I chose them."

If she expected sympathy, she was disappointed. Instead he said, "But he didn't take you to Somalia."

"No. To the flat. We were watched all the time. I wasn't allowed to talk to anyone. I kept thinking all I had to do was be patient, that my chance would come. That the men guarding us would get bored and careless, and we'd be out of there. But the right moment never came. They never got careless enough."

"Never? Not in four years?"

She met his gaze without flinching. "Never. We were safe, we were even comfortable; life of a kind went on. I thought of you all the time. I knew what you'd be going through. There was nothing I could do without putting the boys in danger."

"And the video call?"

"Graves turned up at the flat one day. He said to pack everything up, we were leaving. He took us back to the builder's yard. He said you'd surfaced again, that he needed to put you back in your cage. If I refused to help, I'd never see the boys again."

"So you said yes."

Cathy hesitated. "I didn't say no. I waited to see what he had in mind. Several days passed. Finally Graves said you'd found the

Cambridge flat, and he'd fixed up a video link so I could talk to you. But I had to pretend I was in Somalia."

"Did you know what he was proposing to do? The deal he was going to offer me?"

For the first time Cathy's voice wavered. "No. I thought knowing we were alive would be enough to keep you in line. I only knew . . . when . . ." The sentence petered out.

"Did you watch?"

Her eyes dipped. "He made me. He said it was important, to both of us. That he needed to know it was done, and I needed to know why you'd done it. For us. The boys and me."

"Then you flew out to Somalia, ready to come back to a hero's welcome."

Cathy nodded. "Graves had false papers for us."

"And then you were back in England, and the boys were with you, and Graves was talking to CTC. Why didn't you tell Detective Inspector Gorman everything that had happened?"

"I meant to. When I'd got my breath back." She looked up at him, her eyes begging for his understanding. "I just couldn't face any more questions. It's why I came here. It was a spur-of-the-moment thing, I just needed to get away. I'd spent four years doing exactly what I was told, not daring to do anything else. I wanted to be somewhere I could do what I wanted for a while. No watchdogs, no police, not even your well-meaning little friend. Just me and the boys."

"So Graves was never here."

She looked surprised. "He doesn't know about this place. How could he?"

"Only one way," admitted Ash.

The silence opened like a pit between them. Ash did nothing

to fill it. Finally Cathy whispered, "Is that what you've been thinking? That we were *lovers*? That I chose him over you, and that's why I took the boys and let you think we were dead? Gabriel—*is that what you think of me?*"

It would have been seductively easy for him to deny it. To say of course not, she'd misunderstood, he was sorry, he loved her, he'd always loved her . . . But what if the Cathy he'd always loved was a myth? He needed to be sure more than he needed to be comforted.

"I don't know what to think," he said simply. "For four years I thought you were all dead. Now it turns out you were living in Cambridge. Stephen Graves threatened you, and you were so afraid that in four years you couldn't find one opportunity to grab the boys and go to the police. That is what you're telling me?"

She nodded guardedly.

"I don't believe you," said Ash.

Another long, painful pause. Cathy propped one hip on the corner of the table and crossed her arms. When Ash looked at her, he saw two people: the woman he loved and had married and held sacred in his heart all through the broken years, hiding in the shadows behind the older, stronger woman who felt like a stranger. Of course she was older; they were both older. He wanted to love her again. He wanted to believe her. But not quite enough to lie to himself. To tell himself that the story he was hearing made sense.

Cathy said quietly, "I've told you what happened, Gabriel. I can't make you believe it."

They regarded each other across the tiny expanse of the houseboat's saloon. Four years of tragedy compressed into a space two meters by three. No wonder the air felt electric, as if a storm was imminent.

Finally Ash said, "No. There's something you're not telling me. You know I'll find out. You know this is what I do. You might as well tell me now."

She shook her head. Her eyes held him, unwavering. "You're wrong. It wasn't complicated, it was simple. I believed that our lives were in constant danger. I did what I had to do to keep us alive. I'm sorry if you think I should have handled it better. But I was catapulted into a situation I had no way of dealing with, and Graves created that situation but you bear some responsibility, too." There was a note of accusation like acid in her voice. "Your work is why Stephen Graves tore our lives apart. Your precious work. None of it would have happened if you'd known when to back off; if you hadn't been so goddamned *dedicated*!"

"You blame me." His voice was like a scratchy chalk. "Do you think I don't blame myself? That I haven't *been* blaming myself every minute of the last four years? Do you think I haven't regretted the things I did, the things I didn't do? I'm sorry to the bottom of my soul for what happened. I'm sorry I was a better security analyst than I was a husband. Whatever you did in consequence, the one who let us down was me. I know it, and I will always regret it.

"But what you're telling me doesn't add up. However afraid you were, you didn't live in a nice apartment in Cambridge for four years without getting a chance to raise the alarm. So maybe you weren't looking for one. Maybe you didn't want a way out. Cathy, be honest with me. Were you in love with Stephen Graves? Is that what kept you there? It was an apartment building, not a prison—you could have knocked on any door and had help in minutes. But something stopped you. Was that it? You didn't take the first opportunity to get away from Graves because you didn't want to?"

Ash's dark eyes searched hers till Cathy broke away with a

dismissive shrug. "I've told you all there is to know. It's easy to look at someone else's dilemma and think you'd have handled it better. Maybe you would have, Gabriel. I'm not saying I have much to be proud of. Except that I survived, and so did our sons. Maybe, if I'd been braver, we wouldn't have done."

He shook his head slowly. "You were always brave. From the moment I met you. You took London by the throat while I was still wiping my feet on the doormat. No one ever succeeded in making you do anything you didn't want to."

"They had guns!"

"But I don't think they were pointing them at you for four years. So there was something else. A reason to live as the cooperative Ms. Anderson, and not run for help when the chance arose, and to tell the story Graves needed you to even after you were released.

"Oh dear God!" Understanding hit him like a train, breaking him in a million pieces. His lips went to parchment, dry and pale, his limbs to water. His fists clenched, white-knuckled, on the handrails on either side of the companionway. "Oh Cathy. Please . . . please tell me it wasn't money. Tell me it wasn't as simple as *that*. Graves offered to cut you in on the deal, and you bit his hand off?"

CHAPTER 34

THIS WHOLE CONVERSATION HAD BEEN PUNCTUATED by awkward silences. Where one or the other of them had stopped breathing for a moment, waiting to see which way the fish was going to jump, and if it was going to pull the angler into the river. Some had gone on almost too long to bear. Long enough that the gritted teeth started to pain the jaw, that the skin crawled with electricity, that the unblinking eye itched like a burn.

None of them, Ash now discovered, had been in any way meaningful beside this one. This was like the world holding its breath. Every muscle in his body clenched tight as he waited for her response. At first he waited for her to gasp and for tears to spring to her eyes, but the moment for that passed. Then he waited for her to slap his face, all the power of her hurt and anger behind the blow, but the moment for that passed, too. Finally he was waiting for her to speak—to marshal words adequate to the occasion, in the low, precise voice of bridled fury, and furnish an explanation that would fill him with remorse and regret and infinite relief.

But the moment for that passed, too. After that, he didn't

know what he was waiting for. Cathy wasn't avoiding his gaze any-more; she was returning it, level, calculating. Waiting for him to blink first. Waiting for him to rush out an apology she could take her time about accepting. And it took all the strength Ash owned to keep from withdrawing the accusation, even though she hadn't bothered to deny it.

Finally, incredibly, she chuckled. "Oh Gabriel," she said, and the amusement in her voice was quite unfeigned, "when did you become such an insufferable prig?

"No, really," she persisted, seeing his stricken expression and tempering her assault not at all. "You weren't always this boring. Or maybe you were and I was too young to notice. I was only twenty-five when we married. It didn't seem that young at the time. Looking back, it seems much more than twelve years ago.

"And you were clever. I knew that the first time we met. I think I was a little seduced by it. I thought it would be a fine thing to marry a clever man. But then, I thought you'd do rather more with it than jockey a desk and add up columns of figures all day. I know it was important, but it's not exactly *sexy*, is it? Not the sort of thing a girl can boast to her friends about. 'And guess what he did *this* week? He figured out that the Lithuanians were *giving* more for the gas than the Estonians were *charging* for it! What do you think about that, then?'"

Now she was waiting for him to answer. And she had to wait almost as long before he managed to say, "We were happy. I know we were happy."

"Gabriel, we *were* happy," Cathy agreed, as if handing him a consolation prize. "For a time. Until I started to realize just how much I was missing, being married to a man who was born middle-aged.

"It was London that did it," she reflected. "That was the big mistake. If we'd stayed in the Midlands—if, God help us, we'd settled in Norbold—maybe I'd have been satisfied with you for the rest of my days."

"You loved London!" Ash protested.

"I *did* love London. That's what I mean. Suddenly I saw how much more there was to life. Suddenly I was meeting people who weren't just clever but interesting as well. It doesn't take much to be an intellectual giant somewhere like Norbold. In London, you need to have a bit more to offer.

"And now"—she smiled indulgently—"you're looking like a puppy dog whose squeaky toy has been taken away. I'm not blaming you. It wasn't you who changed, it was me. We grew apart, only you never noticed. I felt trapped and desperate, and you never noticed."

"The boys . . ."

"The boys gave me something to do. But it was only a matter of time before I realized the package wasn't indivisible. I wouldn't lose my children if I pulled the plug on my marriage."

Was he clever? Struggling to get his mind around these revelations, Ash seriously doubted it. "You mean you were never kidnapped? You just left me?"

She shook her head, her pale eyes merry. "How astonished you sound! Do you honestly think you were such a treasure that no woman in her right mind would have turned her back on you? Gabriel, I was ready to leave you long before Stephen Graves came along. All I was waiting for was a catalyst of some kind. If a distant aunt had died and left me an inheritance, that would have done. If someone had offered me a job I wanted to do, that would have done. Well, Stephen offered me a way out—a nice flat, a new identity, enough money to fund a stimulating lifestyle. I'd like to say I agonized over it, but I didn't really. I had everything to gain and nothing to lose."

"What . . . ?" The word came out so thin Ash barely heard it himself. He cleared his throat and tried again. "What happened?"

Cathy gave a negligent shrug. "I told you what happened. We were kidnapped off the street. We were kept under armed guard at that builder's yard for a fortnight. And then . . ."

"He made you an offer you couldn't refuse?" The words tore Ash's throat on the way out.

"Well, actually, no," admitted Cathy. "I made him one. It worked for both of us: he got what he needed, and I got what I needed. He looked"—she laughed at the memory—"pretty much how you're looking now when I suggested it. But I was sick of that bloody yard, the boys were climbing the walls. I had to find some kind of a solution. I told him I'd do everything he needed me to do if he made it worth my while.

"His first thought was that I was lying. That I was working the chain loose before making a bid for freedom. Of course he thought that—he'd have been stupid not to. He started thinking maybe I could be trusted when I explained that being kidnapped was not the worst thing that could have happened to me just then."

Ash's mouth was almost too dry to get the question out. "You persuaded Graves to cut you in on the deal?"

"Persuaded." She thought about the word. "Yes. Yes, in the end he was persuaded. He recognized that if he turfed me and the boys onto the street with enough money for a taxi, we still weren't going back to you. A whole realm of other possibilities opened up."

"Are you telling me you *were* lovers?" He didn't want to hear her say it. But he knew he needed to.

Her voice ran up in a light rill of laughter, all cool unkind-ness. She seemed to have abandoned any hope of winning his sym-pathy, decided her best course lay in unmanning him. "Men are such *romantics*! Stephen's the same. He will keep talking about love! I'd rather think of it as a happy convenience. But then, I married for love, and look what a letdown that was."

The corners of her mouth turned up in an impish smile. "I don't suppose this is what you wanted to hear. But you demanded the truth, and this is it. I left you because you were boring me rigid. Fate presented an alternative and I took it. I'm not low-maintenance, Gabriel, I never was, and I wasn't prepared to spend the rest of my life learning to be. Stephen represented financial independence. I was never going to turn my nose up at that."

"So what next?" asked Ash weakly. "You play house together? You know he's on the run?"

That seemed to surprise her. "Really? I thought they'd bought his version of events. Someone figured it out? Ah . . ."

There hadn't been much comfort for Ash in this conversation. Cathy's expression, when she realized that her husband had in the end outflanked her lover, was about all there was going to be. "Hazel had her suspicions before I did," he said. "Of course, she wasn't hindered by supposing she knew the people involved. When she made me think the facts through dispassionately, it be-came obvious that Graves was working with the pirates. And that, probably, you were, too."

"Well—*thinking* always was your forte." She managed to make it sound like a vice. "It doesn't matter. All we have to do is stay off the radar until interest in us dies down. Anyway, I couldn't have stayed in Norbold, with your little friend and that no-neck policeman trying to question the boys every time I turned my back.

I thought we'd be safe here. I thought the only one who'd remember this boat was already dead. But at least you haven't told anyone else."

He tried to keep his tone neutral. "No?"

She regarded him with a fine disdain. "If you'd told the police, they wouldn't have let you come here. You had to choose. You could send in an armed response unit and see me in court. Or you could keep your suspicions to yourself until you'd talked to me. You're on your own here, Gabriel. There is no Seventh Cavalry waiting in the gulch."

She knew him so well. Ash cleared his throat. "Cathy, you said it yourself—you're not low maintenance. Do you really think you can have the kind of life you want—the kind of life that was worth throwing me to the wolves for—with the police looking for you? You can't go back to Somalia, even if you wanted to. You'd be arrested there. The pirates were being rounded up even as you were flying home. The local authorities weren't really up to the job, but Philip Welbeck is a resourceful man. You'd be amazed what strings he can pull. Stephen Graves has no friends left in the Horn of Africa."

"Stephen's a resourceful man, too," retorted Cathy. "He'll take us somewhere no one will follow. I made it clear to him. If he wanted us to stay together he'd need to offer me something better than I could achieve on my own. He said he'd do whatever it took to keep me happy. Wasn't that sweet?"

"You believed him?"

"Oh yes," Cathy replied immediately. "I told you, he loves me. He thinks we're going to be together for always."

"But you don't?"

"Always is an awfully long time."

It wasn't that any of this was coming at Ash out of a blue sky. At intervals, though, the enormity of what she was confessing broke through the defenses his mind had fashioned, and rage and grief erupted through the breach. "People died! Cathy—the men flying those shipments died! Twenty-nine pilots and engineers who disappeared along with their planes and cargoes died to keep you in comfort in Cambridge!"

"Yes, they did," she agreed. "But I didn't kill them."

"And me." His voice was thick with bitterness. "I thought I'd got you killed. You and our sons. It tore me apart. You must have known that. You must have known what you were doing to me."

"Gabriel"—she sighed—"you're not the first man to have a bored wife walk out on him, and you won't be the last. Don't be such a drama queen."

"I thought you were dead!"

"Well, I thought you were dead. So we're even. Can't we leave it at that? Go home now, back to that dreary house in glum little Norbold, and get on with your life, and I'll do the same."

Even after everything that had passed between them, she had the power to amaze him. "You think we can carry on as if nothing much happened? As if we reached a fork in the road and went our separate ways? You think Graves can smuggle you and your money out to some Caribbean island with a history of turning blind eyes, and I'll keep your secret? I won't haul you back kicking and screaming if it takes another four years and some whole new extradition arrangements to do it?"

"Ah." Cathy looked pensive, and a little annoyed. "That's a pity. I'd rather hoped you'd be civilized about this."

"*Civilized!* . . ."

"Because if I can't trust you, perhaps I shouldn't let you leave after all."

The effrontery of it beggared belief. "You really think you can stop me?"

Cathy smiled again. "No." She glanced back over her shoulder. That was when Ash first realized that Stephen Graves was standing behind her, in the open door of one of the sleeping cabins. It took him another three seconds to see the gun. "But I think he can."

CHAPTER 35

S O MUCH HAD CHANGED since these two men last met. They regarded each other in speculative silence. Ash was trying to find room in his head for the reality that Stephen Graves had not only stolen his wife but had also corrupted whatever moral sense she'd once had. Graves was struggling with the fact that Ash was alive.

He'd thought it was the perfect crime. You don't kill someone; you persuade them to kill themselves. No inconvenient fingerprints at the scene, no murder weapons turning up in the trash, no late-night dog walkers to see you hurrying out to your car. He'd seen—or believed he'd seen—Gabriel Ash blow his brains out, and it had been like a great weight lifting off his shoulders. He'd walked away from his home, his business, and his family without a backward glance, because he'd thought a better future beckoned. A future of luxury and self-indulgence, bought with the profits of his ingenuity and shared with a woman he believed was his soul mate. A woman who would turn heads in any gathering but was otherwise so like himself it was almost scary.

Now, in the course of a few minutes, the weight was back— not on his shoulders, but crashing down on his head. Gabriel Ash wasn't dead. He was alive, and he was here, and whatever Cathy thought, the man was far too intelligent to have come alone.

The man *used* to be intelligent. Then his intellect had imploded and he'd spent several months sucking his thumb in a mental institution. Perhaps all was not yet lost. Stephen Graves moistened his lips with the tip of his tongue, his brain working overtime, certain—*certain*—there was still a way out. "We can make this work. For all of us."

Ash waited until the silence groaned. Then he said, "No. We can't."

Graves's voice took on an almost supplicatory note. "There's enough money in the pot for three."

Ash found himself smiling. It wasn't bravado, the last wave of a gallant flag as he faced the firing squad. He was smiling because a truly astonishing thing had happened. He'd found the answers he'd come looking for. After four years, he knew what had happened and why, and who was responsible, and—most miraculous of all—it wasn't him. He felt the layers of guilt and anguish peeling away from his mind like an onion shedding skins. The relief was enough to leave him weak. But also, as near as he could categorize it, happy. Yes, he'd lost his wife—but it seemed he'd never had the marriage he'd thought he had, because she really wasn't the person he'd thought she was. Finally recognizing that, he was able to let her go. There was nothing more to be done than put that whole phase of his life behind him and move on. The sense of release the knowledge brought was transcendent.

He said, "There isn't that much money in the *world*."

Cathy was looking between them, sharply, trying to work out which was the cat and which the mouse.

Graves gave a fractional nod. His whole body was tense, his

eyes uncertain. The gun in his hand didn't seem to be controlling the situation as it should. "All right. That was a mistake. I understand that. It was never money you wanted."

"No," agreed Ash.

"But I have something that you want."

"Yes."

Cathy Ash said through clenched teeth, "Don't even think about it. Either of you."

Ash looked at her half in surprise, half in amusement. "You? I'm sorry, Cathy, you aren't worth anything to me anymore. Go with Graves. It doesn't matter to me. You won't make each other happy, but that's hardly my concern. He's clearly willing to spend money on you, and perhaps that'll fend off the boredom for another year or two.

"Eventually, though, he'll need things you won't be able to give him. Honesty, commitment, some sense of loyalty. It'd be fun to be a fly on the wall when you have *that* discussion. Because when you're facing murder charges, you can't just agree to disagree. You hold each other's futures in your hands. And I wouldn't trust either of you with my car keys. I'm pretty sure that, sooner or later, one of you will end up killing the other. I'm just not sure which."

Ash knew he'd struck a nerve from the way Graves reacted. As if someone had touched him with a cattle prod. Because, somewhere inside him, Stephen Graves already knew everything Ash was telling him. He didn't want to admit it, even to himself, but he knew that betrayal is like sex: it's easier the second time. A woman who would do what Cathy Ash had done to her husband would do the same to him as soon as someone richer or prettier came along. Graves had left his wife, his family, his home, and the business founded by his uncle, for Cathy. But he'd always known, at some level, what she was. He'd found her exciting. He'd thought they could bestride the earth together. But Ash was right. She would use him only as long as it suited her, and then she'd betray him, too.

"I know what you want," he said, his voice hollow. "Take them."

"*No!*" screamed Cathy, her slender body convulsing with rage.

"Take them," repeated Graves sharply. "Take them, get in your car, and drive away. We won't try to stop you. Only, don't call the police for twenty-four hours."

Suddenly Ash had something to lose again. It wiped the smile off his face. "Why wouldn't I?"

"Because if you do, we'll be caught," said Graves rapidly. He'd always been good at this: thinking on his feet, when the stakes were so high that he couldn't afford to lose. It was how he got involved in the piracy in the first place. "And everything will come out. Everything I've done, but also everything Cathy has done. Now, I'm sure you'd like to see justice catching up with me, and maybe you don't care if it catches up with your wife. But what about your sons? They'll never forgive you for opening *that* can of worms and dumping it over them. And for what? To see us in prison? You might find the satisfaction wears thin when you can't take your sons for a kick-about in the park without some tabloid hack trying to photograph them. Imagine the headlines. Imagine the excuses when they want to bring their school friends around to play, and their friends' parents would much sooner they play with someone whose mother *isn't* a celebrated criminal."

For much of the last four years, Ash's life had meant nothing to him at all. It had been a burden he would have been happy to lay down. Now all that had changed. If Graves was serious about letting Ash walk away with both his life and his sons, handling this wrong could cost him everything. It made him afraid.

Then there was Cathy. As she listened in mounting disbelief, her face grew dark with fury. This wasn't something she and Graves had discussed. And it wasn't something she was going to agree to. "Shoot him," she said, her voice hard.

Graves glanced at her. "There's no need. He isn't going to make things difficult for us. He's going to make them easier. Aren't you, Gabriel?"

"How do you figure *that*?" demanded Cathy.

"With just the two of us, we can disappear. I have money, I have connections. We'll be fine. But with two little boys in tow? We'd be spotted. Or one of them would say something to draw attention to us. And what about their future? How long do you suppose they'd be content to trail around after us, upping sticks every time we think someone might be taking an interest in us? Gilbert's eight now. What about when he's fifteen? What about when he's twenty?"

If Cathy had had the words printed on a T-shirt, she couldn't have made it plainer that she'd never considered the possibility that she and Graves would still be together in seven years' time. "At fifteen, and at twenty, and at forty, they will still be my sons. I'm not giving them up. Shoot him. If you want me, if you want us to be together, shoot him. *Do it now!*"

And that was when, with the monumentally bad timing of the very young, Gilbert Ash ducked his head inside and whined petulantly, "What are you all talking about? I'm hungry. What's going *on*?"

Cathy froze. She knew what she'd just said; she wasn't sure if her son had been close enough to hear her. She didn't think, even if he had, he'd realize who it was she wanted shot; but, like smoking and drinking, inciting murder probably isn't something you should do in front of children.

Stephen Graves froze. He'd known these boys for four years and never once had shown them a real gun. Now he was surprised with one in his hand, pointed—if the child but knew it—at his own father. He wasn't sure if he should try to hide it, or if that would only draw attention to the thing.

Ash didn't freeze. He rose slowly from his seat on the companionway steps and turned. Turned his back on the gun and his face to his son. "Gilbert, I need you to do something for me. Do you know why I feel I have the right to ask?"

There was a long pause while the boy considered. He had Ash's eyes: deep, dark, intelligent, stubborn. Finally he said, in a small, stubborn voice, "Are you my father?"

Ash nodded. "Yes, I am."

He wasn't the sort of boy to throw his arms around anybody. He made no move of any kind. "Mummy told us you were dead."

"She thought I was."

"Why did you leave us?"

That went deeper into Ash than a knife. It took him a moment to catch his breath. "I didn't leave you. You were taken away from me. I've spent the last four years looking for you. I was afraid *you* were dead."

"Can we all be together now?"

Ash wasn't going to lie. Whatever relationship he was going to have with his sons, it wasn't going to begin with a lie. "No. Your mother's got herself into some trouble, she needs to go and sort it out. You're coming home with me."

"I don't *know* you!"

The sharpness twisted in his gut. "I know. But I know you. Your favorite color is green. You have—unless you've grown out of him now you're eight—a gray plush elephant called Mungo. You got him for Christmas when you were three. Even when you were three, you thought an elephant was cooler than a teddy bear.

"You learned to talk absurdly early, and never went through a baby-talk phase. Your first teacher was Mrs. Sellars. When I picked you up after your first day at school, she said she'd never met a four-year-old who knew what *diplomacy* meant. But you're even better at numbers. Nobody remembers teaching you numbers; you seem to have been born knowing them. I imagine you're doing trigonometry now, are you, and maybe calculus?"

He was rewarded by a hint of a grin from the pale, intense boy.

"Guy, now, he's the opposite. He was a very placid baby. He'd lie in his pram for hours just admiring the view. He didn't start talking until he was nearly two—but once he started, there was no stopping him. He'd chitter away like a budgerigar for as long as anyone was prepared to listen. He won't do as well in tests as you will, but he'll never be short of friends. He takes after his mother that way. You're more like me; God help you."

Gilbert Ash looked at his father; looked uncertainly at his mother; looked back up the jetty to where his brother was playing on the grass. Still admiring the view. He bit his lip. "You want us to go with you?"

Ash's throat was tight. "To my house in Norbold. You stayed there when you came back to England."

"It's a bit . . . crappy. . . ."

"I know it is. I haven't been very well. We'll smarten it up now it's going to be a family home. What color do you want your room? Let me guess."

"Green," said Gilbert with a shy grin.

"This is nonsense!" exclaimed Cathy, exasperated beyond bearing. "Of course you're not going with him! You're coming with me. Both of you are coming with me."

"Tell you what, Gilbert," said Ash quietly, "let me talk to your mother for a minute. We'll sort it out. Will you take Guy and go up the hill and sit in my car? The big gray one. I'll be along in a few minutes. Sit on the backseat, and don't play with the controls."

He had no way of knowing if the boy would do as he was asked. But Ash knew for sure that if he himself tried to leave the boat now, there would be bloodshed. Any of them, boys included, could be hurt or killed. Gilbert backed away from the hatch. Ash moved slowly until his body blocked both the exit and the view.

Graves broke the silence. "He's right, you know. They'll be better off with him."

Cathy stared at him as if he'd said something obscene. "I am their *mother*! Of *course* they're coming with me."

"If they come with us, we'll be caught. I'll go to prison, so will you. He'll get custody anyway. If he takes them now, we're free and clear."

But she was past listening to reason. She spun on him with violence in her eyes. "You coward! You're a big man, aren't you, when you're directing mayhem from behind a desk. When you can make a phone call and people thousands of miles away will do your dirty work for you. You've already killed a lot of people, Stephen. You may not have pulled the trigger, but you planned it and you ordered it and you profited from it, and that makes you a killer in every way that matters.

"Now I need you to do one thing for me. Just one, but I need you to do it, and I need you to do it now. I need you to kill my husband. After that we'll do anything you want. We can split up, and I'll get the boys somewhere safe and we'll meet up later when everyone's tired of looking for us. Or we can split the proceeds now and never see each other again. It's your call. But you'll do this one thing for me. I've done everything you needed, and now I need something in return. I need you to kill Gabriel Ash."

There was, Ash thought, a look of godforsaken understanding on Graves's face. As if he, too, had finally realized just who it was he'd yoked himself to. He'd admired her ruthlessness, but until now he'd never quite made that last leap of intuition—that when her own interests required it, she'd be equally ruthless with him. He'd thought they could play a sort of Bonnie and Clyde version of Happy Families on the proceeds of five years' worth of international crime. He'd thought it would be exciting. He knew now there was no future for them. That he'd thrown away everything he had for money and nothing else.

He started to raise the gun. Then he held it out sideways. His voice was expressionless. "You want him dead, you do it. I've nothing against the man. Except that he's cleverer than I am, and that's no reason to kill someone." He managed a gray smile in Ash's direction. "It's funny. I thought it was. I thought we'd be safe if you were dead. But it's too late for that. Killing you won't make any difference now."

"It'll make a difference to *me!*" snarled Cathy.

"Then do it." Graves shrugged. "Me, I'm out of here. I'll take the car, if you don't mind. If you shoot him, you can take his. If you don't, I imagine transport will be provided for you." He headed for the steps. Ash moved aside to let him pass.

Perhaps it wasn't the wittiest joke ever made. But for a man in Graves's position, with the cinders of his world settling softly around him, it was brave to attempt a joke of any kind. It should have earned him something—a moment's appreciation, a faint grin, something.

In fact, it got him killed.

As Cathy's fingers closed around the gun he'd given her, the scale of the disaster overwhelmed her. She'd thought she was free and rich, and the jewel in a besotted man's crown. The future she'd envisaged included palmy shores and expensive hotels, and possibly a small yacht, and the kind of security from consequence that only a great deal of money can buy, but always—*always*—with her sons beside her. She hadn't distinguished herself as a wife. She hadn't made a conspicuous success of being a mistress. But nothing would shake her conviction that she was a good mother.

To challenge that view of herself was to court her bottomless fury. Think she-eagle with chicks; think lioness with cubs. The eyes filled with blood and the claws came out, and it is entirely possible that she didn't even know what she was doing until it was done. But Cathy Ash was a fiercely protective, angry woman who felt her children were being threatened, and the two men she blamed were right in front of her, and one of them had put a loaded gun in her hand. There was never a chance that she *wasn't* going to use it.

A gunshot at close quarters is a louder thing than anyone raised on television drama ever expects. Two reports filled the cabin of the little houseboat and went rolling away across the water like staccato thunder.

Stephen Graves fell the way a tree falls: slowly at first, gathering momentum as he went. He was on the top step when the bullet with his name on it hit him in the back. It wasn't big enough to throw him forward. He stopped, and looked back vaguely, and one hand reached up behind him as if trying to scratch an itch.

But the bullet had torn open two of the chambers of his heart. The blood that should have been pumping to his brain was pooling inside his chest, and it took him longer to fall—bouncing off the handrails, and off Ash, who tried to catch him—than to die. By the time his body slumped to its awkward rest at the foot of the companionway, his eyes were already still and blank.

Ash stared at him, openmouthed, his own eyes stretched with shock. He stared at Cathy, gun still in her hand. It occurred to him that he didn't know if she'd meant to kill Graves, if she'd been shooting at her inconvenient husband, or if the fact that she'd fired twice was significant.

That was when the inside of the houseboat started moving around. Not so much up and down, which might be expected in something afloat, as in and out. Beyond the galley, the cabin doors were washing in and out like driftwood on a tide. So was the woman in front of him.

Ash recognized that this was not a normal state of affairs. Even so, it took him an absurdly long time to find an explanation. There was blood on his shirt. He blinked at it, owlishly, wondering where it had come from. Of course, Graves in his death dive had tumbled over him. But that didn't explain the visual disturbances he was experiencing. Tentatively, testing a theory, he pressed one hand against his ribs. The blood kept coming, seeping between his fingers.

"You shot me," he said stupidly.

"Yes."

Cathy was still pointing the gun at him—at arm's length, as if she meant it, so that from Ash's perspective the black mouth of the little handgun looked as big as a cannon. He held his breath. She'd said she wanted him dead, and he believed her. Perhaps both shots had been intended for him. Perhaps, if her aim had been truer, they wouldn't be having this conversation.

But there were more rounds in the gun. If she'd meant to kill him rather than Graves, it was the work of a moment to rectify the situation. He ought to try to stop her. Run, or rush her before she had the chance to fire again. But the weakness from the hole under his hand was spreading outward through his body: quite literally, he could not have fought her to save his life. He stayed where he was, waiting for her to put him down like an injured horse, one bullet between the ears.

She sighed. All the fury seemed to leach out of her along with the breath. She lowered the gun until it was pointing at the floor. "Oh Gabriel, how did we come to this?"

"I think"—he was having to enunciate carefully now to get the words out at all—"they call it 'irretrievable breakdown of marriage.'"

Cathy laughed out loud. There was a hysterical trill to it. Perhaps afraid that the gun would go off again, accidentally, as reaction caught up with her, she placed it—well out of his reach—on the table. "It's hard to argue with that. Are you badly hurt?"

He was too tired for anything but honesty. "I don't know."

"Let me see."

Ash didn't want to move his hand, was afraid that both the blood and the pain would quicken if he did. But Cathy prized his fingers away, tore open his shirt, and considered the wound beneath. Just below his ribs, dark blood was pumping freely from two holes a handspan apart.

"It's gone straight through," she said judiciously. "How's your basic anatomy—is there anything vital around there?"

He didn't know, either. And he didn't know what she'd do if he said there wasn't.

Cathy looked at him. She looked at the gun. She blew her cheeks out in exasperation. "I know what I said. I didn't want you coming after us. I still don't. But maybe it doesn't matter now. With Stephen dead, you won't be the only one looking for me. And, in a funny sort of way, though you've driven me crazy most of the time I've known you, I'm not sure I want to kill you after all. I think the world might be a poorer place without you in it somewhere.

"Tell you what: let's leave it in the lap of the gods. If you can get help before you bleed out, maybe you'll live. If you can't, you'll die, but I'll know that I gave you a fighting chance." Having reached a decision she was comfortable with, Cathy spent a minute throwing belongings into a couple of bags, stepping over the dead man's legs as she did so.

"Is that what you'll tell the boys?" mumbled Ash. "That you gave me a fighting chance?"

"I won't tell them anything. They think their father died three weeks ago. Why would I tell them anything different?"

"Because Gilbert knows!"

"He knows you *said* you were his father. He also knows there are strange men out there who tell lies to little boys. I'll tell him you were lying."

"I'm never going to see them again, am I?" Ash heard his own voice break.

"No," said Cathy. "But you'll know they're safe. I'm sorry, Gabriel. I'm sorry that I've hurt you. But it's time to forget about us."

"*Forget* . . ." It came out as a sob.

"I'm sorry," she said again, and then she was gone.

In his mind Ash followed her. In his mind he moved quickly enough to block her exit up the companionway, kept her there and reasoned with her, calmly yet forcefully, marshaling arguments about the welfare of the boys and her own best interests. In his mind he knew he could win her over, and she would leave alone. But when he tried to do it for real, his body let him down. The pint of his blood that had pumped doggedly from the holes in his side seemed more vital to his ability to function than the other seven still coursing through his veins. When he tried to stand, his knees wavered and dropped him, gasping with pain, back on the steps.

Driven by despair, he tried again; this time he managed to stay on his feet. But he couldn't climb the steep steps, not with one hand clamped against his ribs. He needed to grip the rail on either side. Immediately he felt the queasy sensation of his warm blood cooling on the outside of his skin. But there were only half a dozen steps; he could stay on his feet for half a dozen steps. There was still all to play for if he could reach her now. . . .

And then it was too late. He heard the car start up, the revs climbing as it scaled the hill. At the brow the engine noise diminished quickly and silence washed back. Ash was still only on the second step. He felt the life drain out of him as the sound of Cathy's car went away, and the evening sunshine, reflected into the little boat by the surface of Ullswater, faded as if someone were drawing one curtain after another. As the last curtain closed he was already falling, the way Stephen Graves had fallen, the floor and the crumpled body coming up to meet him. But he didn't remember hitting them.

CHAPTER 36

THE BLEEDING STOPPED EVENTUALLY. But not before every piece of fabric Ash could reach had been saturated in his attempt to stanch the wound.

Certainly he was still bleeding when he woke up on the floor of the boat, cold to the bone, partly with shock but also because night had come and Ullswater is a northern lake, chilly by default even in summer. Shuddering with distaste, he disentangled himself from the dead man's twisted limbs and sat up against the galley units, breathing the wholly disconcerting smell of his own blood and waiting for the boat to stop spinning.

His wits were slow returning, but two things he knew as soon as he'd figured out which way was up. One was that his sons were gone. The other was that he could still die if he couldn't find some way of summoning help.

He had a phone. It was in his car, at the top of the hill. If he could have reached it, he probably wouldn't have needed help.

The short night passed. Dawn filtered into the boat. He was still alive, still sitting on the floor, surrounded by bloody cloths, with only a corpse for company. Then there were footsteps on the deck and, bizarrely enough, Hazel Best and Patience were there. He lifted an arm as heavy as a sack of grain, and put it around the dog's shoulders while Hazel strapped him up. As she worked, he talked, in a dull, distant, soulless voice, telling her what had happened as if it had happened to someone else.

When she was finished, she went on deck to call an ambulance. Hazel's phone was, of course, in her pocket, where it could do her some good in an emergency. Patience went with her.

They were longer than Ash expected. But then, his sense of time was shot to hell. He waited, not so much patient as apathetic, until Hazel came back alone. The dog had plainly found something more interesting to do than sit with a man just this side of comatose.

Hazel took a duvet from one of the cabins to cover the dead man on the floor. She checked Ash's dressing again. It was almost clean. She sat back on her heels. Ash couldn't think why she was smiling. So he wasn't going to bleed to death. To a man who'd lost what he'd lost, it didn't seem much reason for cheer.

Finally, irritably, he said, "What?"

She stood up. "Some people to see you."

He hadn't heard the ambulance. Perhaps that wasn't surprising. Even in an emergency the big vehicle could only have crept down the steep, stony lane. The boat rocked very slightly as someone stepped aboard.

Patience sprang nimbly from the top of the companionway to the bottom. Slower, hesitantly, the two boys climbed down the steep steps.

Hazel thought she would treasure the look on Ash's face for as long as she lived. For several seconds it seemed that he literally could not believe what he was seeing. His pale lips rounded in the *wh* shape that almost all questions begin with, but no sound came. Perhaps he couldn't decide which to ask first. So he just stared at them, mouth open, eyes wide in astonishment, and joy rose through him in an intemperate tide.

When the ambulance arrived, he suffered himself to be taken away, still understanding almost nothing of the miracle that had come to him. Hazel, driving behind with the two boys and the dog, spent the journey coaxing a coherent story out of Gilbert.

W hen Cathy hurried from the boat, throwing bags into the back of her car, she was spurred to fresh anger by the discovery that her sons were not waiting for her. "Will you stop messing about?" she shouted, turning on her heel to gather the hillside in her gaze. "I haven't time for your nonsense. We have to leave here now."

But they were nowhere in sight. Hiding? There was nowhere to hide. Unless . . . Seeing the vehicle parked higher up the slope, her eyes narrowed and she started her own car and drove up the lane to where Ash had left the Volvo.

It was a good guess. Gilbert was in the driver's seat, Guy in the back. They watched her intently through the closed windows. She snatched at the door handle. It was locked.

"Open this *at once!*" she snapped. "*This minute!*"

Gilbert shook his head.

It was so unexpected that for a moment she didn't know what to do next. They were little boys, not angels, and they didn't do everything she said and sometimes they did things she said not to, but she wasn't accustomed to open defiance.

She caught her breath, bridled her temper. Frightening them

would only add to the delay. "Come on, Gilbert, there isn't time for this. We need to leave. Everything's in the car. Bring Guy and let's be on our way."

Her elder son shook his head again. He'd locked the doors, and nothing in his expression suggested he was going to unlock them anytime soon. Cathy was mystified and alarmed. She didn't think Ash was mortally wounded. When the shock passed, he would come after them. He was much bigger and, in the normal way of things, much stronger than she was: if it came to a tug-of-war, he would win. She needed to be away from here while his knees were still trying to bend both ways.

"Honey, please," she wheedled, "what is this? You can't want to stay here. With him? You don't know him!"

Gilbert's voice, small to begin with, was further muffled by the glass. But the words were unmistakable. "He's my father."

She'd need more time to persuade him otherwise than she could spare right now. "And I'm your mother! I love you. I need you to come with me."

But Gilbert shook his head again. He said nothing more, but his expression spoke volumes. His obstinacy would have bent girders.

In desperation, Cathy hammered on the glass with her fists. The boys shrank from her, but the car remained locked. She was crying with grief and frustration, but tears don't open every door. She couldn't think what else to do. A professional car thief might have been able to break in with minimal time and effort, but he would have the right tools and, more than that, the know-how. Cathy didn't even have half a brick. She looked around urgently, but nothing suitable presented itself. She still had the gun, but she wasn't about to fire it into the car where her children were sitting.

She supposed there would be a wheel brace somewhere in the boot of her hired car, but her luggage was piled on top of it and she felt time breathing hot on the back of her neck. At any moment Ash might emerge from the cabin, and the God-honest truth was that she was afraid to face him. Four years ago he would have died rather than hurt her. But now? She didn't know what he might do, knowing himself betrayed, seeing his sons on the point of vanishing once more.

She returned to her car and drove away.

S he drove away?" whispered Hazel, appalled, jerking her attention back to the road as she felt her own car veer over the center line.

Beside her, Gilbert nodded. His eyes were cast down to his knees and he didn't look at her, consumed by the shame of being abandoned by his own mother. Of knowing there were things that were more important to her than her children.

"So you stayed in your dad's car? All night?"

Again the solemn, wordless nod.

"Why? Ah . . ." Ash had asked him to take his brother up to the car and wait for him. That's what he had done. Admittedly, he'd ignored the other instruction, which was not to play with the controls, but if he hadn't locked the doors, Cathy would have taken her sons away. He'd made his decision; then he'd waited for his father to come, as he'd said he would.

And if Ash had bled to death in the little boat? If Hazel had not come, nor had anyone else, would they have stayed in the car until they, too, died? Hazel shook her head in wonder, by no means confident that they would not have.

There was still something she didn't understand. "Gilbert," she said gently, "why did you decide to stay with your father? When your mother wanted you to go with her. I mean, it was a brave decision, when you've been with her all these years and you hardly remember him."

Still Gilbert refused to look at her. He mumbled, "She made us lie. About where we'd been."

"That must have been difficult," Hazel said softly.

"It wasn't her, it was him," the boy said in a fierce rush, answering the inbuilt urge to defend his mother. "Uncle Stephen."

"Uncle . . ."

"We had to call him Uncle Stephen. He isn't really our uncle."

"No."

"And now he's dead," Gilbert added with a certain relish.

Hazel winced. So they'd guessed what she'd hidden under the duvet.

"Is my father going to die?"

At least she had a proper answer to that. "No. He's going to be all right. In twenty minutes he'll be in A&E, getting stitches in his side, then they'll stick an antibiotic in his bottom"—predictably, that made the little boy smile—"and send him home with us. Everything's going to be fine."

"Did my father shoot Uncle Stephen?"

There were only two possible answers, and she wasn't going to lie. "No, Gilbert, he didn't."

"Ah." It was somehow a very adult sound. "Then Mummy did."

Maybe, without actually lying, Hazel could soften the truth. "I think she thought she was protecting you."

"*I* think she was protecting herself."

And that was why, faced with a decision no child should have had to make, Gilbert Ash had backed the father he hardly knew over the mother he knew only too well.

Hazel had been over-optimistic. The hospital wanted to keep Ash long enough to be sure that he wouldn't start bleeding again as soon as they said he was fine.

While he was being admitted, Hazel took the boys for something to eat. All they'd had since the previous afternoon was some biscuits they'd found in Ash's car. Hazel didn't say so, but she was fairly sure they were the ones he bought for Patience.

The boys tucked into everything put in front of them, then filled their pockets at the chocolate machine.

While they were occupied, Hazel did something she was aware she should have done sooner: tell Saturday.

It wasn't yet midmorning. The phone rang for two minutes before the teenager dragged himself out of bed and down into the hall to answer it. "Yeah—what?"

"Saturday, it's me." Silence. "Hazel," she added, pointedly. "I'm in the Lake District. I should be back sometime tomorrow."

"Yeah? Good." He still sounded half-asleep.

She took a deep breath. "Gabriel's here."

"Yeah? Well . . . there's no show without Punch."

"*What?*"

"I mean, you can't have much of a funeral without the dearly departed. But hell, you might have asked if I wanted to go."

He'd misunderstood. Of course he'd misunderstood: for perfectly good reasons, the fact that Ash had survived his apparent suicide had been kept from even his friends. "Saturday—Gabriel isn't dead. He's not exactly on peak form, either, but he's a long way from dead. It was all an elaborate hoax, to persuade the men who were holding his sons to send them home."

A long, long silence. Hazel could almost hear the gears of

Saturday's brain spinning. Finally he demanded, "Are you for real?"

"Yes," she said. "Yes, I'm absolutely for real. He's alive, he's a bit shop-soiled, but he'll be fine in a day or two. I'm hoping to bring him home tomorrow."

". . . Alive?"

"Yes."

"Gabriel. Alive."

"Yes."

Another long silence. Then: "I thought so."

Hazel laughed out loud. "Yeah, right!"

"I did," protested Saturday. "I didn't know how, but I didn't believe—didn't really believe—he was dead."

"I didn't want to believe it, either," said Hazel. "But I knew, or at least I thought I knew, what I'd seen."

"Nah." She heard him shaking his head at the phone. "She'd have known if he was dead."

Hazel frowned. "Who?"

"Patience," he said, as if she was being dim. "Patience would have known. Dogs are smart that way."

"Yes, they are," she agreed. "Anyway, I thought I'd better warn you, so you don't have a heart attack the first time you see him."

"Did he get his kids back?"

"Yes." Hazel felt herself smiling. "Yes, Saturday, he did."

"That's all right, then." And with no more ceremony than that, he put the phone down; and Hazel knew as surely as if she could see him that he was heading back to bed.

By the time she took Ash's sons up to the ward, Ash was tucked up in bed, still pale but glowing with happiness. Unless it was the local anesthetic getting into his bloodstream. At the sight of his visitors, he slid over to one side of the bed and patted the other, and the boys, increasingly confident, went to sit beside him.

Hazel took the chair and, smiling inwardly, watched them starting to learn about one another. This wasn't her moment; all she could be was a bystander. But she was happy for Ash, satisfied at how things had turned out; and if she was aware that the situation was still unresolved, that getting what he'd longed for was no guarantee that he'd be able to hold on to it, and that there would be sensible, experienced, dedicated people in Norbold's social services department who would raise both eyebrows at the notion of leaving two small boys with a man universally known as Rambles With Dogs, now wasn't the time to mention that, either.

After fifteen minutes she excused herself. "I'll go check on Patience. I'll be back for you in half an hour, boys—your dad ought to get some rest soon." To Ash she said, "I'll find somewhere to stay tonight. With luck we can all go home tomorrow."

His deep, dark eyes were liquid with gratitude. "I owe you so much. One day I'll make a start on repaying you."

Hazel grinned. "There's no hurry. First of all, get better."

The grin slowly faded, though, as she headed down the stairs alone. What she was thinking was, I think you're going to need a lot more help, my friend, before you're in a position to do anyone else any favors.